WAS HE GOING TO KISS HER?

Now?

He was.

His lips caressed hers. Lightly at first, then with a firmer press when she responded instinctively to his touch. They didn't cling. It was too soon. Too dangerous for that.

Instead, the kiss said everything. *I'm attracted!* And *I wish . . .*

Then, like a hurricane, they came together. Tongues meshed, bodies entwined. She wanted to touch him everywhere. She wanted to feel his hands, his arms against her bare skin. She could feel every inch of him, every surprising inch of his response to her.

Oh, God, what was she doing?

BOOK YOUR PLACE ON OUR WEBSITE AND MAKE THE READING CONNECTION!

We've created a customized website just for our very special readers, where you can get the inside scoop on everything that's going on with Zebra, Pinnacle and Kensington books.

When you come online, you'll have the exciting opportunity to:

- View covers of upcoming books
- Read sample chapters
- Learn about our future publishing schedule (listed by publication month *and author*)
- Find out when your favorite authors will be visiting a city near you
- Search for and order backlist books from our online catalog
- Check out author bios and background information
- Send e-mail to your favorite authors
- Meet the Kensington staff online
- Join us in weekly chats with authors, readers and other guests
- Get writing guidelines
- AND MUCH MORE!

**Visit our website at
http://www.kensingtonbooks.com**

DARK AND DANGEROUS

Jeanne Adams

ZEBRA BOOKS
Kensington Publishing Corp.
www.kensingtonbooks.com

Contrary to popular belief, writing is not a solitary occupation. It takes the support and love of family, friends, and fellow writers to get to the amazing point of publication. To that end, I thank my parents James and the late Ann Pickering with all my heart. You gave me a love of books, as well as abiding love and the unspoken knowledge that I could do anything to which I set my mind. To my wonderfully supportive sister Susan, you rock! To my brother John and his fiancé Benn; and to my brother, David, and his family, thank you. Thank you as well to my dear stepmother Dr. Lorraine Clark and her family for their delightful support.

To my wonderful husband Ralph, and my sons, there is absolutely no way I could have done any of this without you. I love, appreciate, and thank you for everything!

I'm also deeply grateful for the joy of brilliant encouraging friends (Leah, Malena, Babo, Kaz, Neela, Mattie, Vas, and Susan) as well as fellow writers who have so long supported me. From my first critique group, led by the amazing Donna Gulick, through the Wicked Sisters (thanks Leah, Barb, Judi, and Terri!), to my current outstanding circle of dedicated writers, The Romance Bandits (http://RomanceBandits.blogspot.com): I celebrate you, and am blessed to have you in my life.

To my superb editor Kate Duffy, thank you for your faith in me and in Dark and Dangerous.

Chapter One

The windchimes began to peal, a musical jangle. Dana had just set her book aside and turned out the bedside lights. Listening, she felt a twitch of intuition. For her, the tingle of unease was as good as a certified letter when it came to danger.

There had been no breeze, not even the barest hint of wind when she'd let their dog, Shadow, out for the last time at eleven. The cool spring air, redolent with the scent of new growth, had been still.

Getting out of bed, she flicked the television on for light. Tossing the remote on the bed, she walked to the inner hallway; continuing to listen, preparing to act.

The clanging of the chimes picked up speed. *Fools,* she thought, even as her heart raced, and she realized what hovered outside her house.

Shadow began to growl. Everything seemed to slow down, separate into moments. They had come for her, for her son. She'd been dreading this and yet expecting it.

It had only been four hours since she'd sat with Xavier, reading from one of the *Harry Potter* books at bedtime. Now, she would have to wake him, to run.

They'd had to scurry away in the night before, or leave with bare minutes of leeway, but then they'd had help. The FBI or WitSec—the witness security program—had been there.

Donovan had found them again, and this time she was on her own.

As scared as she was, the clangor of the bells almost made her laugh. Almost. For all her ex-husband's cunning, for all the expensive black-market military hardware he bought with his drug money, he didn't have anyone smart enough to think about those windchimes.

Thank God.

Warned by the wind. If that's not cosmic justice, I don't know what is. How soon he'd forgotten. He'd trained her well to take near-paranoid precautions. That hard-won expertise worked against him now and ensured she knew trouble had arrived.

Being forewarned only helped her if she took action, she reminded herself, thinking furiously. There was no time to get to the van, and even if they did, the helicopter would be armed. They would be sitting ducks on the country roads. There was no time to go to the safe room in the basement, either.

Donovan's men would be on the ground by now.

She did have time to activate her other protective measures, pitiful though they were. Still growling, Shadow—one of her more traditional defenses—obviously sensed the peril and stood ready for her commands.

"Roust your lazy asses! We're movin' out!" The shout reverberated through the old warehouse that served as the headquarters for Donovan Walker's assassination and retrieval team.

Tonight was it, then. The adrenaline instantly pumped into his system. After months of training, it was time to get Dana Markham and her child. Finally, he would get what he needed to close the cage on Donovan Walker. *Finally*.

Caine Bradley heard the discussion start outside his door, and an almost palpable tension sprang into the air. He tapped his keyboard, his fingers flying over the slim laptop in a blur. He hit SEND as Spike, the brawny thug who nominally ran their team, flung open the door to the Spartan room where Caine worked. The flick of a key returned a porn site to full screen.

To show his complete disdain for Spike, Caine didn't even acknowledge the dramatic entrance.

"You jacking off in here again, Pollack?" Spike growled, shooting a glance at the computer.

Leaning back, Caine eyed the man who knew him as Pollack, not letting on that he'd just sent an email to his FBI counterpart that would end Spike's career. And maybe his life, if he didn't surrender when the trap was sprung.

That pleasant thought made it easier to keep his cool. "You should try it, Spike," Caine replied laconically. "Might improve your disposition."

"Put a lid on it, pretty boy. You impress the Boss with that wiseass chatter, but not me. Get your sorry ass in gear. We're a go."

Caine set the laptop aside and rose from the cot. In less than two minutes, the computer would be useless, its hard drive wiped clean. Clad in black fatigue pants and boots, Caine stretched his upper torso, bending from side to side to loosen the coiled muscles in his shoulders. He couldn't help the nasty smirk that arose as he noted Spike's unspoken unease.

Looming forward, he used his tall frame to his advantage, intimidating the shorter, bulkier man. He shifted his weight, and Spike recoiled. It was a mere half a step, but there was no erasing it. Caine's smirk turned to wolfish delight. The obvious shift in the power balance needed a verbal nudge as well.

"Since you go for itty bitty titties on itty bitty bodies, I'd think a robust ride like that," Caine pointed at the lusty, buxom woman on-screen, "would be too much for you." Spike's predilection for little girls was one of the many reasons Caine hated him. He couldn't wait to see the horror on Spike's face when he realized who his nemesis *really* worked for . . . ah, priceless.

"Drop dead, Pollack," Spike snarled. As far as comebacks went, it was weak. Caine snickered to himself.

"Same to ya, Spike. Hell has a spot waiting for you."

Society called it wrong, but sometime soon Caine wanted to see Spike very, very dead. In lieu of that, he would settle for bruised, bleeding, and handcuffed. The mental image was so satisfying, he broke into a full-blown grin.

The humor must have been even more menacing to Spike than anything else, because he hastily turned to go.

"Quit stalling and get your fuckin' pansy-ass moving. We're due at the wharf in less than fifteen," Spike blustered to cover his retreat. He checked his watch and glared. "And counting."

"I'm on it," Caine replied, without stirring.

Although he stomped out, Spike never quite turned his back. That evidence of cowardice, along with the slammed door, had Caine shaking his head in both disgust and delight. He was a superb undercover operative because he didn't really care if he lived or died. The department shrink called it a death wish, but Caine didn't want to die, he had too many karmic debts to pay. Of course, dying in the line of duty would pay many of them. So if that was the outcome, he was up for that too.

The only regret he had was that pushing the buttons of pitiful, disgusting criminals like Spike was too easy and he'd gotten too good at it over the years. As a form of entertainment, it left a lot of room for improvement. There were times that he worried that he had come to enjoy it too much.

The other factor was that one of these days, it was probably going to get him killed.

Dismissing the possibility, he got to work. From nooks and crannies he pulled knives, a thin wire, several small boxes filled with miniature tools, and finally, from under the cot, a long, razor-edged Bowie knife.

Within five minutes, he stood on the loading dock with three other men. They were armed and dressed in the same dark clothing. All of them, Caine included, had night vision goggles. Caine would bet his life, however, that none of his current companions knew just how well equipped he was.

A glossy, midnight-hued Humvee arrived, and they piled in.

"We really goin' this time, Spike?" one man asked. They'd been drilling, thorough military-style maneuvers, for this event. The big Boss wanted his son, failure was not an option.

"Yeah, long as Pollack does the job taking the kid, this is it. Now shut your trap, I'm driving here."

Caine crossed his arms and slouched in the seat, his mind working at a furious pace. As one of Donovan Walker's mercenary assassins, he had been designated for the recapture of their primary target—Donovan Walker, Jr., now known as Xavier Markham, the boss's son. For Caine, this assignment was the culmination of three years of undercover work for the FBI.

So many things could go wrong. His contact, Tervain, might not receive the message and get Dana and Xavier to the safe house. His fellow mercenaries could screw the pooch and either kill the decoys or Dana Markham and the kid before he got in. The men would murder him if they believed he was a turncoat. The woman, if she survived, or the police, might shoot him if something else went awry.

His sole mission, when it came to it, was to keep Donovan Walker, murderer, drug lord, and mob boss, from regaining possession of the two things he most wanted: his wife—preferably dead—and his only child.

They rumbled over the dock to the waiting freighter. He saw the faint vibration in the hull shiver the tie ropes, which meant she was under power. No doubt once the team departed, the ship would too. No boat, no questions, no evidence—a classic Donovan Walker strategy.

"Holy shit!" The man next to him jerked forward, craning for a better view.

Following his gaze, Caine got the first nasty surprise of the night. His stomach sank when he spied the sleek military helicopter resting on the deck. Menacingly beautiful, the machine's matte paint absorbed the light. This was something neither he nor anyone in his organization had foreseen.

His mission was well and truly screwed.

"When he told us we'd have a shit-kickin' ride, I never expected no helicopter," the thug in front exclaimed. "Donovan rules, for sure."

"Shuffle out, Pollack," his seatmate said, shooting him a quick elbow. Damn, he'd been caught staring like a green kid.

Idiot.

"Chill," he said, returning the elbow with interest as he scanned the docks. "You jump out of a vehicle and run for a ship you're gonna attract a bullet."

"You'd know," came a voice from behind them. A high-pitched, almost boyish giggle accompanied the words. His seatmate's lip curled.

"Let it go." His words blocked the other man's hasty retort. He tensed under Caine's restraining hand, but said nothing more.

"The annoyance," as they called their accomplice in the rear jump seat, began a singsong chant as Caine resumed his scrutiny of the scene. "Walker rules, Walker rules." The noise cut off abruptly as Spike popped the driver's door open and jumped down. Caine released the breath he'd been holding. The man behind them was nuts, literally, but a hell of a disabler. His nimble, mad mind held the wiring diagrams of virtually every alarm system ever made. So far, no configuration had stymied him.

The disembodied chant resumed. A fanatical follower, the annoyance had tattooed the drug lord's name into his forearm. In odd moments, Caine had caught him stroking the inked image, muttering over and over that he would do anything to serve. Anything.

It creeped Caine out to think about it.

"Fuckin' weasel." His seatmate vocalized Caine's line

of thinking. Skill kept the annoyance alive. His crazy cackling was nerve-wracking, especially in close quarters. After the past few months shut up in the warehouse, they all wanted him as dead as Jimmy Hoffa.

Spike returned and jerked the door open. "Move it. Time's a-wastin'."

Caine dropped down from the vehicle's high seat, felt the vibration of the ship's engines through the soles of his boots. The wind slapped the water onto the pilings, and the ocean's tang teased his nostrils. The breeze ruffled his dark hair, reminding him to put on the black knit hat he had tucked in his hip pocket. He saw others doing the same as they made their way to the swaying gangway.

"Party time," Spike said to the waiting captain as he led the group across the deck. Within minutes they were in the helicopter, and the pilot had the engines revving. Power thrummed in the air as the rotors circled. The go-ahead signal thumped on the machine's heavy hide, and they lifted off.

Their target was two hundred miles inland. They would fly along North Carolina's Outer Banks, turning west over the scarcely populated border counties, to avoid the radar at Cherry Hill Air Station. Heading north, they'd cross the line into Virginia's heartland, well beyond range of the searching electronics at the naval base in Virginia Beach.

Under the scope of military radar, the jet engines ate up the miles as the helicopter headed for the outskirts of Richmond. Caine visualized the route. He wished he'd known about the helicopter. There was no way, now, that his FBI colleagues would make it to Dana Markham's house in time to remove her and put decoys in place. He'd been sure it would be at least another two weeks, but had put an emergency plan together as well.

With this, even the emergency plan was shot to hell. The timing, set for driving, would be skewed by at least four hours.

Dana, formerly Mrs. Donovan Walker, and her son were on their own. As the city lights faded behind him, Caine thought, *God help them.*

With no hesitation, Dana strode into her son's room, the dog padding at her side. She slipped a hand over his mouth before shaking his shoulder. They'd practiced midnight escapes, so once she woke him he'd know what to do. As he drew breath to scream, she whispered his name, forestalling it.

"Xavier, he's come."

"Outside?"

"Whisper," she returned, mentally praising her astute ten-year-old while simultaneously praying for his safety. "It's a helicopter, running in silent mode. They'll probably have thermal imaging and sound detection on board, so if you talk in a normal voice it'll be picked up. Let's give 'em something to hear, exactly the way we've practiced. Tell me in a regular voice that you had a nightmare."

"Mom. Hey. Must'a had a bad dream. Sorry to wake you."

"You okay?" The play-acting was killing her.

"Yeah, yeah."

She leaned low. "Go to the hall bath, use it. On my

word, lie on the floor and get as close to that cast iron tub as you can manage."

"What—"

"Just do it." She didn't want to tell him that bullets wouldn't go through cast iron the way they would sheet-rock. Besides, Donovan didn't want to hurt Xavier. On the other hand, he wanted her—the woman who'd sent him to jail—dead, so he could claim his heir.

They rose together. She slid her arm around his waist and hugged him to her side.

Sparing a moment, she cursed the day she'd married Donovan Walker. Nothing made her regret Xavier, but if only she hadn't told Donovan about the boy and then naïvely, foolishly believed in happily ever after.

"Got to go to the bathroom," he said, right on cue.

"Okay, I'll wait and tuck you in."

"Mom . . ." She sensed his fear as he paused in the bathroom doorway.

"I know, I know, you're a big boy. Don't tell me. I'm your mom. I get to do these things." *And please, God, let me do them for a long time,* she prayed. Smiling, she blew a kiss, and mouthed the words, "I love you, Xavier."

Hardening her heart to the anguish she saw in his expression, she leaned down to press her face into Shadow's fur. The shepherd was trained in Schutzhund, German guard training. She whispered her orders in German.

Shadow stiffened under her hands and, before she'd finished speaking, he'd angled his body between Xavier and the door. Ninety-five pounds of muscle, teeth, and power protected her child. In the glow of the nightlight, Xavier caressed the dog's ears, and she caught a glimpse of his countenance, white and strained.

Turning away, she leaned on the wall. With a deep

breath, she mustered her strength. Her strategy was sketchy, but there was no time to improve it. Dread stretched her nerves. Knowing every second counted, she hurried to the guest bedroom, opened the closet, and plucked two small remotes from the box she pulled off the shelf.

There was no telling how many men he'd sent. Any minute now they'd move in. The helicopter couldn't come too close to the house, because of the trees. One man, then, would stay in the chopper. If it was a four-seater, she'd have three to deal with; a six-seater would mean four or five.

Since her ex never wasted resources, her bet was four, which meant a trio on the ground. After all, in Donovan's mind, it was a woman and a kid. How hard could it be?

She needed to go toward her bedroom to keep them guessing. If they had heat-seeking technology, they might wait until she went to the rear of the house. It would be their chance to kill her and not hit Xavier.

Everything she'd learned taking advanced firearms courses and survival skills classes blurred through her mind, a refresher course on high-speed. If this, then that; the mentally projected scenarios changed like the devil's vacation slides.

A shiver ran down her spine. Every trap she'd set would have to work perfectly to get three intruders. If she was lucky, the chopper pilot would bug out after the first explosion.

God, let me be lucky.

In the long wakeful hours, so many nights since she and Xavier had run, she'd worried and prepared. The FBI couldn't convince her Donovan was dead, murdered by his "associates." She knew better. They'd never found a body. He'd talked with her in better times, about faking his death. She knew he'd done it, gone under. Waited. He'd plot and scheme no matter how long it took, then one day, when he believed everyone had relaxed, he'd come for Xavier.

It gave her no satisfaction to realize she'd been right.

The toilet flushed.

She passed the bathroom without a glance at her son. She knew if she did, if she focused too closely on what was happening, she'd lose her nerve.

Stepping around the doorframe and into her room, she paused. Hand on the triggering remotes, she waited for them to make their move. She would give no shot across the bow, no warning that she was aware of their presence; nor would she give any quarter, not when it came to her son's safety. But with so few options of her own, she wouldn't make the first move.

If she'd pegged it right, the ground team would be going for the alarm system. They'd attack when they saw her or when the system went down.

"Three, two, one . . ." she counted in her head. No more had "one" left her lips than the sound of machine gun fire blasted through the night. She dove for the hallway floor, pushing two buttons on the remote.

The roar of the guns didn't quite block out the screaming.

Her first trap had sprung, no doubt electrocuting their alarm disabler with his own wire cutters. Simultaneously, she hit another sequence, setting off small charges in the huge planters on the patio. Shrapnel would be flying with the bullets now.

Glass shattered under the steady barrage, and she heard the television crash to the floor. At least one man still stood, since the rounds continued to tear through her room.

Struggling to be still, she focused on separating the noises outside. Dimly, through the tumultuous wail of the activated house alarm, she heard the renewed clangor of her garden bells and managed a grin. The chopper was on the go. Pressing another sequence, she exploded the barrel at the rear of the lot, spraying the air at her property line with nails, bullets, and chunks of rock. A series of chuffing clangs told her she'd at least hit the helicopter. Now she heard the engine's whine, the whump of the blades. The pilot had slipped out of silent mode and was bugging out.

"Xavier, stay still, there'll be another blast!" she shouted. Adrenaline rushed through her as she set off another charge. It demanded she leap into action, run to protect her son. She could almost feel the waves of fear and longing rolling from her boy as he wailed.

"Mommmmmmmm!"

"Stay on the floor," she hollered.

The house shuddered with the force of the detonation. She clawed at the carpet for balance, pleased, even in her terror. *That will teach you, you monsters, to try to take my son.*

Along with the ringing in her ears, Dana heard sirens. She closed her eyes in thanks, for the barest moment, that help was on the way. They weren't clear yet. She sensed it in her bones. The helicopter was gone, the machine gun fire had ceased, but someone on the ground team might still be alive. That someone could do a lot of damage before the cavalry arrived.

"Xavier, if you love me, stay where you are." Using the

wall, she struggled to stand, steadying her nerves for what came next.

"Mom, no!" His voice quavered.

"Do as I say. The police are coming, don't go with them unless you see me first. It might be a trap."

"The police? Mom—"

"No argument, Xavier," she called to him as she snatched an H and K MP5 submachine gun and extra ammo magazine from the hiding place in the linen closet. She raced downstairs, knowing she had to get them before they reached Xavier.

Rounding the corner into the family room, the first thing she saw was the red-gold flames devouring the bushes beyond the broken windows. The sofa smoldered, and smoke smudged the ceiling above it. *Shit, shit, shit,* she cursed in her mind. She had to find any ground men, deal with them, and get Xavier out before the whole room caught fire.

Heart pounding, she tiptoed through the wreckage with as much stealth as she could manage. She couldn't lose it now. At the door, she flattened herself against the wall, twisted to peer out, then jerked back.

The crackling glow of the blaze lit an unholy scene. On the patio, her teak furniture was alive with fire, as were the vines and trellises on the walls of the house. Fortunately, the brick and siding dampened its progress, and the structure wasn't involved yet.

Two of her huge planter pots were smashed and overturned, the bases disintegrated by the charges she'd implanted. The terrace was blackened by the blast. Beyond the pots, illuminated in the eerie light cast by the burning chairs, she was both relieved and sickened to see a twisted, charred shape lying by the wildly sparking alarm box. Another motionless form lay in the yard.

In front of the blown-out wreckage of the French doors, protected by the other two planters, lay the body of a third man. He was still alive, still twitching. Glass crunched underfoot as she ducked through the mangled wood frames to stand above him, her gun aimed at his head. This man had come to kill, to destroy. Could she shoot him? Anger rose to swamp any trace of remorse. Yes, she could.

Her finger tightened on the trigger as he stirred. Through the haze of her rage, a warning bell rang in her mind. *Don't do it,* it said, and the clamor of that inner voice rose to a shout. He rolled, and she followed the movement. When he looked up and saw the gun, he froze.

Caine opened his eyes to the second nasty shock of the night, followed hard by the third. The woman standing over him held a gun pointed at him with deliberate intent. He knew she saw a hated henchman sent by her ex-husband to kill her and take her son.

With the utmost care, he opened his hands, palm out, in a display of surrender. Death stared at him down the barrel of a gun, not for the first time, but he saw it more keenly than he ever had before. Hot blood ran freely over his brow, a wet, warm trail. His head hurt. He knew he was fading. He wanted to live, needed to. Had to . . . He had to tell her. . . .

Holding onto consciousness with gritted teeth, he struggled to remember the code words, the phrase that would reveal who and what he was.

What the hell was it?

Chapter Two

"I come from Salem with news. . . ." The man lying on the ground blurted the words as his hands fell limply to the stones. With a jerk, Dana raised the gun.

Holy crap, he was FBI.

"How the hell . . . ?" she wondered aloud. "Doesn't matter." She cursed under her breath as she bent to beat at his smoking clothes. The growling note of heavy engines and the fire crew's sirens could now be heard distinctly. From the sound of it, they'd be there within minutes. Should she hide him? Would the police know how to handle it? She had seconds to decide.

The tight grip of his hand, clamping over her wrist had her swinging the gun down in reaction. Fortunately for them both, she had good reflexes and belayed the strike before it landed.

"I have to get out of here, they can't find me. I can't blow my cover."

"You're injured. You need a doctor," she protested.

"It's not bad. Help me up. I'm sure I can stand. If the police expose the covert op, you, your son, and I will be toast before the week's out."

Conviction rang in his voice, so she took him at his word. He had the code, which meant he was Federal and knew Tervain. Since Dana had devised the cipher for this sort of situation herself, she had to at least listen. The main objective was to protect her son.

Leaning heavily on her arm, he rose. When he tried to walk, however, he almost collapsed.

"You can't run, not with that leg." She pulled his arm over her shoulder. "Which means you can't get off the property before the cops and firefighters get here."

Making her decision, Dana turned them toward the house. She didn't want to leave him in her hidden room, especially injured, but if he insisted on secrecy, so be it. "Come on, I have a panic room, we have to hurry."

They made their way through the debris and headed for the basement door. Even at a hobble, they got down quickly. She didn't turn on the lights at the bottom of the stairs, concealing her actions as she slipped a key from its hiding place on top of a picture frame. "Follow my lead, and you won't bump into anything."

Through the blown-out basement windows, she heard the sirens come closer. From the noise, she guessed they were turning into the driveway. She hadn't opened the gate, so they'd be stuck there for a moment. Even so, she didn't have much time.

"Hold onto the wall," she ordered, shrugging him off to brace on the wall. With three deft motions, she shoved a wall hanging aside and opened the locks on a concealed door. "Go in. There's food and water, lots of first aid supplies. I'll come for you as soon as I can. Don't expect me for several hours at the very least. Clean up, get out of those clothes if anything in there fits you." As she turned away, he grabbed her arm.

Off balance, she stumbled into his chest. With no rhyme or reason, she felt a surge of attraction, heat. What the hell?

She tried to pull away, but he held her tight. "Already falling for me," he rasped, and gave her a cocky grin, which faded to grim seriousness as he tugged her close in a one-armed, comradely hug. "You're one gutsy lady, Dana Markham."

He released her and hopped forward into the box-like room. As she closed him in, their eyes met.

"Hey," he called, and she halted the door's swing. "Thanks for not shooting me."

Her last image of him was of a tall shadowy form, braced on one leg, the other carefully held off the ground.

Slamming the door, she twisted the locks. A surprised laugh escaped her.

Giving herself a mental shake, she pocketed the key and kicked into high gear. She had no time for pondering a hug and a devil's grin, even if the devil did have great lips.

And a hard, muscular chest.

Her traitorous mind added that last bit to taunt her. Why on earth had she noticed either of those things?

Running across the basement, she paused at the stairs when she saw blood on the carpet and at the basement door. Darker imprints from his boots were barely visible, thank goodness, and she scuffed her shoe over those.

The movement left a dark smear along the carpet. Lifting her foot, she checked the leather. A slit gaped along the side and the sock and skin underneath were sliced as well. It didn't look deep, but blood oozed over the leather as she watched.

Well, hell. Her stomach pitched, and a near-hysterical giggle escaped her lips.

"I kill two guys, deal with a fricking FBI agent, and my own blood wigs me out." Her wavering voice echoed in the stairwell, making her realize how close to a full-blown panic attack she was.

She had to lock it down and get Xavier out. Then she could engage in a fit of the vapours. But not now.

"Get it together, girl," she ground out the self-admonition as she dashed through the kitchen.

Her mind whirling, she worked out her story. The blood on the rug was easy to explain as her own, a check of the downstairs. If he'd left the blood trail, it would have been impossible to conceal.

Running now, she called for Xavier and Shadow to come. The sound of their rushing feet gladdened her heart. Rounding the corner into the foyer, Dana was in time to meet her son's desperate hug and keep the fire chief from breaking in.

Throwing open the door, she and Xavier began the first of a long series of explanations.

An hour later, huddled in a blanket, Xavier sat on the bumper of the ambulance while the EMT tended to Dana's bloody foot.

"You really need to go to the hospital, ma'am, to get a tetanus shot." The EMT had said the same thing, or a variation thereof, repeatedly since she first started working on the cut.

Smiling, Dana thanked the woman and declined again. "Since you're sure it doesn't need stitches, I'd rather have you deal with it so I can be here for the fire department or police with any questions."

"But you'll need to stay off of it, and your shoes, they're ruined—"

"I know, and I will. And," Dana quickly forestalled the other woman, "I'll go right away for that tetanus shot. My doctor should be able to get me in for that tomorrow. Besides, as I said, I'm needed here."

With a final twist of tape, the woman finished her bandaging. A waver of headlights caught Dana's eye, and she squinted through the glare of emergency flashers. Two dark sedans pulled along the driveway and parked next to the police cars. Four people approached, silhouetted in the glow of the fire truck's headlights.

From his perch, Shadow's leash in hand, Xavier watched as well. He shifted restlessly, and she knew he recognized what, if not who, had arrived. Federal agents. When he glanced her way, she was ready with a reassuring smile. "They'd come as soon as they heard, of course," she said softly. "They warned us something was coming."

They didn't have to wait long for the agents to approach the parked ambulance.

"Mrs. Markham," an older man spoke first, automatically flipping a leather wallet open to show his credentials. "I'm Agent Parlier with the FBI."

He didn't quite mask his surprise when she held out her hand for the identification. Pain and deceit, Donovan's enduring legacy, had taught her caution. Thanks to him, she'd recognize forged ID. Scanning it, she searched for telltale signs. Seeing none, she returned it and let the muscles in her neck relax a fraction.

"And your associates?" she questioned.

At his nod, a man and a woman approached to present their credentials. "Agent Booth and Agent Sears." From behind him another man came forward as well. "You know Agent Tervain."

Relief flooded her as Tervain's familiar face appeared in the light. Parlier and his agents seemed competent, but she knew Tervain, trusted him.

"Thank you." She handed the wallets to each of them. "I'm sure you've guessed what happened here tonight." Her voice was grim, and she knew it held accusation as well. She directed her comments to Tervain as much as to the others. "So much for your assertion that you were tracking him closely. Then again, as of a month ago, you weren't even willing to admit he was alive, so I shouldn't be surprised. At least you believed me, Tervain. That's something, I guess."

Agent Parlier had the grace to look embarrassed. "Yes, ma'am. Why don't you tell us what happened?" He seemed to finally notice Xavier. "Agent Booth can walk your son over to the house, maybe they can get you the socks and shoes the EMT mentioned."

At her raised eyebrow, he admitted he'd asked the EMT about Dana's injury. It annoyed her, but she let it go. However, she wasn't going to dismiss Xavier because the agent believed her son to be a young, impressionable boy. They were in this together and she never forgot it.

"Xavier, do you want to stay here for the recap or go to the house? Your choice." When he met her eyes, she nodded and held out a hand. "We're a team, always."

"Always," Xavier repeated. He rewarded her with a relieved grin, and he grasped her hand and started the complex handshake routine they had developed in fun.

That completed, he stood, back straight and head erect. "I'll go to the house and get your shoes." He flipped a measuring glance at the agent who was to accompany him, then peered at Dana. "Is she gonna be able to get me and Shadow past the fire and police lines?"

Shadow. Now that was a problem. The dog might alert someone to their visitor in the hidden room if Xavier went wandering through the house. "There's a lot of glass and debris, honey. Since the agent will be with you and is, I presume, armed?" She waited until the woman flipped her jacket open to show a gun. "Why don't you leave Shadow with me?"

Xavier searched her face, trying to see if she was warning him in any way. She gave a minute shake of her head and a smile to reassure him. Evidently satisfied, he handed her Shadow's leash and headed off toward the house, the agent in tow.

"Nice boy you got there."

She leveled a stare at Agent Sears, and within seconds the agent averted his gaze. Parlier cleared his throat, turning her attention his way. "Uh, Mrs. Markham, we do need to chat. Agent Sears, if you'd make sure we're undisturbed? Agent Tervain, if you'd take notes?"

Propping one foot on the heavy bumper, Parlier leaned in. His smile was friendly, but his eyes were flat. Cop eyes.

"Now, start at the beginning, and don't leave anything out."

Gritting her teeth at the condescension in his tone, Dana told her tale. When she outlined her defenses, the agents exchanged surprised glances.

It irritated the shit out of her.

"Contrary to your assurances," her voice dripped sarcasm. "I knew Donovan wasn't dead, and I knew he wouldn't rest until he found Xavier. When you finally admitted it, I took quite a number of precautions. I can also tell you this won't be his last attempt. What are you going to do about it?"

"If I might interrupt?" Tervain's piercing gaze flicked from her to Parlier and returned. The frown on his saturnine face cautioned her to silence. "Do you know, Mrs. Markham, if anyone actually made it into the house? As you and I discussed last week, we discovered Donovan was still alive and we traced the organization. The data was classified, so I wasn't at liberty to tell you we'd embedded a man on the inside."

The emphasis he placed on his inability to discuss the matter told her Parlier didn't know about the code phrases she and Tervain had arranged. Interesting. Why would one sector of the FBI keep secrets from another? When he continued speaking, she filed the info for later consideration.

"Our last transmission from the inside agent indicated they'd discovered your location and had been given orders to hit your house next week. We were planning to relocate you and Xavier tomorrow."

Anger rose, hot, hard and soul-deep. "You knew they were coming?" she grated, her hand shooting out to grab the man's tie and draw him to her. At her side, Shadow's rumbling growl made a counterpoint to her staccato words. "You knew and gave me no warning? You risked my son's life?" She had yanked him so close she saw the flecks of black in his blue irises. "You bastard."

Agent Parlier touched Dana's hand, trying to loosen her grip to give Tervain some air. At Shadow's deepening growl, Parlier desisted. Talking fast, he attempted to justify their actions. "We were supposed to have several more days at least, possibly even weeks. Instead, the agent was barely able to let us know the time had been altered to tonight."

His voice was reasonable, calm. But as he continued, she detected a note of concern, as if she might not release Tervain. "Mrs. Markham, please. Our agent either couldn't tell us or didn't know Walker had the helicopter. They got here far faster than we had any reason to believe they would. Had we known, even an hour earlier, we'd have had you out of here, and put decoys in your place."

"Decoys?" Dana knew her eyes must be blazing because both agents recoiled. "Decoys? That wouldn't have been worth shit," she snarled. "He'll come at me until I'm dead and Xavier is his. If you had a man on the inside, why the hell didn't you kill Donovan and end this, once and for all?"

Rubbing his throat, Tervain answered. "It doesn't work that way, Mrs. Markham. You know that."

Parlier forestalled her nasty comment. "He's right. We have to follow procedure and the law, even when we don't care for it."

"We're committed to taking him down, Mrs. Markham. We've discussed this. You know how much we want him. It's a priority. Perhaps I should have emphasized that more."

Puzzlement was fast matching her anger. She knew Donovan was a priority. Why was Tervain reiterating it, emphasizing it yet again, when they'd talked just last week? He seemed to be trying to distract her from pursuing her questions, but why?

"It's even more of a priority now, Mrs. Markham. They also hit the decoy house, the one we had created and put in place to distract them from you. Two agents, one woman and one who was to play your son."

"And?" There was a reason he'd told her this, but she couldn't fathom it at the moment.

"All dead."

Her heartbeat faltered, her chest clenched in pain and she dropped her head, fighting tears. More dead at Donovan's hand because he couldn't, wouldn't let her go. Her freedom, her life was worse to him than anything, since it was she who had betrayed him. That betrayal had set her free in one sense, and doomed her in another. He would never let her go, let her live, while he too was alive.

"Mrs. Markham, we have to know," Parlier interjected, urgency in every line of his body. "Did you see our agent? Did you have contact with anyone? Our inside man should have been with this team."

As she lifted her head, Tervain met Dana's stare, nodded, unseen by Parlier. As further encouragement, he added, "Everyone on the ground is confirmed dead. They've put out the fire, by the way. There's one dead by the alarm box and one in the main part of the yard. Your booby traps, I presume?"

When she nodded, Parlier jumped in. "The police are already talking about a ground search. I need to know what you know before I give them the go-ahead."

Whatever was going on here, it would wait. She needed to get the agent some help. And she needed to get Tervain alone.

She would grieve the agents who'd given their lives for her, and for Xavy, later.

"Let them search, they won't find him. He's in my panic room in the basement." When their faces lit with relief, she continued. "He's hurt, but I didn't have time to work on him. He didn't want the EMTs or police to see him."

The tension seemed to drain out of Parlier and Tervain smiled. "Excellent. We have to get him out, but we need to get the cops and firefighters out of the house before we do."

A variety of comments jumped to mind, none of them complimentary. She remained angry that they'd kept her in the dark about Donovan. *Then again,* the mental voice of reason chimed in, *she had known anyway, so what was the big deal?* "I'll let him out as soon as you clear the house."

"No need for you to go—"

Cutting him off, Dana spoke. "Yes, actually there is."

"If you'd let us—"

"No, sir, I won't. We've been in protective custody twice before. I'm sure you're going to want to put us there again. As *nice* as your staff can be, and the US Marshals as well, a secure location isn't home. This time, I'm not leaving my house without some of our things. You clear my taking stuff from the crime scene with the cops. While you do, Agent Tervain and I can go to the house, get your man."

Beyond Parlier's line of sight, Tervain grinned. When his compatriot turned, his expression revealed neutral patience.

"You heard the lady, Tervain," Parlier snapped. "Don't walk. Get the car and drive. I'll get the locals out of the way. Load up and get them to a hotel. If Agent Bradley can walk, send him over the fence at the rear of the property, pick him up on the road, if not, the car."

"Yes, sir," Tervain's reply was clipped, virtually military. He trotted off and, within a minute, he returned with the car. He offered Dana his hand and a boyish grin. "If you and your protector will hop in, we'll get this show on the road."

Putting aside her frustration, Dana accepted his help and the ride.

When they drove up in front of the house, Parlier got out and headed right for the fire captain. Before she got to the front door, the firefighters and officers were walking away from the house. Parlier was making good on his word.

Glancing around, she winced for her poor flower beds. With the equipment and water, they were beyond saving. Xavier and Agent Booth met them in the foyer. Xavier carried a pair of Dana's sneakers, socks, and a fully laden backpack.

"Mom," her son's voice held both concern and relief. She hugged him as he hurried over. She sat down momentarily to put on the socks and shoes, leaving them unlaced to accommodate the bandage on her foot.

"Xavy, I see you've gotten a couple of things. We've got clearance to take what we need with us this time, if you want to get anything else from your room." She saw his relieved grin, and he plopped his pack on the floor and sped up the stairs. Agent Booth, caught off guard, hurried after him.

"He's learned to move fast," Tervain commented.

"We both have, as you well know."

Tervain nodded and said, "Let's get going."

So he wasn't ready to clue her in. Exasperating, but predictable. Changing the subject, Dana spoke briskly. "I'm going to put a few things in a bag here in the laundry room." She pointed to a room off the kitchen. "After that, I'll see if there's anything left of my room and my clothes."

"But we need to get you out of here, and Agent Bradley—"

"Can wait for ten more minutes. I know you want us out of here fast. I'm also aware that you don't really want to wait for me and Xavy to pack anything."

The sheepish look on Tervain's face told her she'd guessed right. Limping away from him, she grabbed another backpack from its hook on the laundry room wall. She did her best to ignore the smoke that smudged the cheery walls she'd painted herself. The gentle smell of detergent and fabric softener was overpowered by the acrid stench of burning insulation. Even through the walls, she heard the atonal hiss and buzz of emergency radios.

Putting the filled pack next to Xavier's, she followed him upstairs. The breakers had flipped, and the lights were off, but the white glare of the fire department's emergency lights lit the room. It was a picture of destruction.

A lump rose in her throat at the wanton devastation. Forcing herself not to cry, she got to work. The closet doors were relatively unscathed. Flicking them open, she grabbed her "run-bag." It was already packed with money, sundries, and several changes of clothes for both Xavier and herself. Setting it out, she pulled another duffel down and loaded clothes, her cosmetic kit, and jewelry into it.

Picking her way across the fractured wood and avoiding tufts of mattress that littered the floor, she reached under the bed to retrieve a locked metal box.

"The boy and Agent Booth are packing some favorite books. They'll go right to the car when they're done," Tervain said.

"That's good." Dana slipped past him to peer into Xavier's room. "Honey, don't take everything. Get what you need for right now and for a few days. We'll come home again."

At his hurried assent, she headed for the foyer. Tervain did the same.

"Do you think it's wise to tell him you'll be back?"

"Agent, we may be going with you into custody for now, but you can't keep us. I'm going to file my insurance claims and have my house rebuilt. If he's going to keep coming for me until you catch him or kill him, I sure as hell am going to pick the battleground. I think tonight's an example that on my turf, with my rules, I stand a lot better chance of surviving."

Framed in the basement door, she faced him, and anger welled within her once more. "So far, *my* precautions have kept my boy and me alive. Your people haven't done squat. So, yes, I'll tell Xavier that, because it's true."

Tervain remained silent as they made their way downstairs. Concealing her actions with her body, Dana unlocked the door. Hand poised on the knob, she knocked in a sequence of twos and threes saying, "Everyone's high in Salem tonight."

From inside came the sound of a lock being drawn. She twisted the knob and dragged it open. A light burned in the room, so he'd gotten the mini-generator working. Agent Bradley stood propped on the wall by the door, his gun drawn.

"Hello again, Mrs. Markham. Oh, and I guess I need to say that 'Nineteen people sure can swing.'" He provided the counterphrase with a grimace of distaste. "Who the hell came up with these passwords, the Marquis de Sade?"

Chapter Three

"Before de Sade's time," Dana quipped, ignoring the gun. Going into the room, she pulled her Swiss Army knife off the shelf and tucked it into her pocket.

"I guess you got my message." Caine's wry comment was directed at Tervain.

"Not fast enough for this, dammit."

"Parker and Soli?"

"Taken out in the first round. There wasn't a whisper at the decoy house before they hit. We've got a leak. Or a plant inside."

"I figured that, when we flew here instead of the decoy house." Caine tucked the gun away and hopped to the door, ready to head out. "Soli covered my ass in Afghanistan. She was a good agent."

Dana's heart twisted at the thought of the dead agents, but she ruthlessly shoved her horror away. She knew from painful experience that once she'd been found, she needed to change locations. Quickly. In spite of her bravado about coming back, she wanted to leave. Soon. So it was her turn to remind everyone to hustle.

"They were good agents, and they wouldn't thank us

for standing around, letting Donovan have more time to get at us."

"Right." Tervain snapped to the matter at hand. "Caine, how fast can you travel?"

With a pained expression, Caine shook his head. "Not fast. My head's stopped ringing, but I've got a gash in my thigh. It's not bad, but it needs a stitch, maybe two. If there's a choice, I'd rather not run on it."

Tervain turned to Dana. "Let's get him to the car."

She nodded, juggling the options with lightning speed. "If you've got a leak, you don't want Booth or Sears in on this. You get Xavier and our bags loaded and send Booth down the hill to Parlier. I'm strong enough to get your agent to the car. Turn off the porch lights. He's tall, but with the dark clothes, he shouldn't be visible."

They both looked at her, consternation written on their faces. "How do you know so much about this?"

"Are you kidding?" Her laugh was sharp as a razor as she pushed past them and motioned them out of the room. "You know who I was, regrettably, married to. How do you think I'm still alive after six years of running from that bastard?" She shut down the lights and generator, locked the door, and slipped the concealing panel into place. "Okay Tervain, what's the plan? Are you sending Booth away?"

"She's right," Caine said, pushing off the wall to loop an arm over Dana's proffered shoulder. "The fewer who know, the fewer who tell."

"Agreed. I'll tap the horn when we're set." Tervain was already heading to the stairs as he spoke.

"We'd better get started." Caine's voice was as deep and silky as the night. "The trip up the stairs may be slow going."

"I know. We'll lean on each other since my foot isn't in great shape either."

"Your foot?"

"I cut it when I came to find you on the patio," she explained as they hobbled to the base of the stairs.

"Ouch, that's a bad bargain."

"We're both a bad bargain, Agent Caine."

"Bradley. My name's Caine Bradley." It came out on an "oomph" as they limped from one riser to the next.

Partially supporting him, Dana was glad for the sturdy railing. The man was heavy. She grunted again, bracing as he realigned his weight to turn on the landing. A glance at his profile revealed a crooked nose over generous lips and dark skin, stained with soot. A long, thin scar scored a line down the side of his face. Injured and covered in smoke residue, he still exuded menace, as if he were one of the bad guys. This certainly wasn't her picture of someone working on the side of the right.

Then again, her libido recognized a hunk when it was pressed up against one. Her pulse was doing a jig. Rolling her eyes at her irreverent hormones, she struggled to the top of the stairs with Caine.

Within minutes, they were secreted in the dark sedan and speeding away into the night. Dana's emotions took a depressing swing as she sat slumped in the front seat. Despair rolled over her in waves. Would she and Xavier ever be safe, would they ever be free?

Running one hand through her damp hair, Dana desperately tried to relax. Her other arm, wrapped around her sleeping boy, was beginning to tingle from lack of circulation. They'd been at the rural motel for an hour, and it was now a couple of hours before dawn. She'd managed a quick shower while Tervain stood guard and the physician they'd called in had treated Caine.

As Parlier returned the doctor to wherever they'd found him, Dana, Caine, and Tervain discussed options. All the choices were unpleasant, and they finally agreed to sleep on the various ideas. With the insouciance of youth, Xavier had slung one arm over Shadow, snuggled into the curve of Dana's arm, and promptly fallen asleep.

Alone in the dark, reaction hit her hard. Fighting down her shudders, she soaked the pillow with silent tears. Her body ached from the exertions of the night and from holding herself rigid to suppress the wracking sobs which struggled for release. All the "might have beens" ran through her head, haunting her with specters of Xavier's death and the annihilation of all she held dear.

The loss of the decoy agents was equally painful. Their faces, drawn by her imagination, flashed before her mind's eye, reproaching her for living, for surviving. She wanted to rail at them that she might be alive, but she was still in bondage. No option they'd discussed would allow her to be free, to ensure that Xavier would be free. Nothing was guaranteed but a continued life on the run.

Exhausted by her horrid visions, she tried to focus on the next direction. The agents had argued about what to do. They wanted her to go underground again. The difficulty was, as Caine pointed out, she'd been as deep undercover as they could make her, and it hadn't protected her. They'd admitted that her wits and foresight had saved her, as well as Caine, but had no solutions for how to make it foolproof.

Xavier grunted in his sleep, snuggling closer. As he

turned, his head rolled off her arm. The rush of returning blood flow distracted her, but only for a moment.

Caine was the one who'd broached the scariest plan. The thought of the confrontation he proposed made her blood run cold in her very bones. Rather than think about it, she considered the man. Obviously, he'd been undercover for more than the three months since Tervain had contacted her and set the decoy house. He'd been sent to watch Donovan, but her ex had been a step ahead. She wondered how it must feel to lead the kind of double existence he did, acting the villain to catch a monster.

In spite of his job, he seemed to have a sense of humor, a boyish streak, she decided, remembering his joking in the basement room. Dark humor perhaps, but humor. She smiled at the memory of his hug and the "thanks for not shooting me" line.

It had been a good, strong hug. Her mind wandered toward Caine's hard body, his dark eyes.

Ruthlessly, she shut down that mental journey. She had no business thinking about him, or anyone, that way.

Instead, she forced herself to redirect, to think about their next gambit. Knowing her ex's temper, Donovan's fury at the near-miss would be lethal and drive him even harder to get his son. Her first impulse was to take Xavy and run. Just as quickly, she discarded the idea. She needed the FBI. She couldn't find a place to hide, manage Xavier, and keep track of Donovan all at the same time.

Could she trust the agents to put Xavier first? No. They wanted Donovan badly enough that they'd risk her son if they had to. Could she do it on her own? No.

The impasse kept sleep at bay.

Caine's idea wasn't any worse than living with one ear cocked for stealth helicopters or ever awaiting a knife from behind. She examined his proposal. If she took his suggestion, Xavier would be protected while she deliberately served herself as bait on a platter. But *would* Xavier be safe? Who *would* Xavier turn to if it all went wrong and Donovan got to her, killed her?

A noise from the next room cut short her pondering, and Shadow emitted a low growl. She sat up. In an instant, Caine was beside her. He gripped her arm and gave a quick squeeze before shielding them with his body.

"Stay still." The words were a mere whisper of sound. She silenced the dog as Caine crouched, his bulk a darker shadow in the black of the room.

"Caine," a voice whispered, as the door opened then closed again. "Caine?"

"Tervain?"

"Get them out of here. Parlier should have checked in two hours ago. I can't raise him. It might be nothing, but my gut says something's wrong. With this situation, we can't take any chances. Go for the mountain house. I have your cell and Dana's. Stay there till you hear from me."

"And if we don't?" The question was terse, and Dana felt the tension radiating from the man next to her.

"Go under, as a family. There are papers in the lockbox at the house, they'll work for you both. Take the Escalade. No lights and move fast. If the worst happens, contact Hopkins, and pray he's not the leak." There was a metal clink and the door shut.

Dana's every nerve went on high alert. She slid out of the bed, put on her jacket and shoes. Tying the laces, she sucked in a pained breath as the fabric tightened over her bandaged foot. Caine's hand closed around her wrist.

"Xavier?" he questioned.

"Still asleep. Should I wake him?" Their bags were by the door where she'd left them. The one thing she'd allowed Xavier to unpack was his bear, and that was clutched in his arms. She could scoop up boy, bear, and baggage and be out the door in a flash, Shadow at her heels.

"No, not yet. If you need to use the bathroom, do it. It'll be several hours before we have another chance."

Taking stock, Dana decided she'd better go. He touched her arm. She jumped. The man must have the eyes of a cat. "Don't flush."

Stifling an irrational snort of laughter, she nodded. Trailing her hand along the bedspread for guidance, she quickly made her way to the lavatory. On the return trip, she held out a hand to feel the way. Within seconds, she connected with a hard, cloth-covered thigh. "Sorry," she whispered as a blush warmed her face. Two inches to the left would have been really embarrassing.

"Take the keys and the bags. I'll get the boy."

She started to protest, but bit her lip instead. It was faster and easier for her to carry the bags and take Shadow. At twice her size and strength, even with an injury, Caine would manage Xavy better. As hard as it was to depend on someone else, she held out her hand for the keys. When her searching touch grazed his bicep, she froze. His fingers slid down her arm and a laden metal ring jingled into her palm.

"Shadow, with me," she whispered.

In two strides she was at the door. With the deftness of practice, she slipped the backpack onto her shoulders and looped the duffel bag and purse straps into the crook of her elbow. She put her hand on the knob.

A surge of body heat announced Caine's presence behind her, and she shuddered. She hadn't heard him at all, not even a rustle of sheets as he picked up her son.

"Which way?"

"Go right, out the door. Ten paces to the end of the building. Down the stairs, hard right at the bottom, and through the breezeway. Car's two slots down."

"An Escalade, Tervain said. That's a big Caddy SUV, right?"

"Dark blue, tinted windows, DC plates."

Tightening her grip on the keys, she slowly turned the knob, silently releasing the latch. "Ready?"

"Go."

Opening the door a fraction, Dana peered into the erratically lit parking lot. The balcony rail was iron and allowed a clear view to the area below. The lone motion came from the moths circling the yellow sodium lights.

Heart pounding, Dana slid the security bar over, propped the door open, and slipped out of the room. Quiet as a mouse, she and the dog headed for the stairs. It took everything she had not to check over her shoulder. What if Caine was the leak? What if he was taking them to Donovan?

With ruthless precision, Dana excised that mental blip. There wasn't anything she could do if he was. She'd thrown the dice and had to go with the roll. Her gut told her Caine was one of the good guys. Given his countenance and demeanor, he was more of a black knight than a white one, but he was a knight nonetheless.

The scramble of those musings got her to the car. She unlocked it with the key, not trusting the unfamiliar gadgetry. It would suck if the power locks flashed the lights or sounded the horn. Should she get in? Crank the engine? Why hadn't she simply taken Xavier and run? Where was Caine?

The last question had barely surfaced when he appeared, sliding past her so she could open the rear driver's side door for him to set Xavier on the seat. Xavier was awake, his eyes wide with fear. She pressed a finger to her lips, reinforcing the silence. When he nodded, she smiled at him.

Still tangled in the blanket from the bed, the boy scooted into the car, and Shadow followed. Caine piled the bags onto the seat and floor and eased the door closed.

His hands clasped her upper arms, he pulled her forward and leaned down. Close as an embrace, his breath shivered the skin of her neck. Every sense in her body responded to him. She cursed her hormones and their wretched timing, and tried to focus when he spoke.

"You drive. Left out of the lot, onto 64 West."

Releasing her, he walked around the end of the truck with the barest trace of a limp. She climbed into the spacious vehicle at the same time as Caine. Their eyes locked, and she saw grim determination carved on his features. She slipped behind the wheel and found the switch to kill the dome lights, all the while wondering what the heck she was going to do with this odd, disturbing man.

Within minutes they were out of the lot and onto the road, heading west. In the rearview mirror, she studied Xavier's white face, and the darkness beyond it. Reaching behind the seat, she searched for his hand. "It's going to be okay, honey. We're going to another safehouse. Agent Tervain is worried about a leak, so we're going into the mountains until he can figure out what's going on." His fingers were limp for a moment, then strengthened as he gripped her hard.

He let go before saying, "Okay, Mom."

The car was quiet for several minutes. She heard Xavier shifting around. "You all right back there?"

"Yeah." A pause, then, "Mom, what about him?"

"Who?"

"Agent Bradley. Why's he going too?"

They had introduced Xavier to Caine last night simply as one of the agents. She hadn't had time to tell him anything else. It took a very little time to fill in the blanks. Xavier asked a few questions, sharp ones that proved he'd figured out most of what she hadn't said and a bit more as well. She sighed. It was a sad fact that her little boy knew so much about the worst of the world at ten than most suburbanites realized in their whole lives.

Throughout the entire exchange Caine remained mostly silent, adding a spare comment or two as clarification for both Dana and Xavier.

"How much further is it?" The typical kid question had her smiling in spite of the circumstance.

She looked over at Caine, and he cast her an answering smirk. "It's about a hundred seventy miles, so about two and a half hours, maybe three depending on how much back-tracking we have to do."

Reflexively, Dana checked the gas gauge and considered where nearby cities might be. Three quarters full. If they were going west-northwest, they were headed into the Virginia mountains. Beyond Charlottesville, probably. Maybe more north toward DC, or farther west, toward Tennessee. She ran the options and routes in her mind.

"We gonna get to go to the bathroom?"

Caine glanced over the seat and nodded.

"Yes, we'll stop at some point for gas. You need a bathroom break now, or are you okay?"

"I'm okay." Xavy paused a minute, then said, "Did you get our stuff, or did we have to leave it?"

"We got it." She smiled at his delighted response. "No rummaging around though. Try and get some sleep, honey. Are you belted in?"

His faint snicker reassured her, and she grinned in response. Quick to discover the car's secrets, Xavier was soon reclining the seat and arranging the purloined blanket to his satisfaction, using his duffel as a pillow. A swell of pride filled her. He was resilient, her boy. Resourceful. She wished he didn't have to be, but thanked the good Lord that he rolled with the craziness of their situation.

She mentally revisited her choices and wondered how life would have been different if she'd made other ones along the way. It all circled around to Xavier. If she'd done things another way, he wouldn't exist, and that was untenable. She suppressed another sigh, recognizing that this was always her pattern, and the conclusion was always the same.

A creak of leather from the passenger seat reminded her that she wasn't alone. Caine made no comment about her driving or the banter with her son. Nor did he break the silence. As they passed out of the well-lit streets, she flicked on the lights and turned onto I-64. As the miles flew by, she let herself wonder about him. Who was this man, this black knight, as she had dubbed him? Maybe it was time to find out.

"Have you worked for the FBI for a long time, Agent Bradley?"

"Fifteen years."

She waited for him to elaborate. When he said no more, she tried again. "Do you have a family?"

"No."

Uh-oh, bad topic. She could tell by the short bark of his reply. She searched her mind for another conversational gambit. The reflection of a highway eatery sign reminded her that he hadn't eaten at the hotel. The other agents had brought her and Xavier a snack before leaving.

"Are you hungry? Should we find a drive-thru?"

From the corner of her eye, she saw the faint glimmer of teeth. Was that a smile?

"No. We need distance between us and the hotel. For now, drive. I'll tell you where to turn." He seemed content to ride in silence. After an hour on the road, the quiet jiggled her nerves. All the horrid outcomes she'd wept over circled around to haunt her again.

"Mind if I turn on the radio?"

"No."

"A man of few words," she muttered and switched the knob. It was tuned to a talk radio show, so she pressed scan, tapping the button until she found music.

"All the hits of the seventies, eighties, and nineties," the DJ's voice crooned.

That would work.

"What do they say now that it's the two-thousands?"

Dana didn't realize she'd made the comment out loud until Caine's chuckle rumbled in the darkness, making her swerve.

Flustered, she laughed as well.

"Sorry. I talk to myself a lot."

"Doesn't bother me. Can't say I've wondered about that particular thing, however."

"I don't know why I did. Anyway, I guess the stations that play twenty-first century tunes don't care. They're too busy fending off iPods and Napster-type download companies and worrying about market share."

"True."

Somehow the exchange broke the tension, and she began to relax. The absence of small talk or any direction bothered her, and kept trying her patience, but she tried to let the darkness and the car's rumble soothe her. She found herself humming along with a song, her mind empty of anything but the words.

"Exit here."

"This takes us to this cabin?"

"No."

"And we're going off here because . . . ?"

"I said to."

That did it. Dana's irritation rose to the breaking point. Her earlier logic flew out the window. She took the exit and jerked to a halt on the shoulder.

This time, it was her turn to be monosyllabic. "Get. Out."

If she hadn't been totally serious, his baffled amazement would have amused her. She reached over and unlatched his seat belt. "Now open the door and go." She unlocked the doors. "You're a super spy guy, you'll be fine. Get out."

"What in the hell are you talking about?"

"I'm talking about you getting out of the car right now. I'm bloody sick and tired of being lied to, pushed around, and kept in the dark." Her temper at a boil, Dana turned in the seat to face him. "No thanks to your organization, we're on the run. Again. And now it's not only from Donovan but possibly one of *your* people as well. Yeah, I needed that added bonus," she snarled, her voice ripe with sarcasm. "So, if you're going to be all mysterious and 'need-to-know' on me, then you can hitchhike your sorry butt back to whatever cave you crawled out of. Xavier and I have been saving our own asses for a while now. We can take it from here."

"Mom, what's wrong?" Xavier asked in a sleep-filled voice.

"Nothing, sweetie. We're simply letting the nice man go."

"Dana, lock the doors, put it in gear, and get going."

"Fuck you," she said conversationally, ignoring his scowl. He could force her, probably hurt her. Her mind was busy building scenarios, planning how to get him off balance, fend him off when he attacked.

"I'm a lousy lay."

The comment brought her up short. It didn't compute. "What?"

His grin, wide and flashing, disarmed her, and her anger melted into confusion. "That changed your state, didn't it?"

He was making fun of her. She mentally stiffened her spine. "It doesn't change anything. Since I'm not going to sleep with you, I don't give a shit if you're Superman in bed. Get out of the car. Now."

"Lordy, you have the mother voice going strong, even when you're mad." He shook his head and she saw the continuing glint of his smile. She wanted to punch him. He must have seen the venom in her glance, so he held his hands out in supplication.

"You're right, you need to know. We're going to a

cabin in western Virginia, in the mountains near the state line. I want to get off here, double back, check for pursuit. If it's clear, we'll take the parkway and smaller roads. I know the turns, not the road names. Once we get there, we wait for word."

Leaving the decision in her court, he merely watched. The seat squeaked behind them. A quick glance in the mirror showed her Xavier was awake, listening.

Part of her wanted to throw Caine Bradley out on his ear for being cocky, dangerous, and working for the FBI. The sane, logical part of her was on a mental rant. He'd given her what she wanted. He'd told her the plan as he knew it so far. She'd had to force his respect, demand he treat her as a partner in a difficult situation. But he had. What kind of example did she set if she threw him out now?

A childish one, she decided, hating that it was true. Dammit, she *wanted* to pitch him out on his ear and screech off into the night, laughing.

Instead, she put the car in drive and eased the big vehicle down the ramp. Turning at the bottom, she cruised smoothly back onto I-64, and heard his seatbelt click. From behind, her son's sleepy voice called, "That's seventy-five cents you owe me, Mom."

Oh, hell. Even thinking the curse word made her wince. "You're right. I'll give it to you later."

"'Kay." The word slurred as he conked out again.

"If I see even a hint of a smile on your lips, Agent Bradley, your a——, your posterior is out the door." She turned to him, daring him to crack a smile.

"Not me. Had a humor-ectomy. Mandatory when you join the FBI," he quipped, his face as straight as a poker.

She couldn't prevent her own snort of laughter. "Yeah, right. And I'm assuming that followed the lobotomy?"

As rejoinders went, it wasn't very pithy, but she didn't care. The mental image of the vast organization and their line of humorless servants fit all too well when she considered it.

Silence descended once more, and this time it was Caine who reached over to turn up the music. A long slow ballad wound its way through the car's excellent speakers.

"Pass by two more exits. We'll go into the filling station, wait five minutes, go back one."

"Why?"

"There are three cars on the road with us, four passed the other way. If anyone else pulls off the highway with us, or comes down within five minutes, we're being tracked somehow."

"Can we get coffee?"

"If there's a drive-thru."

She glanced at the clock, it read six twenty-five. The sky was pale gold over the tops of the foothills. Hopefully the McDonald's would open early at this junction, if not, she'd take truck-stop coffee over none at all.

Coasting down the incline, she turned toward the brightly lit station. Fifteen or twenty big trucks sat quietly in the sleeper lot with that many or more fueling or idling along the fringes of the road.

"Drive around by the self-serve pumps, and go to the farthest one." He slipped a wallet out of the glove box and held out a credit card. "Use this card. I'd be a nice guy and pump the gas, but the way I'm dressed is too memorable."

For some reason, her errant mind supplied a full-blown image of the way his black shirt clung to his heavily-muscled chest, and her fingers tingled as they had when she'd brushed his thigh in the hotel room.

"Yeah, I guess you do sort of stand out," she mumbled, parking by the pump he'd indicated.

Confused by the unusually vivid images, she stared blankly when he got a Baltimore Orioles baseball cap from under the seat and thrust it at her. "Tuck your hair in this and zip your jacket. Slouch when you walk to disguise your height."

Nodding, she put on the hat, opened the door and eased onto the running board. She was about to jump down when he spoke again. "Dana?"

"What?"

"You going to tell me why you owe your son seventy-five cents?"

Chapter Four

A tense silence descended as Donovan stalked to the vast windows overlooking Miami. The blood and broken glass behind him testified to the heat of his wrath. The depth and length of the silence in the wake of his destructive rant proved how seriously his men took his vivid words and murderous intent.

He could see the men reflected in the glass, glancing nervously around, checking the exits like a bunch of Nancy-girl, sissy cops. Idiots. No one with *cajones* in the lot of them. Jesu knew, the only ones with any sense or skills were dead or caught in the attempt on Dana.

"I will have my son," he said with intense certitude. "You will find him. Again. You will get him."

"But boss . . ."

Donovan was on the man in two strides, before a third word could pass his lips. The knife pressing against his throat was small but sharper than any razor.

"*But?*" Donovan roared. "You dare to say this to me?"

The fear glinting in the man's eyes was so satisfying, so energizing, Donovan wanted to draw it out, feed on it, drink it in like a fine wine. It made him stronger, eased the anger. He smiled.

That must have been worse, for the man quivered in his hands like a virgin on her first night with a lover. "There are no '*buts*' here, Emil. This you will do. You will do it quickly, and you will do it well. You have doubts?"

Eyes struggling to see the knife, Emil cautiously shook his head. "No, Donovan. I know you're right. Sir."

"Good. Then we are agreed."

The knife pricked the barest bit and the terror that leapt into Emil's face made him chuckle. "A memento, Emil. Remember that there are no excuses. You fail, you die. By my hand or," and he had to laugh at the thought, "my wife's."

With careless ease, he wiped the blade on Emil's white shirt and returned it to its hidden sheath. He loved doing that, making it disappear as if it had never existed. To emphasize it, he stretched out his arms, palms up and empty. "There is no recourse, for any of you. I will have Dana. I will see that she pays for her sins against me, and my son, my Donovan will be with me once more. It's long past time for him to learn what he needs to learn."

"Uh, sir?" another man spoke, but even as he did, his eyes flicked over Donovan, searching for the knife.

Amused, Donovan chuckled. "Sir? We have worked together too long, Patrick, for me to be 'sir' to you. What is it that you would know?"

Confusion tripped the man's tongue, and Donovan's smile widened. This cat and mouse game with his underlings was one of the things he loved best, one of his greatest amusements. They never knew when the lash would strike, when the blade would slip free to slash them, or when he would give them a bonus, or gift them with property or women.

"Uh, yeah, uh . . . um, Donovan. We're gonna have to find another disabler. We know the annoy—Petey's dead. And Spike too."

"And if Spike weren't already dead, I'd kill him myself," Donovan said conversationally, delighted with the near-simultaneous flinch he saw in each of the men as he bluntly declared Spike's uselessness. "I told him no noise. No using automatic weapons. He took chances with my son."

The fury rose again in him. There was nothing else to throw. The breakables in the room crunched under his feet. He refused to start on the furniture or windows. No. He must, he *would*, control his rage that much. Words would work just as well.

"Nothing. Nothing is more precious than Donovan, Jr., do you understand this?"

There was a chorus of "Yes, sir" and "Yes, Donovan."

"He is to be untouched. How will I regain his trust after the poison Dana has fed him if you frighten him beyond his wits?" Donovan raved. "Patrick," he pointed to the man, and Patrick winced as if Donovan's finger were a whip. Donovan enjoyed the image and let the quiet do his work for him once more.

"Yes, Donovan?" the man finally said nervously.

"You have a son."

Ah, that pause which screamed a million protests.

"Uh, yes, I do."

"A life. A good one, for yourself, your beautiful wife. Your son."

"Thanks to you, yes." This a bit bolder. Good. It was

good that Patrick remembered who to thank for his fortune, even for his wife and son.

"Yes. You know best of all why I must have Donovan back with me. You know why he must not be frightened."

Patrick nodded cautiously. "Yes, I do. Boys are easily frightened, and their mothers have a strong hold."

"Exactly!" Donovan nearly yelled the words, and the men shifted uneasily. It was like watching a play. He could predict their reactions, one by one. He was going to miss Pollack. That one had been different. He had been dangerous in his difference, but that had added spice.

There was a chance he was alive, but little certainty. The pilot had seen him go down, but not die, before he had to leave, thanks to Dana's little bombs.

Donovan had to admire her, a fierce admiration for an enemy's skill, even as he cursed her and wished her deader than Pollack, deader than the annoyance she had so neatly electrocuted. He grimaced as he turned back to the blue-sky vista, deliberately showing the men his back, using his body language to demonstrate his disdain for them.

Dana had done him a favor, in a way. Spike was obviously too stupid to live if he couldn't follow simple instructions. Donovan would have had to kill him for his crass disobedience, even if the mission had succeeded. And the annoyance.

"We won't need another alarm worker. Especially one like Petey. Madmen are useful, to a point. That one had passed his 'point,' so *my wife*," he added special emphasis to that, "has done us a favor.

"Patrick," he said it casually, still facing the windows. Donovan had no fear of these who remained. Animals they might be, but he was their pack leader by right and they would no more think to harm him than they would harm Patrick's son. "You put together the new team. Use the property in Baltimore. They haven't gone far, not yet. They're still on the East Coast for the moment."

"You got it, Donovan. Um . . ."

Wait for it, Donovan thought. *The supplicant must ask the leader for direction. If I order him, I'm a boss. If he asks me for help, he's bent knee to my leadership and will forever be mine.*

"Um . . . do you want me to put out word for additional men?"

"No." Donovan's delight surged within him. Once again, those lessons from the old masters of war, Machiavelli and Sun Tzu, served him well. "Leave that to me. You assemble an assault squad and set up a base in Baltimore. Check with Paulina about what property up there is vacant. She'll know."

"Yes, Donovan."

"The rest of you, Patrick speaks for me. If he tells you to jump off a bridge, you do it." He whipped around, met each man's eye. "Do you understand me?"

A bleating, ragged set of affirmatives straggled through. "You may go. Patrick, you stay for a moment."

The others filed out, Patrick waited. All he needed was a cap to twist in his hands, and he'd look like a nervous messenger from an old Robin Hood movie, facing the nefarious sheriff.

"Watch out for Emil. I shamed him, so he'll pick a fight tonight to reestablish himself. Head it off. I don't want to lose him. If he won't listen though, you know what to do."

"Yes."

"Give my regards to your wife."

"Thanks."

Donovan returned to watching the boats in the canal below. When he heard the doorknob turn he spoke.

"Patrick?"

"Yes, sir?" Perfect. He'd responded perfectly. *God, my timing's amazing.*

"Hug that boy of yours, Patrick. Appreciate that you have him. You, out of all of them, understand what I'm missing." A threat and empathy in one fell swoop, tying Patrick even more to his quest. If he was right, Patrick would give it away in the tone of his voice when he answered. . . .

"I do. Understand, that is."

Dead on. Patrick would die before he returned to Donovan without the boy.

"Thank you."

Patrick hesitated a few seconds before leaving, waiting to see if any other orders fell from his master's lips. Much as Donovan ached to see his own son again, to hold him, to watch him sleep as he had when Donny, Jr., was small, this power, this control over others that he had learned through that loss, almost made up for it. Almost.

The door closed behind his minion, and Donovan was alone once more.

The dawn breeze was cold and stung her cheeks as Dana swiped the credit card Caine had given her through the station's pump. With casual ease, she catalogued everything she saw, from the skinny young man perched behind the station's counter engrossed in a novel to the gaggle of semis parked in the lot.

Four rows away, a sleepy eyed blonde in hospital scrubs gassed up. A pen stuck out of her ponytail, standing over her head like an Indian feather. As Dana watched, she drove off, still yawning.

Glancing at the surrounding businesses, she searched for signs of watchers, for anything out of place. Then she went one better. Closing her eyes, she listened with *all* of her other senses on alert. There were no hits on her internal alarms. She got none of the quasi-queasiness that usually presaged danger. Satisfied, she opened her eyes.

With a yelp of surprise, she stumbled back. Caine Bradley was standing in front of her. She hadn't even heard the car door open. Cursing herself for being tired, she recovered.

"What are you doing?" His hissed whisper was accompanied by a plastic smile.

"Nothing." She returned the play-acting with her own smile. "Get in the car. The station attendant's looking out. Don't make him any more curious."

With a casual pat to her back, he returned to the passenger side.

Commanding her heart to stop its pounding flight-or-fight mode, she grumbled to herself. "And he's one of the good guys, on our side." She shook her head and finished with the pump. "Christ, he nearly gave me a heart attack." The fact that he made her uneasy wasn't about good or bad. It was about her response to him in other ways. But that didn't bear thinking about either.

No, she decided, shooting him a glance as she climbed into the car, Caine disturbed her because she couldn't read him, couldn't *see* him with those other senses she relied on so much—her intuition, her gut instinct. For the first time in a long time she'd seen someone as attractive. Why the hell did it have to be him?

And he's a fricking Feebie, Dana, she reminded herself. For all she knew he was one of the dead men Donovan had loved to find and convert to his cause; agents and special forces guys who knew how to disappear, go under deep. Donovan had managed to find and seduce a number of those men. They'd been weary from the burden of secrets they carried, the things they had seen.

As in the proverbial sale of a soul, once immersed in Donovan's world, those men found themselves at the mercy of and beholden to someone more ruthless than any regime or dictator they'd ever faced.

There was no end to the payment, short of death.

With those bleak considerations circling in her mind, she followed Caine's murmured instructions, pulling through the just-opened McDonald's drive-thru for coffee and biscuits.

He looked back, and she did as well. Xavier hadn't stirred.

"Will the boy eat biscuits cold?"

"If he won't, Shadow will."

At the sound of his name, the dog poked his head over the seat and licked her elbow, the one thing within easy reach. She broke off a piece of her biscuit and slipped it to the dog. She heard the heavy whump of his tail slapping the leather seat.

"Shhhhh," she admonished. "Jump back up and lie down, boy." With a last lick, the dog complied.

"Well trained," Caine commented.

"And well loved. He's a good one."

"Will you leave him with the boy if the decoy plan comes through?"

Dana considered the question and took several long gulps of the strong coffee before answering. "On the slim chance that Agent Tervain's plan works out and we take on another agent posing as my son, then yes, I would leave Shadow with Xavier." For some reason, she was driven to tell him her reasoning. "God forbid, if the plan fails, Xavier would at least have Shadow, even if he lost me."

"Poor substitute," Caine said, his voice quiet.

"But better than no one at all."

The sun rose, smudging the mountains with gold and red. In the valleys, darkness still reigned, but she saw from the lightening sky that it would be a beautiful day. How ironic.

"We'll need a dog food run at some point," Dana finally broke the silence. "I have some, but he eats a lot."

"There's a farm and feed store at a crossroads several miles before our turn. I need some other clothes. I'll be able to get some jeans there, some shirts, as well as the dog food. I'll go in alone on that one, so it seems as if I'm traveling solo with the dog."

Morning advanced and Xavier woke, yawning and stretching. "Mom, I have to go to the bathroom."

They were traveling along I-64 West, and exits were scarce. With a glance at Caine, she answered him. "As soon as I see a busy exit, someplace where we can blend in, okay? Can you hold it till then, or do I need to find a roadside stand of trees?"

"Yuck, Mom. I can hold it. Okay if I put on my headphones and listen to some tunes till we get there?"

"Sure." She flicked a look at Caine, but he was mum as usual. With full daylight upon them, the views were lovely. Dana tried to distract herself with them but instead went round and round debating the merits of running, staying, fighting, or giving up. That brought a grimace eased only by an occasional burst of song from Xavier when he got to a favorite lyric.

What would happen to Xavy if she was killed? Could he live with Donovan? Would the values, the sense of right and wrong that she had worked so hard to instill make him a prisoner in his father's house? She had no doubt that Donovan would dote on the boy, but she also knew he would embroil his son in the game as soon as possible.

Although Xavier had a strange existence, ever on alert, often worried, sometimes on the run, he seemed happy. Why couldn't Donovan leave them alone?

"You can take this exit," Caine said, breaking into her bleak reverie. She changed lanes to take the exit. As she descended the ramp, she watched the rearview, trying to spot any tails or followers. She saw that Caine was bending forward to check the side-view mirror.

Turning right under the highway, she chose a burger place at random. From the backseat, her son piped up. "Not there, Mom. Let's go to McDonald's. They'll still be serving breakfast." Rolling her eyes, she returned to the roadway, crossing to the omnipresent Golden Arches.

The restaurant was moderately busy, enough so that their visit would likely go unnoticed. After finishing her turn using the facilities, she paused to grab extra napkins. Men never got enough.

"Do you want me to drive?" Caine asked.

She looked at him in surprise. "Is your leg well enough for that?"

"Not really, but if you're tired, I can manage for awhile."

"Oh, no. It's okay. I'm doing all right, but we'll need to switch before the feed store."

"There's a scenic overlook a mile before it. We'll change there."

Xavy overheard this and wanted to know the game plan. She filled him in as they drove, outlining what she knew.

"So we're gonna wait at some cabin? What happens if Donovan finds out where we are?"

She heard the fear in his young voice. He called his father Donovan, never my father or my dad. Just Donovan. It hurt her that he couldn't know a real, honest man as his father. She also knew that he was in run mode, as she was. Again her heart clenched at the burdens he took on at his young age.

"Right now, it's the best plan. Agent Tervain is trying to plug the leak inside—"

Caine broke into her explanation. "We'll stay for a day, maybe two. If we can't get info, we'll head out, keep dodging and dancing. There are documents and some money at the cabin, supplies too." He had turned in the seat to face Xavier. "Your mom and I agreed to wait at least a day for Agent Tervain to contact us, try to work within the system."

"That true, Mom?"

Even as she reassured him, she realized he'd doubted Caine's veracity and wouldn't believe the other adult until she confirmed. How sad was that?

"And if that falls through?" her boy asked quietly, sounding old beyond his years.

"Honey—" she began, but was quickly overridden by Caine.

"We keep going until he can help us." The two eyed each other over the smooth leather seats. "We've got some options."

"What kind of options?"

She started to speak, but Caine laid a warm hand on her arm, forestalling her. Never taking his eyes off the boy, he detailed some of their possible scenarios.

"First, we wait for Agent Tervain. If we don't hear from him in a day or so, we go to plan B."

"Which is—"

"Change our identities to travel as a family. Hair color changes, clothes, that kind of stuff." Caine smiled. She caught the toothpaste white gleam of it from the corner of her eye and turned to stare. He glanced at her, then returned his gaze to Xavy. "Maybe we'll punk you out, go bright blond on ya'. Whaddya think?"

In the mirror, she saw the sharp surprise on her son's face. "Hey, Mom . . ."

"Yes, we can," she read his question before he asked it. "Whatever it takes. Blond and buzz-cut might be nice," she said, deadpan, waiting for the explosion.

"Awwwwww, no, man," he rose to the bait. "Not a buzz." To Caine, he added, "She's just saying that. She always says it. She's not going to go for the jarhead cut, are you, Mom?"

She grinned. "Naaaah, but your uncle would resent that jarhead remark, being a Marine himself."

"Yeah, yeah, so you say. Am I ever gonna meet him?" It was always the same answer each time he asked, and he knew it.

"One day, I hope. Even if we didn't have to be . . . careful you couldn't meet him now. He's in Iraq."

"Is he why you pray for the soldiers every night?"

"Yes, he is. I would anyway, but he's the biggest reason."

"He's younger than you, right?"

"I'm really old, of course."

"Mommmmmm, you know what I mean," Xavy rolled his eyes.

"I know. Yes, he's younger. Two years."

"What's he do, again?" Xavy seemed eager for the distraction of idle chatter as he wolfed down breakfast, slipping bits to the dog as they talked.

"I don't really know." It hurt all over again, as it always did, when she thought of her brother, James.

"He's a demolitions expert," Caine said, speaking to her now, rather than to her son. "He's in Baghra working with a team of contractors to dispose of captured ordnance and caches of obsolete weaponry. It's stashed everywhere. Some of it dates to World War II. It's going to take years to find and discharge the munitions."

Tears stung Dana's eyes as she heard this small piece of news. That Caine knew when she didn't hurt, but she shoved it aside, wanting to hear more.

"Discharge . . . Wow! Does that mean he explodes stuff, like for a job?" This, of course, from Xavier.

"Every day."

"Double wow," Xavy said, awe in his voice. "I bet he's got some stories."

"Bet he does," Caine agreed.

They talked some more about explosions, munitions, and Jimmy's job before Xavy tired of the subject and returned to his music.

"I guess it runs in the family," Caine said with a smile.

She turned at this comment, staring. "What?"

"Blowing things up. You did a damn fine job at it, back at the house."

"Thank you for telling us about Jimmy," she said, ignoring his comments because she couldn't tell if it was a real compliment or a sarcastic one. "It means a lot to me. How did you . . . I mean why . . ."

"I checked. I knew you were Donovan's prime objective when I took this mission, but he's devious, indirect if he can't be direct. If Donovan knew about your brother, I figured he'd use it. He knows, of course," he glanced at her and she nodded. "But Iraq requires a longer reach than even Walker can muster."

He was quiet for a moment then added. "If I can, I'll keep you posted."

She said the sole thing she could get past her tight throat. "Thank you."

"Go off over there, the scenic area on the left."

The sudden order startled her, but she reacted quickly, sliding into the turn lane. Crossing the median, she parked in an attractive, well-maintained lot with numerous placards at the various vantage points.

"I need to stretch, try to limber up. I don't want to limp into the feed store. Nothing more memorable than a limp."

She couldn't tell by his bland delivery if he was joking, but it made her smile, nevertheless. She and Xavy got out of the car, and she passed the keys to Caine. Xavy had Shadow's leash, and the pair walked to explore a bit of meadow beyond a low wall.

Checking on Caine, she sucked in a surprised breath when she saw him. He was bent double, his long legs spread, his elbows resting on the ground. He leaned left, then right, to loosen the hamstrings, she presumed. *Oh, did she presume.* She nearly choked watching the muscular ripple of his taut backside. The trousers molded to his legs, and she had a sudden physical memory of his muscular thighs.

"Mom!" Xavy's shout brought her into the moment like a whip crack. Caine was at her side in a flash, before she even answered.

"What?"

"Wow, Mom! Deer." The delight in his voice was so real, so ten years old, that she couldn't chide him, even as her heart pounded a mile a minute.

"Beautiful, aren't they?" she called, willing her voice to come out at a normal level.

"God, I thought something had happened," Caine muttered, beside her. She saw him quickly re-holster a gun at his waist.

"Just ten-year-old stuff," she said, hand to her pounding heart. "But he scared the devil out of me too."

"We need to go."

"Yeah. Um, do you feel okay?" She could feel the heat from his body. He was standing so close, it made her skin hot. Her heart rate, which had begun to slow, picked up speed again.

"Did you, um, get stretched out?" She had an immediate mental picture of his muscular thighs. Damn it. She could hear how funny-squeaky her voice sounded, so it was no wonder he looked at her strangely. His eyes flickered to where her hand lay, pressed to her breast, and something changed in his face. He looked . . . hungry.

Then the look was gone.

"Yes. Some reason for the question?"

"No, no. Just asking."

It was an awkward moment. Something changed then,

a softening, an easing. She couldn't tell if it was her, or him, or both.

"Hey Mom, lookit," Xavy broke in, holding out an enormous pine cone. "I've never seen one this big, have you?"

She blindly reached for what her son held out. It registered after she had it in her hand. "Wow, it is huge, isn't it? Got to be what? Fifteen inches long?"

"It's humongous. It's a mutant or something."

"Mutant pine trees take over western Virginia," Caine said, his voice unnaturally deep. "Film at eleven."

She laughed in spite of herself as they all piled into the Escalade, but this time both Dana and Xavy got in the second door and they put Shadow in the passenger seat.

"Once I pull into the lot and go in, you both have to stay down. I'll be as quick as I can. Don't worry about me unless I'm gone more than an hour." The car slowed, and she heard the dinka-dinka of the turn signal. "If that happens, there are extra keys here." He opened the center console and dug around for a moment, then handed a second set of keys back to her. "Head for DC, call Tervain, go to headquarters."

"I know the drill, and let's hope that won't be necessary."

"Amen, sister. Amen."

As he said the last, he turned and the tires crunched on the gravel lot. From her prone position, she saw the tall forms of storage buildings rising over a low, one-story store.

"You ready?"

"For what?" she replied, puzzled.

"To be alone out here."

She had to laugh. "I'm not alone. Xavier, Shadow, and I are a team. You'll be the one who's alone."

Chapter Five

Alone. Yeah, Caine thought, as he strode into the feed store. He was alone. He didn't mind operating outside the bounds of a mission, but this one was seriously fucked. Nothing was on book, and it was perilously close to a free-for-all. *That* he hated. Donovan was alive and free. He hoped Tervain was alive. And clear. Who knew if Parlier was down, MIA, or even compromised?

At least Spike and the annoyance weren't available tools anymore. He pondered the situation as he climbed the steps to the store. Who would Donovan use to come after Dana?

"Afternoon," the clerk called. Her friendly smile wavered as he spun toward her. Dammit. *Don't frighten the natives*, he told himself.

"Hey, how're you today?" He managed a smile and a casual wave. "You got any paintball supplies? I'm headed out to the course over in Bryce, and some of m'caps busted, got on my clothes."

"Oh, well, yeah. Over there along the back wall. There's a little bit. We got a local group, so we carry some things."

"I met one of them I think, over in Herndon a while

back. He said you carried stuff if I was up this way. It's why I stopped."

"That's great that he recommended us."

"Hey," Caine shot her a warm smile, flirted with her a bit. "If he'd told me how pretty the ladies were running the place, I'd've stopped before."

"Oh, pshaw, boy," the older woman said, laughing at his over-done posing. "Go on with your joshing."

"Caught, but not joshing," he pantomimed being shot in the heart. "Back wall, you said?"

"Yup, over yonder, by the dog food."

"Oh, good, I need that too."

Scanning the walls, he found what he needed. Picking up a pack of the paint gun pellets and shouldering a fifty-pound bag of the kind of dog food Dana had described, he made his way back to the counter. He'd noted the clothes on sale, but didn't want to jump into that right away. It wouldn't be in character.

Instead, he dumped the bag and the paint pellets on the counter. Looking down, he spotted work gloves. "Hey, you got Mule Team gloves. These are great," he said, slapping a pair into his hand. "I can't get these over in Alexandria."

"Got Mule Team shirts too. They're on sale."

"Really? Where?" He let the girl point them out, then pulled out four shirts, three denim, one black. From the pants, he found three in his size, all khakis.

"Got some Levis on the far rack too, sir," the older woman mentioned, holding her hands out to take the shirts and pants for him. "They're on sale as well."

"I can always use another pair of Levis. I don't think any of the paintball stuff got on my jeans or socks, but just in case . . ." He let that hang as he snagged three pair of jeans.

He was headed back to the counter when his phone rang. It was a special ringtone.

Shitfuckgoddammit. Not now.

"Mind if I try these on?" he asked the older woman. "Can't remember my size."

"Dressing room's back that way," she motioned, looking at him quizzically since he wasn't answering his phone.

"Girlfriend," he said, rolling his eyes and grinning. "I was supposed to call her last night."

"Better answer that boy, or she'll make you pay."

"Yeah," he pulled the phone from its holster and went into the dressing room.

"God dammit, Donovan," he growled into the receiver, his voice pitched low and deep, so neither clerks nor customers could overhear. "You didn't tell me she'd fucking have explosives."

"You were supposed to be ready for anything, Pollack," Donovan answered coolly. "Even a bomb. She does have a degree in chemistry. You knew that."

"Fuckin' bitch you got there. I can see why you want her dead. Spike's out. Petey too."

"I'd heard. Do you have her?"

"Trackin' in. Feds copped her, but that's no big. I got a bead." He cupped his hand around the phone to further muffle the sound as if he were being surreptitious. "Doc's here, I'm getting stitched. Can't talk. Call you later."

He disconnected with a heavy heart. It would have been better if Donovan thought him dead. That he'd even called meant Donovan knew he was alive with his phone intact. HQ was going to have to figure out who Donovan had bribed at the cell phone company and what kind of technology he'd wired to make that happen. Dangerous and terribly useful.

"Y'all all right in there?"

"Yes ma'am," Caine answered, acting as if he were pulling his own boots back on. "Hey, you got any work boots?"

A pair of work boots were handed over, wrong size, but right type. After he finished in the dressing room, he managed to change the boots in the box to his size, piling three pairs of heavy socks onto the stack for good measure. Delighted with his excess, the ladies folded everything into a large shopping bag as he chatted with them, continuing to keep it light and flirtatious.

"You need help getting this to your car? I can call Billy from the back," the older woman offered.

"No thank you, ma'am," he flattered. "I can manage."

He hefted the bag and, with the dog food on his shoulder, headed for the exit.

"Let me get that door," the younger woman hustled around the counter to open it.

He gave her a warm smile and winked at her. "Thank you, ma'am."

Knowing the women were watching, he took his time crossing the lot, making sure he didn't limp. His leg ached with the effort, but he didn't feel any dampness or pain where he'd been stitched. Going to the back of the Caddy, he lifted the hatch, dumped in the dog food, and stowed the bag.

"Stay down, the clerks are watching from the door," he warned Dana and Xavier.

As he moved to the driver's side, he raised a hand and

saw the blushing young clerk wave back. The older woman had already gone inside.

Good. They'd remember a lone male, a nice man with his dog, going paintballing in Bryce. A guy from Alexandria, they'd say if they even remembered that. He'd bet the girl wouldn't remember that, but she'd be able to describe him physically better than the older woman. Hopefully, neither had gotten a good look at the car or its plates.

Waiting was dreadful, Dana decided as she listened to cars and trucks come and go in the parking lot. Another few minutes went by, and she began to get antsy. Shadow whined and his tail thumped twice which meant Caine was on his way. Shadow only reacted to people he knew. She loosed a breath.

Closing her eyes she tried to let her anxiety go, but she couldn't. The tailgate lifted and something heavy thudded down, along with Caine's warning. There was some rustling as well, then the breath of fresh air was gone as the rear hatch closed. It wasn't until Caine climbed into the driver's seat and started the engine that she unclenched her hands and let her muscles relax.

"Everything go okay?" she asked.

"Fine. I got a few looks, dressed this way. I told the clerks I was going paintballing and she did the 'Oh, that explains it' kind of comment. I got the dog food. They carried the right brand. I also got a few pairs of jeans and some shirts. They were on sale, so I didn't have to make up any reason about why I was getting more than one."

From monosyllabic to garrulous. It seemed as if Caine was talking a lot.

"Caine, are you okay? How's your leg?"

"It hurts. Why?"

"You're talking. A lot. You haven't said anything for hours and hours, and suddenly you're Mr. Chatty. What's going on?"

He was silent for a long minute. "I got a call."

"Tervain?"

"No," his voice was dark, sharp.

She sucked in a breath. "Donovan."

"Yeah."

"Shit."

He was quiet, then said, a touch of humor lightening his voice. "I believe that's another twenty-five cents you owe."

Closing her eyes, she let out a shaky laugh. "Yeah. What'd you tell him?"

"That I was tracking you and Xavier. Told him I was going to grab you soon, then stash you. He'll call back tonight, give me my orders."

"Oh, God."

They rode in silence for a while. She finally wrapped her mind around the knowledge that Donovan essentially would be in the house with them later that evening. She hated it.

"You can sit up now," Caine said. With a sigh, she did just that. Shadow whined and stood, turning in the seat to peer at her, his tail waving in the front window.

"I can't imagine what oncoming cars think of that view," she said, as much to the dog as to herself.

"Dog waves at passersby?"

"Ha, as good a title as any. How much farther?"

"Not too much longer. I want to do some doubling back before we make the real turn."

"Okay," she said with weary resignation. The cabin was

probably within a mile or two, but it would take forever to get there, with all the doubling back and switching roads to avoid detection.

"You want to climb up here and send the dog to the back to take your place?"

"Sure." She patted the seat calling Shadow to jump over. With a happy bark that made her ears ring, he landed beside her and licked her cheek. She checked Xavy and, to her astonishment, he was asleep once again. She patted the seat once again, encouraging Shadow to lie down. Burying her cheek in his fur, she hugged him. "You can go back with your boy if you want to or stay here. I'm going up front."

He bestowed another lick, then jumped back as she climbed over the console and into the spacious front passenger seat.

"Do you always talk to the dog as if he were a person?"

"Yep, and I always pay my son twenty-five cents when I break the rules and cuss."

"There's the turn," Caine said, nodding toward a nondescript, one lane, gravel road. He passed it, scanning the surrounding lanes and turnoffs. Several miles down the twisting route, he turned around. Cruising back, he whipped into the driveway and under the sheltering trees. Out of sight of the road, a cattle grate preceded a barred fence.

Peering into the woods, Caine rolled down the window to press a code into an elevated keypad. The gate rolled away and he drove carefully in, avoiding large dips and rocks in the road.

"Why such a crappy road?"

"No one can approach at speed. Line of sight shot from the front porch, so stay down. And alert."

"Charming appointment for the weekend home," she said sarcastically.

He gave a wry laugh. "Yeah, great for the discerning buyer."

"How long do you think we'll have to be here?"

"Depends on Tervain." They drove behind the house and he reversed the car, putting its nose out so that they could make a run for it. "I'm just—"

"I know."

He gave her a long, appraising stare. "Yeah, you would."

She didn't want to think about what that meant. "Hey Xav, rise and shine, dude. We're here."

"Where's here?"

"The cabin."

"Cool," Xavy said, taking in the view. "It's big."

"I'll secure the house." Caine unbuckled his seatbelt and eased a gun from under the seat. "Get behind the wheel, leave it running. I'll come onto the porch and wave. If I don't come all the way out or you get spooked, peel out of here. Got it?"

"Got it," Dana said as she climbed over to take his place behind the wheel. She'd never realized that taking precautions could be so much easier with two adults. Xavier was never left alone. She and Xavy had practiced this exact maneuver; she'd even taught him to drive. Sort of. Enough to get to a police station, if anything happened to her.

"I hope it checks out and we can stay," Xavy murmured, craning his neck to see the upper story of the house.

When Caine came fully onto the porch, waving vigorously, Dana let out a pent-up breath. "I guess we're good to go. Let's go see what's inside, get the lay of the land."

"'Kay." Xavy enthusiastically clambered over the seat,

opened the door, and jumped to the ground. Shadow bounded down and blocked Xavier from going any further. "C'mon Shadow, give," the boy complained.

The dog was off leash, and the territory was unfamiliar. He was doing what he'd been trained to do. "It's okay, Shadow. *Siest*," she gave him the off-duty command.

Barking, Shadow ran out into the yard dashing around in an excess of canine delight. Xavy ran after him. The dog turned the tables, chasing the boy. They switched places three or four times before Xavier collapsed giggling. Shadow pounced on him, and they rolled together in the grass, a laughing, barking, mock-growling pile of boy and dog.

Leaning on the doorframe, she watched them play. It was a photo moment that made her wish for a camera. The thought had her thudding back to her own little hellish reality.

Pictures didn't survive witness protection. You didn't keep photos where you sported a different appearance than your current alias. No family pictures, no baby pictures, no school photos, no candids. She took them, periodically. Then squirreled them away in her lockbox, hiding them until the one day in which they could, please God, stop running.

"Call them in," Caine's deep voice broke her trance. He'd donned opaque glasses when driving, but had now taken them off. His dark eyes glinted in the light as he searched her face. "You okay?" He asked the question softly. The sound carried to her, but not beyond her to the boy innocently wrestling with his dog.

"Yeah. Just wallowing in depressing memories. A shame on such a gorgeous day."

"Truer words," he commented, glancing at the rich blue of the sky. "You're right about the day."

"I am."

"Go in. I'll get the bags."

She walked up the steps to stand beside him. As the distance between them narrowed, she felt the warmth radiating from his body. It crossed her mind that if she were sleeping with him, she wouldn't need blankets.

Instantly irritated—and aroused—by the image, she passed him and reached the edge of the porch. Across the property, in the distance, she saw fencing with barbed wire topping its six or seven foot height. The garage they'd parked beside hid the SUV from anyone spying down the mountain.

She turned and bumped into Caine. "Dammit, will you quit sneaking around?"

"Habit. It's saved my as—hide too many times for me to stop now."

"Well, cough or clear your throat or something. I'm going to react one time, go with reflex, and you're going to end up with a busted nose at the very least. Or I'm going to get one, when I strike first and you react."

He grinned a flash of white. "You're right. Your reflexes are strung pretty tight. Almost as tight as mine."

"Maybe tighter," she snapped. "I have more than myself to think about." She regretted the temper in her words as soon as they left her mouth. "Sorry, sorry," she apologized. "I'm edgy, knowing Donovan's going to call."

"I know." His voice soothed, as did the hand he smoothed down her arm. She didn't move. He evidently took her stillness as acceptance, letting his palm slide down, then up; a caress, a comfort. "I can only imagine," he said, shooting a look at Xavy. "And that pales in comparison to reality, I'm sure."

Somehow his honesty in admitting that he didn't know how it felt was her undoing. Tears welled, then leaked from her eyes. "It's hard," she choked out the words. "So hard sometimes." God, she hated the weakness of tears.

His hand tightened, and she sensed his hesitation. He leaned forward the barest fraction, as if to take her into a hug. In that split second of decision, she wondered what it would feel like, to be held . . . protected. By him.

It would be her emotional undoing, so she gave ground, easing away. "Don't. If I did, if you . . ." she couldn't even say it. "I'd lose it. I'm too close to the edge."

"Got it." His voice was cooler now. "Call the boy in." She started to speak, but he beat her to it. "I'll try to remember to cough or something." He touched his nose, which had obviously seen a fist or two before. "My face has had enough damage."

"Xavier," she called, not trusting herself to answer his banter. "Let's get inside, check out which room you want."

The boy leapt up, dog trailing at his heels. Once on the porch, he glanced at her. "Go ahead. Wipe your feet," she belatedly added as he yanked open the screen and both boy and dog ran inside.

There was a faint, "Wow, cool," and she heard the thud of feet on stairs. Caine had one eyebrow cocked and inquiry on his dark face.

"You coming?" Caine asked tersely.

"In a minute."

"You can't be out here by yourself. You know that."

"I know the drill," she snapped. "I have to get a grip

before we're together in close quarters. Please. I'll be careful."

He hesitated, obviously uneasy.

"I'll get our stuff," she continued. "Then come in, I promise. Just let me breathe for a minute, okay?"

Finally, he nodded. "Don't be long."

"I won't."

With another appraising glance, he went inside. She heard him call out to Xavy, something about lunch. Closing her eyes, she simply breathed for a few moments. Letting her defenses down, she tried to relax, let her senses tell her if they were clear. Unfortunately, it didn't work. She was too conscious of the man inside the house. Her internal awareness pinned onto him like a striking hawk.

There was another factor. She couldn't get past his ability to sneak up on her. It unnerved her and kept her on guard. She expected to open her eyes and find him standing there, breathing down her neck.

The image of his hot body behind her sent her sensual imagination into overdrive. Which spiked her irritation level. Why she had to pick now, of all times, to have a hormone surge over a Feebie was a mystery. With a snort of self-disgust, she loaded the duffels and backpacks into her arms, ignoring the dog food. He'd bought a fifty-pound bag, probably all the feed store sold. She'd let him bring that in.

Toeing open the door, she walked into the cabin.

"Wow, is right," she repeated Xavy's sentiment. The interior featured exposed beams, high ceilings, and a breath-taking view out over the valley beyond. Comfortable, manly chairs were scattered about with a plethora of sports, business, and luxury-item magazines stacked in a basket by each.

A sturdy table boasted a fat, bright red, three-wick candle in the center on a wooden stand. It was the sole homey, girly touch in an otherwise bachelor-type pad. Even the art was of a masculine bent, with elk and mountain lions sharing space with an enormous mountainous landscape full of pine and laurel.

The kitchen was state of the art and seemed basically untouched. The guys obviously didn't cook. She said a quick prayer the bathrooms weren't the opposite of the pristine kitchen.

From a balcony above, a voice called down. "Hey Mom, you have to come see this." She followed the sound of her son's laughter and found him and Caine in one of the bedrooms. The exposed logs were white-washed here, but still masculine, and a black and red plaid spread and pillows adorned the bed. There were red, blue, black, and green hooked rugs on the dark wood floor.

"Check this out," Xavy said, coming over to tug her into the room. "Look."

She saw why he was excited in one glance. It was a gamer's idea of heaven. A plasma television covered a section of the wall, and below it cabinets held games, movies, music, and more.

"They even have the latest XBox stuff," he raved.

Caine held out a module. "This one's new," he said, tossing it to Xavier. The boy promptly plopped down to unwrap it and insert it in the machine. "Try that out while your mom and I check out what's available for lunch."

"You bet. Hey Mom, do you think there might be hot dogs?"

"Don't know, baby," she said, brushing a strand of

dark hair away from his eyes. "Frozen, maybe. I'll let you know."

"Okay. I'm gonna kick this," he exulted, then hesitated. "Is that okay? Do we have time?"

Unutterably saddened again, she pasted on a smile. "It's okay, and we have time. It may be hours before we hear from Agent Tervain. Knock yourself out."

"Excellent," he said, turning to the game.

Caine followed her down the stairs, as she headed for the kitchen. To her surprise, there were hot dogs in the freezer as well as frozen dinners, air-sealed steaks, and fish. There were also, to her vast amusement, five boxes of breakfast sandwiches.

In the refrigerator, there were crackers, a loaf of bread, beer, sugary soft drinks, some spreadable cheese that had a faraway expiration date, and a door full of man-condiments.

Ugh. Searching the cabinets she found soup and cans of vegetables, and there was cereal, cereal, and more cereal. Oatmeal, cream of wheat, grits, bran flakes, corn flakes, every kind of flakes. And sugared cereals galore.

Cereal, but no milk. She was about to call to Caine when he was there, coming upon her as silently as ever.

Hand to her breast to still her heart, she said, "You promised you'd give me a warning. I didn't hear a cough, buddy," she scowled at him, still a bit breathless.

Grinning, he made a fake coughing sound. "Better?"

"No. But it's a start."

"You needed me?"

Loaded question. *Get your mind out of the gutter, girl.*

"Did you say there was a grocery nearby? I can make hot dogs for Xavier, and there are breakfast sandwiches we can make in the microwave, but not much else."

"No." His response was immediate, automatic, and clipped.

"Why?" Logic overrode irritation.

"I can think of two dozen reasons, starting with my orders to keep you and Xavier under wraps at all times."

"We're never entirely safe, Caine. Ever," she met him stare for stare. "It's unlikely anyone could make it here unobserved or that we've been followed. Give me your cell number." They programmed his number into her phone. "Cross check measure taken. Now get going."

They argued about it for twenty more minutes, but to her surprise, she wore him down.

"What do you need?"

"Milk, eggs, butter, peanut butter, jelly. Some ground beef, chips or pretzels or something to snack on. Hamburger buns. American cheese. D batteries."

"Cereal?"

"There's enough cereal here to float a ship."

He glanced at the cabinets, and she opened a door to illustrate her point. His eyes widened.

"Okay, no cereal." He handed her two weapons pulled from a bag he'd left by the door. "You know the drill," he mimicked her earlier phrase.

"Window check, door check, bead on the car as it goes and returns. Got it," she replied and opened the freezer for the hot dogs. "Hit the trail."

"Check," he said, military style, and left the room, and within minutes, the house, silently passing her yet one more weapon before he left.

Preparing two hot dogs and taking them to her son, Dana pondered their strange companion. He was a study in contradictions. At some points all agent, by the book. At others, with his hot gaze turned her way, all man.

"Hey Mom, did you see? I got the high score."

Xavy had devoured the hot dogs and was once again immersed in the digital world of right and wrong.

"Excellent," she replied, tuning in to the game and her son's excitement. "That's a new one. How do you score?"

"Blowing things up, like Uncle Jimmy." His grin was delighted, and he plunged back into the game.

Circling the house in a security check, Dana tried to figure out how long it had been since she'd seen her brother. Dredging her memory, she finally came up with the event. Xavier's third birthday. Donovan had gotten a pony, a clown, and a large moonbounce machine. A host of children, all of wealthy parents from their exclusive neighborhood, had raced, screeched and laughed in the backyard. In the kitchen, Dana had surveyed the chaos with a mix of irritation and delight. Most of the parents were a bit stuffy, a few of the kids bullies or truly princessy and dreadful, but most were average, happy kids. Having fun was the name of the game.

Her brother had come in, in search of a beer.

"Hey girl," he said. "Some party for a kid."

"Yeah, you know Donovan." The excessive display had bothered her, but she'd kept quiet. It had troubled her that Donovan was using the child's party to invite the self-important, up-and-coming crowd. She'd been raised in a simpler way, with basic parties, homemade cake, and pizza as they got older. Donovan claimed it was good for his import/export business, but she also knew he enjoyed the display and the people sucking up to him. "I know it's over the top. You and I understand that, right? It was different for us," she'd said to Jimmy with a sigh.

"*I'm* beginning to," he had said cryptically. His voice

had fallen to a mere whisper. "I've found out a lot about your husband. Do you know him, Sis? Really?"

She'd been deeply disturbed by his implications, and tried to get him to explain, but he'd said no more. He'd never come back to that house. Months later, as she uncovered and understood the depths of Donovan's dirty business deals, she knew why.

When she agreed to testify, go underground, her brother had come.

They'd barely gotten one visit before she and Xavier had been assigned their first identity. He'd hugged her, told her he was proud of her, the choices she'd made.

Tears stung her eyes at the remembered image.

"Mom. Mom," Xavy called twice before he got her attention.

"Sorry, what?"

"Can I have another hot dog? I'm really hungry."

"When Agent Bradley comes back."

"Sounds good. You want to play? There's another control module."

"Sure," she said, sitting down on the floor between him and Shadow.

For thirty minutes they battled away, knocking off monsters, crashing cars and spaceships. Shadow alerted, and she caught the faint sound of tires on gravel. Seconds later the gate release beeped. Peering around the living room window frame, Dana scanned the driveway, weapon in hand to see the Cadillac as it powered around the driveway's potholes. That didn't mean it was Caine behind the wheel, however.

Commanding Shadow to guard, she glided to the back, following the car. Zig-zagging across the kitchen, she released the safety on the second weapon, setting it on the counter.

The vehicle spat gravel as Caine reversed to park it. She watched him search the hills. His gaze swept over the house. Within a few seconds, he had locked onto her position behind the door as if he had a laser targeting system.

He brought two fingers to tap them at his brow in a Boy Scout salute. How had he known she was there? She had no clue. She shifted to be visible in the glass of the door and returned the salute. She, however, used the barrel of the gun.

As he came in carrying the groceries, his phone rang.

Chapter Six

Caine dumped a bevy of plastic bags on the counter in the center of the room and reached for the phone. Its ring told him it wasn't Walker, nor was it Tervain.

Signaling for quiet, he picked up the call. "Yeah?" he growled, using Pollack's persona. Even though he was sure he knew who it was, he was taking no chances on blowing his cover.

"It's Sears. You okay?"

"For now."

"How about the dove and the chick?"

"They're fine," Caine said, glancing at Dana. Faint beeps and bongs told him Xavy was gaming upstairs.

"Good. Still working on finding Parlier. Tervain'll call later. You a hillbilly?"

Caine frowned. Tervain knew they'd headed for the mountain house, but had he withheld the information from Sears? Was Sears the leak?

"Probably."

"Is that . . ." Sears' voice faded as he answered someone else who'd called to him. "Gotta go. Word on Parlier."

Caine returned his phone to the holster at his waist.

"Bad news?"

"No," he said, still thinking about Sears. What was up? "Oh, milk, eggs, etc.," he pointed to the bags. "As requested, ma'am."

"Excellent," she said, delving in. "So are you going to tell me about the call, or do I have to pull the car over again and threaten to throw you out?"

He heard the irritation in her voice first, before the words penetrated. For some reason the reminder of her fierce order to get out of the car in the middle of the night, made him smile. "No, I'll cooperate, Sheriff, I promise," he joked, raising his hands in surrender.

As she put the groceries away, she asked, "Do you want a hamburger, Agent Bradley, or some soup and a grilled cheese?"

"Ouch. So, I'm in the dog house? You called me Agent Bradley."

When she merely looked at him, her hands on her hips, he relented. "Soup and a grilled cheese sounds great. I haven't had that since I was a kid."

"Mom," Xavy called from upstairs. "Call off Shadow, I gotta go to the bathroom."

Dana gave a strangled laugh as she ran to give the dog a cease order. Caine was laughing too, but puzzled as to why she'd actually gone upstairs, rather than just calling the order to the dog. When she got back, he asked about it.

"Shadow's a smart one. Every now and again, if he can't see me, he'll wait before he follows a command. It might save Xavy one day, but it's usually a pain in the neck."

"Hey Mom," Xavy called down the stairs. "Can I get another hot dog now?"

"Yes, I'll bring it to you in a few minutes." Dana got out bread, cheese, and one of the cans of soup, as well as a hot dog and bun. To Caine, she said, "Is tomato okay?"

"Yeah. It was Sears, on the phone. Checking in."

"Why not Tervain?"

"Good question."

The microwave had dinged, and she turned to look at him, a full plate in hand. "Bad feeling or something concrete?" She kept working as he thought, piling chips on the plate and pouring a glass of milk.

"A twinge. Nothing concrete."

"Hmmm. Would you take this to Xavy? I'll finish ours."

"Yes, ma'am," he grinned at her and disappeared.

It took her a full two minutes to recover from the effects of his smile. What was wrong with her?

Banging out her irritation on the cupboards, she got the things she needed. Pouring the soup and cutting a grilled cheese, she found herself hoping he'd stay upstairs for a bit.

And wasn't that stupid? They were going to be living in close proximity for God only knew how long. She damn well better get her hormones in control and quit thinking about his muscle tone. Or his smile. Or the fact that he cared enough to find out about Jimmy. Or how he looked in briefs as the doctor tended his leg.

"Stop it," she scolded herself. "This isn't the time."

"For what?"

She nearly screamed when the soft words came from right behind her. "Dammit, you promised to cough."

He faked one and when she didn't respond, did it again. "Sorry."

"Yeah, right. Sit and eat. Tell me about your hunch."

The words tumbled out of her mouth. "How's your leg? Does it need tending? I've got bandages and antiseptic."

"You were thinking about my leg?"

Oh, if you only knew. "Well, only that it was rude of me to send you up and down the stairs with stitches in your thigh. I mean, what if you injured it further? We need you as healthy as you can be, right?"

"Yep," he said, sitting at the small kitchen island. She saw his quick frown and the wry twist to his lips, but just as soon as she saw it, it was gone. "The leg's doing okay. I heal quick. I got stuff at the store, there should be supplies here too. I've done this before."

"Really? You get injured on the job a lot?" She took a seat across from him.

"Enough that I know what to do."

"Would you like another sandwich?" she asked, noticing the empty plate. He'd finished the sandwich in a few quick bites. "I'm used to cooking for a boy. One's probably not enough for a grown man."

"That would be great."

"No problem, keep your seat. I'll get it."

"Thanks." She felt him watching her as she turned the stove on again. "My mom used to make them that way, with butter. My aunt's never tasted the same. She used oleo."

"Oleo?"

"Margarine. She's from the Midwest, some people out there call it oleo. The way they call soft drinks, pop."

She nodded. "Here you go. Is one more enough or should I make another?"

"This is plenty. I appreciate it." Caine was halfway through the second sandwich when his cell phone rang again.

They both froze, gazes locked, then Caine checked the number.

The change in his face told her all she needed to know. It was Donovan.

"Go to Xavier and stay quiet. I'll be telling him you're tied and gagged, so no noise. Got it?"

"Got it," she hurried upstairs. When Xavier looked up in surprise, she put a finger to her lips and whispered, "Agent Bradley's talking to your father. Mute the game," she pointed to the console. "Good job. I'm going to go to the top of the stairs to listen, okay?"

Xavier nodded mutely, watching her departure with frightened eyes. The impact of his fear followed her to the stairwell. The house's open floor plan made eavesdropping easy.

Caine's voice was rough, with an ugly edge she'd not heard from him before. "Yeah, I got 'em. That wife of yours is one tough broad, Walker. Bitch cost me sixteen stitches, dammit. Fucking bombs. God damn near got me again when I caught up to 'em. Had to kill the dog—"

A moment later she heard a blast of comment from Donovan, even this far away. "Well, hell, Walker, I ain't likin' to go around killin' dogs either. Yeah, bitchin' big guard dog. Bit me, the fucker."

Silence. Then, a laugh. A harsh bark of sound. "You think? I'll tell you what I think. I think she's smart as hell, and she hates your guts."

Jesus, he's baiting him. Why?

"Yeah, yeah, rant all you want, but she nearly killed us all. If Tappen hadn't lifted that Huey off and bugged out, he'd be dead meat too. What?"

Two heartbeats passed as Caine listened. "She thought I was dead, what do you think? Like I said, smart bitch.

And cold. Stepped over me to check on the annoyance. Yeah, took him out at the alarm box. Had it wired. He was still sparking when I took out of there after her and the kid."

Yuck. She shuddered, listening to him describe the scene. She had caused it, but hearing the starkly painted details sickened her.

"It's gonna cost ya, man. She fucking shot me, the bitch. Just a graze, but as soon as I finish with the bandage, I'm gonna smack her around for that one. You want me to go ahead and off her? I can dump the body an' bring you the kid. Nice kid, by the way. Dead ringer for you."

Dana ground her teeth at the remark. She knew he was acting, knew it was said for Donovan's benefit, but the callousness of it pissed her off.

He had his act down pat, that was for sure. It scared her because if he had been Donovan's man, it might have played out just the way he'd described. And Xavier looked so much like his father.

"No, no, we got a contract. You pay me what you pay me. But I fucking earned a hazard bonus. That shot nearly hit my balls. Too fucking close for comfort."

Donovan must have said something equally crude in return, because Caine laughed. "Yeah, but I'm gonna make her change the bandage. Maybe have her . . . what?"

When he spoke again, it was with more anger in his tone and a note of servility.

"Right. Okay, I get it. No touchy. I thought you hated the bitch." Caine paused, and Dana strained to hear, not wanting to miss any nuance of the conversation. "Yeah, I'll get the kid something. Of course not." Now he sounded indignant. "Hell no, I won't scare him. Yeah,

yeah. Fuck, man, I get it, okay? I don't hurt the bitch. I don't scare the kid. I get them to you. Where's the meet? I'm in Virginia. Yeah, Alexandria," he lied smoothly.

A pro at deception. Then again, who was she to talk? She did it too, with the best of them.

"Jesus, dude, I know my biz, that's how. A motel. Of course it's out of sight. Yeah, tied up and gagged. She's too damn tricky to let loose, even to go pee. Hell no, and she had a big, fuckin' gun. Christ almighty, how come you had to go and teach her to shoot? Uh-huh, like I said, I want a fucking hazard bonus, Walker." Another pause, longer this time.

"Couple of days. Gotta make sure the fucking Feebies ain't on my tail. They hit the house 'bout thirty minutes after the shooting started. Me?" Now Caine laughed again, that harsh bark of sound. "Did you know your *wife* has a panic room?" The emphasis told her Donovan had used the term as well. "Yeah, snatched her and the kid and tucked us all neatly away till we had an all clear. Nah, didn't bother with it. Why'd you think it took me so long to check in, man? Can't fricking leap out of there like Batman and drag the two of them away. Then they got past me, had to chase 'em. Took me a while to snag 'em again. Sure as hell wasn't gonna call ya' before I had 'em in hand. Ya' think I'm crazy?"

There was another longer pause this time. Donovan must be on a roll.

"Richmond. Yeah, I know it. Down by the river. Past Shockoe Slip, yeah. I'll head that way in what . . . four days? Christ, I gotta deal with your smart mouth kid for four fucking days? Ha, I'm kiddin' man, he's okay. Takes after you. Smart."

A bit of fawning, eh? Wise. Very wise. It always put Donovan in a good mood.

"Right. Okay, call me. Yeah, this number. Time and place. Remember, hazard bonus, man." He clicked off.

Dana walked back to Xavy, knelt beside him. "Did you hear any of that?"

"Some of it. He sounded mean, didn't he, Mom? Mr. Caine?" Xavy asked, leaning in to her body. "Are we really, uh, okay with him, do you think? He sounded . . . scary. Like, dangerous."

"He did, didn't he?" she put her arms around him and tugged him close. Shadow came and nearly sat on her feet. It seemed all her guys needed reassurance. "It's his job to act that way, like one of the people your father would hire."

"Uh, Mom," her son said, his face buried in her shirt. Voice muffled, he continued to talk. The words tumbled out, fast, as if he needed to say it quickly so he wouldn't chicken out. Or as if he was afraid she'd be upset. "Would you not call him my father any more? Call him Donovan or something else like you sometimes do, or don't talk about him. It creeps me out, like . . . to like . . . be related to him." Xavier raised his eyes to meet hers. His were sober, serious. "He wants us dead."

She couldn't bear to correct him, tell him that his father—Donovan, she mentally corrected—wanted *her* dead, not him.

"How about we call him Walker, the way Agent Bradley does? Will that work?"

"Yeah, that's okay." He loosened his hold as she kissed him, and he realized she wasn't mad at him. "If we have to talk about him at all."

"You need anything else to eat?" she asked to change

the subject, noting the whistle-clean plate and empty glass.

"Nah. Shadow had a few chips. I think he's hungry."

"Yes, I'll feed him. You going to play some more?" She nodded toward the frozen action on the television.

"If it's okay," he said, and her ten-year-old was back, in place of the miniature adult. "I'm rockin' it."

"It's okay. You go rock it and let me know if you get a high score. C'mon, Shadow," she patted her leg and the dog leapt to join her as she went to the kitchen.

Caine sat where she'd left him, gazing out into the beauty of the late afternoon sunlight on the mountains. His face was unreadable, but she sensed a nearly unbearable weariness.

"Agent Bradley?"

He pivoted to face her, and Shadow stepped in front of her, a wordless gesture of defense. He gazed at the dog, then at her face.

"You hear any of that?"

"All of it. I was at the top of the stairs."

"Knew you would be."

To escape the bleakness she saw in him, she walked to their bags and got Shadow's bowl. Dumping in dog food from a Ziploc, she then poured the dregs of the soup over it and tossed in the last bite of her sandwich. Hearing how vehemently Donovan wanted them caused the food she'd already eaten to lie heavy in her stomach.

With Shadow taken care of, she faced Caine.

"Where's the meet?"

"Richmond, at the James River docks. I've got to call Tervain, but we need to talk first."

"Okay," she picked up plates and was about to set them in the sink when he put a hand on her arm.

"I said I need to talk to you."

"I think better when I'm busy. I'll clean, you talk."
Warmth flushed her skin where he'd touched her. A
patch of heat in an otherwise chilling moment.

"He still loves you."

Shocked, she dropped the plates into the sink and
turned. "Who? Donovan?" She pressed her stomach to
quiet the disgust and queasiness his words provoked.
"You're kidding, right? Sick joke, Agent."

"I asked you to call me Caine."

"Okay, Caine. Sick joke, right?"

"No, serious shit. Face it, because it drives him, his decisions. He's more dangerous than ever because he has
to show you he's the man. He believes you belong to
him. 'Til death do you part, you're his."

"That's not love, dammit," she snarled, clanging more
dishes into the sink.

"His words, and no, it isn't. But it's as close as he'll
ever get. He's got other women. They're fluff. You're the
real deal. He was proud of you, you know. Proud that
you'd nearly bested him."

"I did best him, the bastard," she exclaimed, angry
now and ready to spit fire at Caine. "He thinks he got
me, but he didn't, did he?"

Caine held up a hand, halting her tirade.

"No, but thank God he thinks he did. The love thing,
though. It's huge. This is what Tervain didn't want to believe," Caine said earnestly, leaning forward. He lowered
his voice, probably to ensure Xavier couldn't hear him.
"He won't stop till you're dead. Or he is. You know that,
right?"

Dana braced her hands on the counter. Head hanging

down, she took several deep breaths until her voice was steady enough to answer.

"Yes," she said, raising her gaze to his. "But it's not love."

"No?"

"No. It's obsession. I'm a possession, a toy. Once he knew he had a son coming, I became his. It consumed him to think that he'd have an heir, a legacy."

Caine nodded, understanding dawning in his eyes.

"Why did you stay?"

"Stupidity."

"Stop that," Caine said sharply, and she flinched, taken aback by his vehemence. "I may not know every-thing about you, Dana Markham, but one thing I'd stake my life on," he paused, waiting for her to look him in the eye. "Hell, I *have* staked my life, and yours and Xavier's too, on the knowledge that you are not stupid."

It took her a few minutes to decipher the compliment in his irritated words, because she heard the anger first. He was glaring at her, half rising from the stool.

"Thank you," she said simply. Then frowned, adding, "I think."

He gave a shaky laugh, even as anger still reflected in his eyes. "You're welcome."

"The fact remains, whether it was stupidity or naiveté, I stayed. I was pregnant and scared. I married him." She faced Caine, straightening her shoulders. She'd made her peace with this demon. She needed him to under-stand that. "I was raised that you didn't get pregnant until you were married. And God forbid, if you did get in trouble, you *got* married, quick. That was the way it was. Period."

She rinsed the dishes and stacked them in the dishwasher.

"You think they wouldn't have understood?" Caine asked.

"Oh, if I'd gone to my folks, said, 'hey, I'm knocked up, but the father's a monster so I'm not going to marry him,' they would have understood. Eventually."

"But?"

She slapped the door shut on the dishwasher with more force than she intended, making the dishes rattle with the impact.

"I didn't know he was a monster, not at first."

Caine nodded. "Walker didn't come out of the shadows for a long time. If he'd stayed on that level, what he did before your son was born, we'd never have caught him. He was careful, canny. Hell, from what I get, they still wouldn't have caught him without you."

It was her turn to nod. "He was a businessman, a good provider. That's what my parents saw, and approved of, by the way. He was very domineering, but suave and attentive. I hoped he might change. It was young, stupid, I'm-pregnant-and-in-trouble thinking." She wiped the counters, even though she hadn't spilled anything. "Needless to say, nothing changed for the better."

The conversation, depressing as it was, might have gone on, but Caine's cell phone rang again.

She put Shadow in a sit, gave him the command for silence.

Hurrying to the stairs, she called, "Xavy, mute the game. Agent Bradley's got a call."

"Yes'm," he replied, and the beep and clash of virtual battles ceased instantly.

She signaled Caine, and he pushed the button on his phone.

"Yeah?" A pause. "Tervain, what the hell is going down? You okay? What? Aw, shit." Caine rubbed his eyes, and she saw the muscles rippling under the close-fitting black shirt. "Is he going to pull through? Uh-huh. Okay. Yeah, I did. Here's the plan," he said, relating all the things about which he and Donovan had talked.

Dana listened, wondering for the thousandth time how everything had become such a horrible tangled mess. She was drawn back to the present when Caine angled in his seat to see her reaction.

"I don't know how she'll take it, but I'll put it to her. You want to tell her?" He sounded incredulous and gave a genuine laugh, amused and somehow lighter, friendlier, as if he and Dana were sharing a private joke. His eyes twinkled at her. "She nearly blew me to kingdom come. I'm not telling someone who can make that happen to leave her kid somewhere. You tell her." Caine handed the phone to Dana. "Tervain wants to talk to you."

As she took the phone, she heard Tervain saying, "Caine? Caine, you son of a bitch, don't you put her on the phone."

"Too late," she said as she took the cell and put it to her ear. "You got me."

"Mrs. Markham, hello," the agent hastily recovered, sounding overly hearty, like a stereotypical car salesman. "We were trying to formulate . . ."

"I heard. It would have to be one amazing, bullet-proof plan for me to agree to leave Xavier anywhere."

"I know, I know. But if we guarantee his safety while you went on with Agent Bradley," Tervain rushed to spill the concept. "And we had a chance to get Walker, wouldn't it be worth it?"

"Oh, yeah, if all that were really possible. Guarantee his protection, Agent Tervain? The way the Marshals and FBI have managed to do for him and me these last few months? Hmmmmm, that would be a 'no,'" she said, making an X mark in the air with her free hand. "And the possibility of getting Donovan? Let's just say, I'm dubious, shall we? You've managed so well till now. Yes, Agent Tervain, I *am* being sarcastic. I think I have a right, don't you?"

Tervain agreed but kept talking as fast as he could, outlining the plan.

"We'll have a secured location with five, six agents. Constant check in. We're working on a decoy for your son, an agent who's small enough. Maybe a woman in disguise."

Dana rolled her eyes, wondering if the man had gone crazy. "You're kidding, right? Even at that age, girls have a different manner than boys. They walk differently, talk differently—hell, they even chew gum differently."

"It doesn't have to stand up to that much scrutiny, Mrs. Markham. We'll go in to Richmond with the agent in Xavier's clothes, with you and the decoy agent in mock restraints. Everyone's gait changes when their hands are tied. Remember, he hasn't seen your son in what, six years? Seven?"

"Something like that."

"Boys change a lot in that time, you know that."

"Tell me about it," she muttered, momentarily diverted at the thought of how many clothes he'd outgrown, how many sizes he'd gone through.

"So, you and our agent are mock-bound. You two and

Caine arrive at the warehouse, go in. Caine talks to Walker, gives the signal, we close in."

"As easy as that? You think it'll be that cut and dried?" She laughed, but didn't actually find anything humorous about the mental picture he'd built. "We'd be fu–fricking sitting ducks."

"No, no, we'd have the place surrounded."

"Oh, yeah. That worked before. So well, too." She turned the sarcasm on full force and didn't regret it a bit.

"Mrs. Markham. Dana," Tervain pleaded. "We have to try. It's the closest we've been in . . . what? Hell, I don't know, but it's years, not months."

She hated that he was right. "Years, yeah. The reason I'm even talking to you is we both know it can't go on. He'll get me, sooner or later. Sooner, at this rate, given how far he's willing to go, how much he's willing to spend."

She glanced at Caine. He nodded, an agreement based on the conversation they'd been having.

"Then you'll do it?"

"What choice do I have?" When Tervain began to crow a bit, she slapped him down. "Don't get too excited, Tervain. You haven't found a decoy yet. And if you think I'm going in there trussed like a Christmas goose and un-armed, think again."

The sound of grinding teeth came through the phone.

"We've been over this, Mrs. Markham. There's only so many rules I can bend. Hell, I'm in such hot water over what you did at your house I can hardly sit down for the fires on my desk. Do you know how many laws you broke?"

"I do, actually. Three city ordinances, necessitating a mandatory five hundred dollar fine each. Otherwise, none, because everything I used was purchased legally and with no criminal intent."

"You blew up three men," Tervain nearly shouted.

A fast flashback to the image of the dead alarm disabler made her stomach clench. "No, I blew up four flower pots. The men, trespassers, by the way, happened to get hit by flying debris. Agent Bradley won't press charges, will you, Agent?"

Grinning, he shook his head.

"He's not pressing charges, so I'll pay my fine and be done." She paused. "Oh, I did discharge my weapon, but in Virginia, that isn't a crime if your property is being violated."

"That's not the point," Tervain blustered. "It's against the law to—"

"Nope, it's not. I checked. It's on the Internet, you know, as are instructions on how to make a bomb. All the nice rules and regulations for what you can and can't do in a municipality. Pretty comprehensive lists, too. Did you know there's a law in one town that you can't breed mules on Sunday? Antiquated but automated."

"That's ridiculous."

"Hey, I didn't make the law. All I did was read about it."

Caine was doubled over in a vain attempt to control his laughter. It made her grin for a moment before she returned to the topic.

"Back on track here, Tervain. I'm not going into that warehouse unarmed. You cannot restrict the right of a citizen of these United States to bear arms, given a permit. And let me tell you, I've got permits out the wazoo. Oh, and I don't think any warehouse of Donovan's has one of those red, crossed-out circle handgun signs on the door, do you?"

This time, Caine's guffaw was audible, and Tervain

began to curse. Quite inventively, for a man who appeared so stuffy.

"I can't condone that, Mrs. Markham."

"I didn't ask you to, Agent Tervain. I'm simply informing you, not asking your permission." Her tone, all business, had Caine straightening, eyebrows raised. A smile played on his mouth, and there was an approving gleam in his eye.

"Mrs. Markham . . . Dana," the agent began, then trailed off. When he resumed, there was resignation in his tone. "I've informed you of the plan, the details as I know them. Are you in agreement with it, so far?"

"You get a safe house, stock it, and lock it up so tight a mouse's whisper won't get through to my boy."

"Right."

"You get a decoy, and hell, if you get a woman, at least make sure she's flat chested, for God's sake."

"We're working on it."

She didn't even want to know what that entailed.

"You find the decoy, I say 'yea' or 'nay' on whether they'll work or not."

"That's unreasonable, we've got to—"

"All I really have to do is live, love my son, protect him if I can, and die, Agent. I'd rather that be in a hundred years with a pack of grandchildren mourning my passing, but I'll put myself on the line to save my son. My terms, or we don't work. Got it?"

Chapter Seven

There was silence as Tervain absorbed her vehement statement. She hoped he read into it all that it implied. She knew she might die. She knew they might fail. But, by God, she was stacking the deck in her favor as much as possible.

"God help me, yes."

"God being on our side for once would be a plus," she said, feeling the weight of the long day and the sleepless night hurl itself onto her back. "So, I go armed. You don't have to like it or agree to it or even think about it," she said. "In fact, put it out of your mind. Deal?"

At his long sigh, she knew she had him.

"After this goes down, Mrs. Markham, I hope we won't be meeting every few months, other than socially."

"Me too, Agent, me too," she said as she hung up and handed phone back to Caine.

"You're going armed when we hit Richmond," Caine made it more of a statement than a question.

"Is the sky blue?" she asked. "I have Xavier to think about."

Nodding, he stood and stretched. Then he winced.

"I need a shower, fresh clothes. You keep watch. That window," he pointed to the front picture window. "It's the best vantage point. You've already figured that, right?"

"Yeah. What else was going on? You asked about someone being hurt."

"Parlier. You know he didn't check in from the doctor's, which he should have done when he got there. And he didn't come back to the hotel?"

"Yes, that's why we left. Did they find him?" Her heart clenched. Why did so many people have to pay the price for Donovan's obsessions?

"Don't look so stricken. Parlier's a tough old dog. Someone ran him and the doc off the road. The car broke through the guard rail and rolled into a ravine. Took 'em hours to find them even with the GPS."

"It's bad, isn't it?" she said, already knowing the answer.

"Parlier fractured both legs on impact. He lost blood. Probably has a concussion too." His brief delivery didn't lessen the impact of the other agent's plight. "The doctor's still unconscious and has internal injuries but is expected to pull through."

"Some blood? Internal injuries? Dear God, does Donovan have to kill everyone who gets in his way?" Exhausted and overwhelmed, Dana's reserves finally ran out. She put her head down on the counter and wept.

"Hey, hey," Caine said, leaping from his seat to take her into his arms. "Parlier's rallying. He's conscious," he said as he patted her back and stroked her hair in alternating patterns. "We can't be sure it was Walker."

She raised her head, not believing what she was hearing. "You don't believe that, do you? Isn't it a bit too convenient that Agent Parlier is run off the road when we're waiting for him to get us to safety?"

"Yeah," he admitted, tightening his grip so that she was once more pressed against strong, muscular, and very firm male flesh. "It's Walker. Don't know why I tried to convince you, of all people, otherwise."

"Because Tervain wanted you to?" she said, gaining an insight into the conversation. Caine's muscles tensed the barest fraction, and she knew she'd hit the mark. "Gotcha," she said quietly, easing away and wiping at her streaming eyes. "You have a *tell* the way a gambler does."

"I do not," he said, offended and distracted.

"Not a bad one," she conceded, giving herself more distance from the haven of his arms. It was just too tempting. "I caught it because you were . . . uh . . . holding me. You tensed." She sighed and pulled a tissue from a nearby box, glad she hadn't managed make-up yet. With the waterworks she'd just pulled, mascara would be everywhere. "C'mon Caine, be real. You and I know Donovan. Tervain doesn't, not really. He's never been subject to that twisted brand of loyalty and love."

Dana paced the length of the kitchen, stopping only to grab another tissue. "He sucks you in. I know how it is. He did it to me. Parlier's accident wasn't one, so there *is* an inside man. How else would anyone have been close enough to get to Parlier?"

Stopping in front of him, she added, "All the more reason for me to be armed when we go to Richmond."

With a curt nod, he spoke. "I do know it. Unless we can uncover the mole, whoever the bastard may be, we're facing friendly fire too. Besides," he reached out and squeezed her hand. "You can handle yourself."

Friendly fire hadn't occurred to her, so it took a minute to catch up. She sucked in a breath, hiccoughing a bit. "Um, thanks. I do know a few things about guns."

He scrutinized her face, and she was afraid he was going to offer something . . . more personal. *Oh, hell.* To her total relief, he smiled.

"Right. If you're gonna be okay, I really do need that shower."

"Of course. I'm sorry."

"What for? Tervain's the one who wouldn't shut up. Keep watch. I'll be quick."

"I will, and take your time."

With a laugh, he grabbed the bag of medical supplies. "What? You sayin' I stink?" He joked, changing the mood.

"What? No, of course not." Her cheeks flamed. Dammit, she hated that blush. "I meant that I . . ." He was obviously enjoying her discomfort. Seeing the twinkle in his eyes, she mock-snarled, "Hit the showers, Bradley, and quit hassling your protectee." She made shooing motions, and he laughed again as he limped up the stairs with his bag in hand.

She winced at the limp. He was a big boy, part of her brain argued, and could take care of himself. He wouldn't thank her for mother-henning him, treating him as she would Xavier. Then again, if she took a more maternal stance, maybe she wouldn't think about him as if he were prime rib.

Sighing, Dana was about to pick up the gun and go to her post when she heard lighter footsteps on the stairs. Xavy was bringing his plate and glass down.

"High score?"

"Not yet," he said, handing the dishes to her. "I'm going to try again."

"Sure. Before you go, I need to tell you that we'll be here a couple of days, all right? The FBI is trying to formulate a plan. Your fath—uh, Walker, wants Caine to bring us to Richmond. Agent Tervain's working on a plan to put you in protective custody, get a decoy to go with us, and see if we can get this over with once and for all."

"Mom," he protested, fear leaping into his eyes. He grabbed her hand. "You said you wouldn't let them take me away from you." Distress rang in his voice.

"And I won't. The plan's not finished yet. But," she corked the further flow of protest by kneeling so they were eye to eye. "If I think it'll work, if they can plan it to my satisfaction, I may agree."

"Nuh-uh," he squeezed her fingers, frantically shaking his head. "You can't leave me with them."

"Wait, wait. Let me tell you why. C'mere," She led him to the counter, urged him onto the seat, and sat next to him. Holding his hand to keep the contact, she continued. "Here's the deal. I won't risk you. Your . . . Walker wants me because he sees my going to the police and testifying against him as a betrayal, a . . . slap at his manhood. He hates me because I took you away and split up our family."

"Yeah, we've been over this, Mom. I know he wants us back. But we were never a family," he declared fiercely. "We won't go back."

"No," she said, sharply enough to focus his attention. "I need you to understand this, honey." She looked into his eyes. "He wants *you*, so that you can be his heir, learn his business, and inherit it. You're a symbol, a trophy in a way. Do you understand that?"

Xavier nodded. "But you're not. Is that what you're trying to tell me?"

Taking a deep breath, she nodded. "That's it. I'm a trophy, but a different kind. He wants to kill me."

She waited through Xavier's shocked protest.

"I know. But it's true, baby. Think about it. I haven't wanted to push this, to make you think about it. This time, I need you to. We can't keep running. He'll find us again. We have to make a stand. To do that, to defeat him, means we may have to split up for a while."

"But . . . but . . ." Xavy continued. "We could change our names again. We've lived in Virginia for nearly three whole years. It took him a while to find us there. And Mr. Caine, he said—"

"I know, sweetie," she interrupted. "But think it through. If it hadn't been for a lot of luck, this time especially, and some preparation on my part, you and I wouldn't be having this conversation. Please, honey. I need you to really think about it, okay?"

She sat patiently while he did, his protests silenced for the moment. He was a good thinker, her boy. As much as she hated it, as much as she wished it weren't so, she knew he'd see her point.

"There isn't any other way?" The question was both plaintive and resigned.

"Not that we can think of."

"What about if I were bait, instead of you?"

That he would think of this shouldn't have surprised her, but it did. It took her several heartbeats to get past her shock and answer.

"There are a few problems with that, right off hand."

"Like what?" he demanded, arms crossed and a frown on his face. Her stomach clenched. He was truly his father's son in that particular pose.

"You're a minor, so the FBI won't accept your offer, even if I were to agree to it, which I won't."

"But, Mom . . ."

"Hear me out. The other consideration is, if the plan fails with using me as bait, you're still protected. And they have another chance to catch your fa—Donovan when he continues to come after you. If you go as bait, and the plan fails, Walker gets you. There's no second chance to get him. You see?"

Xavier was silent for a minute, then, with a reluctant frown, he nodded. "It's scary, Mom. I don't want to have you out there without me. We're a team. You said so," the pitch of his voice gave away his fear. The young man her son was becoming receded, and the child showed through. He was terrified.

So was she.

"We *are* a team, honey. Always. But, it's like on the baseball field. Sometimes you hit a sacrifice fly to bring another runner in, you know? Both players love to hit, but for the whole team to win, you have to give up your chance at a home run or a base hit to bring in the runner. Make sense?"

Xavier lowered his head, seemingly engrossed in the pattern on his well-worn, high-top sneakers. She could almost hear the gears turning in his head.

"But why can't I be the one to make the sac fly?"

"You're already on base, honey. You get to go play video games, eat popcorn and pizza, and hang out till I hit that sac fly and bring you runnin' home."

He looked up from his shoes, tears brimming in his eyes.

"It's awful, Mom. If we have to do it, I . . . I . . . guess we have to, right?" She nodded and he continued. "But it's going to be hard to be at some cruddy safe house by myself."

"I know," she said, pulling him into a hug and letting him surreptitiously dry his eyes on her shirt. "But we'll get through it, the same way we've gotten through everything else together. We'll each do our part, right?"

"I guess so," he said listlessly.

"Oh, c'mon, let's hear some enthusiasm for the game, dude. If I'm going to be out there hitting sac flies, I better have some enthusiasm," she growled, tickling his ribs until he collapsed onto her lap. The high kitchen stool wasn't exactly conducive to a tickle fight, but she made do.

They wrestled and tickled for a few minutes, renewing the bond that had been strained by fears of the future. When they were both breathless, they called a truce and sat talking about nonsense.

Hearing the water turn on, Dana remembered she was the one on watch. "Hey, honey, why don't you go rummage around in our bags and get me the first aid kit. Agent Caine's having a shower now. When he's done, I'm going to do the same. You need to shower too," she said as she blew and snuffled into the curve of his neck, making him yelp and giggle. "Wheeeeeuuuw! Yeah, you need a wash, stinky boy. I get dibs on the next one, otherwise you'll use all the hot water."

"I don't stink," he giggled, wiggling out from under her restraining arm. "I smell manly." He pantomimed a weight lifter's muscle-bound pose.

"Ugh, manly boy needs a bath, and so do you." The banter lightened the mood, and she scooted him off for the kit. When he'd bounded away, she retrieved the gun and quickly and silently made her rounds. She checked the locks and turned off lights as she slid through the maze of the dusky living room to peer into the shadowy landscape.

Beyond the window, the world was still and quiet as far as she could see. A slight wind shook the mostly naked branches in a random, easy sway. Off a ways, she saw what might be an owl cruise along at tree-top height, then land. It was an elegant, peaceful scene, and she wished, not for the first time, that she painted.

"Woods at twilight," she said to herself, thinking that's what she'd name the painting, if she'd had any talent for painting.

Following Xavy to the second floor, she checked the surrounding area from the higher vantage point of the bedroom windows. He met her in the upper hallway with the med kit.

"Here, Mom. I found it."

"Great. Why don't you and Shadow finish saving the universe, and I'll clean my foot so that when Agent Bradley gets done, I can jump in the shower right away."

"'Kay. C'mon, Shadow."

The dog obligingly followed Xavy into the game room, as she had mentally dubbed it, and she saw him lie down on the floor next to the pillow Xavy had been sitting on. Satisfied Xavy was occupied, she continued into the bedrooms, going from window to window, searching for signs of danger.

It wasn't long before her tour brought her back to the kitchen. She and Caine had just eaten, but Xavier had beaten them to lunch by an hour or more. He'd want dinner before too long.

As she rummaged through the cabinets, her mind wrestled with choices. She'd nominally agreed to being bait for the Richmond deal, but should she head for Canada and a semblance of freedom instead?

Richmond. Canada. The choices loomed large in her mind. Each one fraught with its own challenges and peril. Leave her boy or leave *with* her boy? As she laid out the fixings for spaghetti, she mentally ping-ponged between the two.

Richmond. They might get Donovan, stop the killing, and stop the constant running. There was also a distinct chance, no matter how well they planned and how well armed she was, that she'd be killed. And worse, she could be killed and Donovan might survive to continue his pursuit of Xavier.

If that happened, Xavier would be in his father's hands within weeks. It was her vigilance that had kept them free and alive so far.

Canada was fraught with its own difficulties. She had no friends there, no ties. And if she left the familiarity of the US, she also left behind the network of agents and public assistance, which had kept her incognito and reasonably invisible, thus far.

In the shower, Caine washed off the grime of two days worth of sweat and anxiety. He'd taped a part of a plastic bag over his wound. Screw the doctor and his dictate to not get it wet. If he didn't have a shower, Donovan would be able to find him by smell.

Ten minutes of hot water left him feeling more human. With a grunt of pain, he yanked off the plastic, taking off some skin as well. "Damn," he cursed, pounding softly on the marble countertop. "That freakin' *hurts*."

The wound hurt, and the tape stung. The whole thing

sucked. Dana Markham was too damn smart. She knew she might die. She knew they might not be able to protect her . . . or her son.

The kid. Xavier was pretty cool for a kid. Caine hadn't been around many boys. His sister's children were girls. They weren't into video games, and the last thing his prissy sister would have allowed was a big-ass dog slurping over the kid's hot dogs while they were playing kill-the-bad-guy.

Dana didn't lie to her kid. He gave her kudos for that, admired it. She might hate it, but she told him straight.

In spite of his pain, he laughed. Man, she had been beautiful telling Tervain off. She had scored point after point on the guy, never letting up. Not that Tervain deserved a break, but, to be fair, it wasn't Tervain's fault the mission was screwed. It wasn't any great star on his own record either.

"She told you," he said to himself, thinking Tervain must have been about to have apoplexy when she told him she'd be packing heat on the Richmond deal.

He propped his leg up and bent to deal with his injury. To his dismay, the area was swollen and irritated. Crap. He did *not* need an infection. He smeared a triple antibiotic ointment on the line of stitches, hissing as the cold gel met his tender flesh.

Bandaging took mere minutes, and he rummaged in the cabinets for some oral antibiotics. Thankfully the zone houses were always stocked with meds.

Easing into the new jeans, he grimaced as the stiff fabric ground over the gauze bandage. Lacing the boots was painful too, but it reminded him that he needed to ask Dana if she wanted antibiotics for her foot.

Going down the stairs in his silent way, he was in time to hear Dana tell her son, "He wants to kill me."

Caine listened to the rest of the conversation. When she sent Xavier for the kit, he eased back up the stairs. He needed to think.

It amazed him how much she told her son. How involved she kept the boy. He heard Dana pass the door and go downstairs. He needed to talk with Xavier as well.

"Hey buddy," he said, walking into the game room. Xavy and Shadow were lying on the floor watching television.

"Hey," the boy said, then looked him over. "The jeans are better," he added, bluntly. "A lot less conspic . . . conspic . . . you know."

"Yeah. The word's conspicuous. And you're right. What'cha watching?"

"Oprah. She's got some guy on there talking about this organization that feeds people all over the world. Some kids in Nebraska raised enough money to buy something they call an Ark that helps people eat and, uh, sell milk and stuff for extra money. It's over five thousand dollars. Pretty cool."

"You could probably do something for them too, at your school."

"Yeah, if I go back there, maybe I will. Got a pencil?"

Caine found a pen and paper in the bookcase and handed them to Xavy. "Here."

"Thanks," the boy quickly wrote a Web address and, referring to the TV screen, the name of the organization, Heifer International.

"Funny name," he said to Caine. "A heifer's a girl cow, right?"

Caine wasn't sure and said so. "Sounds right. I've never been on a farm, so I don't know much about it."

"Neither have I but some of my friends live on farms."

"You want to go back, don't you?"

The boy shrugged. "Don't always get what you want, right? Mom says," he cut his eyes toward Caine, very adult now. "She says you and the other guy, Tervain, have a plan. It means I stay hidden while she goes and meets with my . . . Walker. You guys trap him when he comes for her. That right?"

"I think that covers the main points, yeah."

"You gonna kill him?"

The straightforward question took Caine off-guard, but it shouldn't have. Xavier understood the realities of the situation. Dana knew it and treated him accordingly. Caine couldn't—wouldn't—do any less.

"I'm supposed to capture him and take him in for trial."

"I know that. But supposed to and what's going to happen are different, aren't they?"

He imagined Dana saying that very thing. There were a lot of "supposed to's" for them both. *Your father is supposed to love you. Your father is supposed to love your mother, not want to kill her. You're supposed to be able to stay in one place and grow up with your pals. Play baseball.*

"They are, yeah. I don't know if I'll have to kill him or not. Don't know if I'll get a shot. If I can, I'm supposed to capture him. He has a lot to answer for, to a lot of people. Not just to you."

The boy considered this, turning away to watch Oprah for a few minutes. He didn't face Caine as he spoke.

"I wish he weren't my dad. I wish he'd never seen us. That he didn't know who we were."

"I do too, Xavier. I do too." Caine didn't know why it felt right to put his hand on the boy's shoulder and give it a squeeze, but it did.

"I wish he were dead."

Caine didn't say a word. He knew that in a perfect world, he should correct the boy, tell him it wasn't right to want someone dead. Given what he knew though, how could he say it? It's hard to wish prosperity and long life to someone who wanted to kill your mother.

So instead, he sat with Xavier in silence, watching a parade of animals on Oprah's stage.

"These are just a few of the wonderful creatures helping save lives, build communities, and eliminate hunger all over the world," the popular hostess said as the credits rolled. "Consider contributing to our Angel Network, or directly to Heifer International, as you make your charitable plans this year. Bye-bye, see you tomorrow!"

The voiceover announced the evening news, and Xavy picked up the remote. Caine removed his hand, and they continued to sit, the silence less fraught with meaning than before.

"I think your mom's probably getting dinner ready. We ought to go help."

"She said she'd make spaghetti. You're ready to eat?" Xavy said, surprise written all over his face. "You just ate. Man, you eat like a horse."

"You callin' me a ol' nag, boy?" Caine joked. "I'll get you for that."

He reached for the boy, but Xavy danced out of the way, saying, "Horse, horse, horse."

They thundered down the stairs with Shadow barking in hot pursuit.

Dashing through the kitchen, which smelled of garlic and toasting bread, Dana rushed to meet them.

"What on Earth?"

Chapter Eight

"He eats more'n a horse," Xavier said, dashing behind his mom, laughing like a loon. "He said he's hungry again. But he ate earlier. Horse, horse, horse," the boy chanted.

"Am not," Caine protested with a goofy grin, to Dana's amazement. Then he made his hands into claws and growled. "I'm a dragon, an insatiable dragon."

Shrieking with delight, the boy dashed into the sitting area with Caine hot on his heels.

Dana stood, mouth agape, watching the two fool around. Caine never got too close, never crowded the boy. Xavier didn't call any names or do anything too overt. They were having fun, but both were wary and cautious of the other.

Still. She'd never seen Xavier take to someone this quickly. There were so few male influences around him. When she'd first gone under, when she hoped—prayed—Donovan was really dead, she'd dated. It had taken her two years to garner enough courage to accept a date, but it had been fun. She'd managed two or three dates before they'd gone back on the run.

She'd never done it again.

Restraining Shadow, who wasn't sure whether to join in and bark or go after Caine, she watched until she realized it was at a certain point. They were either going to have to take it to the next level of rough-housing or back off.

Men hated to back off.

Knowing it and thinking of Caine's leg, she called a halt to the game.

"Dragon, no boy for you, two weeks. You've been bad," she called out, ending the game in its tracks.

"Hey, says who?" Xavy protested.

"For complaining, small boy who might be a dragon's dinner, you get . . . hmmmmm," she pretended to be considering a dreadful punishment. "Spaghetti."

"And what do I get?" Caine asked, standing up from his dragon-wing crouch.

"I told you," she waggled a finger. "No boy, two weeks. You're on a diet. You eat too much," she said, straight-faced. "Spaghetti for you too. Now go wash, both of you."

"Awww," he said, laughter evident in his voice. "I so wanted boy. Can't I have one, just one?"

She and Xavy both laughed at the childish plea in Caine's request.

"Nope," Xavy answered the question. "When Mom says no, it means no."

The disgusted rejoinder made Dana laugh. "There, you see? From the mouths of babes. Xavier, wash in the bathroom down here. It's in the hall." She pointed him in the right direction. To Caine, she said, "You, kitchen sink. Wash your hands. Prepare to meet a plate of spaghetti."

Caine looked at Xavier and shrugged. "Guess if she won't give any quarter, we'd better obey. But I'll get you next time, buddy, and your little dog too."

"Nuh-uh," Xavy said, dancing away and down the hall. "Shadow's too fast for any old dragon, and so am I."

"We'll see about that," Caine called after him, then limped to the sink. "Thanks for the reprieve," he muttered as he passed her. "I'm not sure I could take him. He is your son, after all."

Amazed, Dana gaped at him, pivoting to follow his progress. He grinned at her. That flash of humor warmed her all the way to her toes. Carefree, easy, and happy, it promised all manner of laughter and fun. The kind of fun, real fun, she hadn't had in . . . well, forever.

Shaking off the spell, she frowned. "What were you two doing?"

"Nothing. Guy stuff."

Xavy came in, just in time to hear that and said, "Yeah, guy stuff. You wouldn't . . ." he trailed off, seeing her face. "Uh, you wouldn't have any, uh, jam for the toast, would you?"

Dana was sure she heard Caine say, "Good save," but she didn't comment.

"I think there's strawberry," Dana said, and Xavy whooped and yanked on the refrigerator door. "But if it's growing green stuff," Dana continued, grinning. "It's destined for the pit of despair. You got it?" She rolled her eyes at his exaggerated groan.

"Aw Mom, Mr. Wood said it's a sugar mold. You can eat it. It won't kill you or anything."

She held a hand out for the jam jar. "Mr. Wood's been a bachelor for forty years, so I'm sure his eating habits don't meet my standards, get it?"

"Yeah, okay. So?" Xavier waited for the verdict. "Pit of despair, or do I get to eat it?"

"Eat it, dude. It's fine."

"All right," he said as he bounced onto a stool.

"The pit of despair?" Caine asked, taking a seat at her direction.

"Trash can," Xavy managed to say around a forkful. Swallowing hastily so he wouldn't face her wrath, he continued, "but it's a movie line, from *The Princess Bride.*"

"Missed that one," Caine said.

"Not a dragon movie, I guess," Dana said, spinning pasta onto her fork.

"No, I guess not," Caine said with a grin.

They spoke of favorite films and music. Xavier brightly joined in to describe his favorite musicians and music. "I get into Bon Jovi, the old stuff, you know?" he piped up.

"I like some of that too, but the Stones. Now, they know how to make some music." Caine offered his opinion.

"Yeah, yeah," Xavy enthused. "I got one of their CDs at Starbucks." He glanced at Dana. "Well, Mom got it, but I copped it and downloaded some of the songs onto my iPod."

"Did you bring your iPod into the house?" Dana asked, sharing a smile with Caine at Xavier's fervor.

"Yeah, it's upstairs by my stuff. I wanted to leave everything together."

Dana left the discussion and the dishes in favor of a shower. Caine had told her he'd manage Xavy and clean up, as well as security watch.

Peeling off her sock, Dana perused the wound on her foot. It wasn't deep, but it was nearly an inch long. She cut new bandages from medical tape, shaped a gauze pad, and slathered on some of the antibiotic cream that Caine had left for her on the counter. It didn't hurt, which surprised her, considering where it was, but she was grateful.

When she was finished with her shower, she called down to Xavier. "I need a manly boy in here on the double."

There was a rumble of voices from below and the pounding of feet. Xavier hurried into view. "Hey, guess what, Mom?"

"What, Xav?"

He grinned. "Mr. Caine says that if we can get to a computer, we can download some old stuff to my iPod. Some Beatles and maybe even some Sting."

"Old stuff, yeah," she said, wondering how Sting could be considered old stuff. "It is good. If you enjoy it, we'll download some songs from his first group, The Police."

"Wow, awesome," he said.

After his shower, he kept a steady flow of questions as he got ready for bed, dressing in sweatpants, socks, and a shirt. "You think Mr. Caine's for real? You think he'll do what he said?"

"Yeah," she said, smoothing his hair. "If he can, he will."

"Cool."

"You ready to get some sleep?"

"Uh-huh. Where are you gonna be?"

"Downstairs for a while. I'll be on first watch. Then I'll be over there," she pointed at the door across the hall. "I'll leave the door ajar, in case you need me."

"Okay. C'mere, Shadow." Xavier said as he patted the foot of the bed. The dog obliged, leaping lightly onto the mattress, and quickly curling up, one eye on Dana to see if she objected.

Dana rubbed his head, making him grin a doggy grin, then did the same sort of head ruffle to her son. "What big, handsome boys. Two-legged and four." She kissed Xavier's cheeks. "Goodnight, Xavy. I love you."

"Love you too, Mom. Say goodnight to Mr. Caine."

"Will do."

She went down the stairs, slowing as she got near the bottom. She didn't know what she was going to say to Caine. He and Xavier had bonded in some strange, male fashion. On one hand, she wanted to warn him off, tell him not to let Xavier get attached to the laughter and the male presence.

On the other hand, for Xavy's sake, she wanted her boy to see how a real good man acted, how he treated others. None of the teachers or coaches Xavy knew were as strong or as potent a personality as Caine Bradley.

Caine heard Dana stop on the stairs and wondered at the pause. He stood in the family room with the lights out, searching the darkness for movement, for the betraying gleam of face or night scope.

To his surprise, although he felt keenly focused, he was calm. The gnawing in his gut, carried since the failed and fatal mission in Tijuana, was absent. The sense of self-loathing that gave him a reckless edge seemed quiescent as well.

It worried the hell out of him. Where was that sharp pang? Where was the angular, predatory snap he'd come to count on?

The boy, he thought. The boy had stolen it away, if just for the afternoon.

A smile tickled the corners of his mouth, even as he continued to watch over the markers he'd mentally set in the shadowy landscape. The kid was sharp, a smart one. To Caine's surprise, he wasn't bitter or cowed by life on the run with his mother. He wasn't playing Pollyanna either, Caine reminded himself, thinking of the kid's comments about wishing his father dead.

Then there was Dana. Just thinking about her got his

juices flowing. Why? He had no idea. She was dangerous, smart, funny, and amazingly sexy all in one package. The way she'd looked, standing over him with that H and K barrel pointed right at his head . . . something in him shuddered. She'd looked desperate but determined. He'd seen what she was made of. Steel. She'd have killed him, if he hadn't managed to get the code words out.

His smile widened as he thought about her look, her body. He still wasn't sure why he'd been so attracted to her there in the basement. Adrenaline maybe.

"Maybe," he muttered to himself, doubting it even as he said it. "Maybe not," he amended, thinking of her firm curves molding to his as he and Dana had made their way up the stairs. Strength, brains, and beauty. It was a hell of a combo.

Maybe that was why he felt lighter, freer, in spite of their circumstances. Maybe.

When she came into the room with her movements sure, despite the gloom, his senses went on high alert.

"See any varmints, Sheriff?" she asked with the accent of an old West codger.

"No, Miss Kitty, no varmints." He eased out of target range of a shot through the window. She moved with a wariness akin to his own, never making a target of herself.

By plopping down in a chair and kicking her feet up onto the well-worn center table, she minimized her target profile even more. "It's good to sit down for a few minutes."

"Xavier in bed?"

"Yeah. He's a solid sleeper, thank goodness. Then again, he's had to be."

"Guess so. Bet you don't sleep so well," Caine observed. He curbed the instantaneous mental images of ways he could improve her rest. He frowned in annoyance at his errant thoughts.

She laughed, but there was a rasp of pain in the sound. "No. Between being a mom and always being on alert for Donovan coming for us, I don't sleep very well. What about you?"

"I don't sleep that well," he answered truthfully, for a change. It felt good. "But if it's my turn to go I'm ready. I rest easy when I rest."

Her smile was a gleam in the darkness, and his heart picked up its pace. The philosophy seemed to surprise her, and she said so. "I didn't picture you as religious."

"I'm not. No church would have me. Then again, most churches are full of politicians and hypocrites," he said cynically. "So I believe what I believe and keep going."

"I can understand that. I miss choir," she mused. "But church membership is another way to be found. I minimize those. The last time I went regularly was before I met Donovan. I went to a Presbyterian school."

"I know. Trinity University."

"Yeah. It's weird that you know so much about me. Makes me feel like I've known you forever," she said. There was a long pause before she continued. "But I haven't. I don't know anything about you."

"There's not much to know," he replied, not wanting to get into this discussion. He was already angry with himself for sharing so much of the load with her. Treating her like a partner. His last partner hadn't survived the experience of being matched up with him, and Caine wasn't eager for a repeat.

He had to get back on top of the situation. Be the professional agent he'd been trained to be. He had to lead instead of just limping along.

"I'd like to know something. If we have to live together and trust each other, then I'd like to know you."

No. If he was sure of anything, he was sure that she wouldn't want to know him. With the life he'd led and the things he'd done, he was damaged goods. What he'd done, he'd done for the government, to help catch people who did so much worse. It was legal, but was it right? He could never be sure.

"I'll tell you that I'm good at what I do. I'll protect you as best I can and do everything in my power to ensure your safety."

"That's not good enough."

What did she want, a pedigree? He shot her a look from where he stood.

"It's all I have," he managed the terse reply as he left the room to check the house.

She was still there when he returned.

"I thought you would have gone to bed."

"Hoped, you mean," she replied. He could hear the smile in her voice. "I'm not trying to make you angry, Caine. I just want to understand something about who you are. I'm trusting my life and my son's life to you."

"I'll lay down my life for you and Xavier." The words were flat and serious. And he meant them. However blurry he'd allowed the lines to be between them, she was still very important. She was the one who had to survive. Dana and the boy.

"Yes," the reply was instant. "I believe you would."

She let the room go quiet, but he could tell she wasn't done. Why couldn't she just leave it alone?

"In his own way, Donovan would die for us too," she

said, surprising him. "Of course, that's only if he couldn't kill us first. Tell me the difference between you. I know there is one."

She was serious. He tried to muffle his anger at being compared, even back-handedly, to Walker. "I don't know what you want to hear, Dana. I'm no saint. Unlike your ex-husband, I don't want you hurt, and I sure don't want you dead."

"Well, that's something, I guess. Have you ever been married?"

He gave the distant woods a last long stare before taking the chair opposite her. She wasn't going to let this go before he answered at least a few of her questions. "No. Engaged, once. She ran a non-profit I investigated. In the end, she wanted someone to take care of her."

"That sounds . . ."

"Boring," he finished for her.

"I wasn't going to say that," she protested.

"No? It was. She married a preacher. Became a missionary." Before he could brood over that failure, one of so many, Dana surprised him.

"Flush toilets," she blurted out.

"Beg pardon?" He was non-plussed.

"Missionary work. Very few flush toilets. Got a cousin," she said, draping both legs over the arm of the chair. "She joined the Peace Corps right out of college. Went to Botswana, way out in the country, digging wells or something. Camp toilets only." She shuddered as he laughed. "No thanks. For a few days camping, okay, but to live that way? Uh-uh."

Somehow, in spite of her probing questions, he was beginning to relax.

"Clean sheets. Chinese take out. People don't know

how good they've got it, do they?" Caine said quietly, thinking once more of Tijuana. His partner had loved Chinese.

"No, in a lot of ways, people in general have no idea how sheltered their lives are." Her eyes were closed and she was smiling.

He felt himself responding to the look of her, the long smooth line of her throat, and her secretive smile. The tightness in his chest—and his groin—made him mad all over again. Who the hell was she, to connect with him so easily? Make him feel . . . whatever.

"Do you have brothers or sisters? Where are you from?" Dana asked.

In his mind, he could hear the same question, from a different woman. A different location. He was drawn back to that dusty hotel in Tijuana, waiting with Carly, his now-dead partner, for the quarry to move. Waiting for something to happen. They'd been bored, passing the time. They'd stupidly thought Walker didn't know they were there and on to him.

Something had happened. All too quickly, the door had flown open, and bullets tore through the room, killing her in an instant. He'd managed to kill all four gunmen, never realizing in his rage that he'd been hit seven times.

"Nevermind," she managed, looking over at him as the silence lengthened. "I didn't mean to get too personal." The bleak thoughts must have shown on his face, dammit. She unsettled him, caught him off guard. He tried a smile, but it must have looked . . . bad. She abruptly sat up.

"Is something wrong, Caine?"

"No. My family's off limits."

She cocked her head, her temper stiffening her posture and gaze. "Sorry if I offended you," she said, snapping out the words, "but since my family *isn't* off limits, and you probably even know what kind of underwear I buy, I hope you'll excuse me for being a little miffed."

"Miffed? Is that a word?" She distracted him. Everything about her distracted him. That was bad. But the images of Mexico faded, replaced with her snapping glance and instant retaliation. When she snarled and rose, probably to stomp off, he relented. "Sorry, sorry. Sit." She spun on her heel, about to blast him again, but he deflected it with one word. "Please?"

She sat, her back ramrod straight, and her arms crossed. Great. Now she was . . . what had she said? Miffed.

"What kind of word is that, miffed?"

"Are you making fun of me?"

"No."

She sighed. "It's a perfectly good word, proper English usage to indicate irritation."

"So, you're a chemistry and biology major who knows her English."

"I minored in literature."

"I didn't know *that*," he said, offering it as an apology. But for what, he wasn't sure.

Suddenly he pinpointed the problem. Trust. It was so simple, so dangerous. He stood up, went back to the window, and looked out into the black night.

Did he trust her? Crap. He didn't *want* to trust her. Not for the usual reasons. For him, trust rendered equality. *You don't trust your protectees*, he heard the instructor ranting inside his head. *They're like two year olds. You protect them. You don't trust them.* Protocol said, "Beware!" but his gut, the warning twitch he heeded most in life, said "she's legit."

He went with his gut. "Did you know that in the beginning The Agency thought you were in on it. Why else would Walker have married a chemist?"

"You're kidding, right?" He heard the genuine surprise in her voice. The non sequitur still hadn't headed off the last of the brewing anger.

He shook his head and made sure he met her eyes so she'd see the truth. "I need to make a sweep. You gonna hang here?"

"Yeah."

"I'll do a last check and then turn it over to you."

"Okay."

Damn. She was still pissed. That didn't help. So far, he was not scoring well on the witness protection part of the gig. And no matter his internal decisions about trust, she hadn't made up her mind to trust him. Oh, she'd still work with him, but not comfortably. He'd tarnished, if not permanently damaged, the easy camaraderie from earlier in the evening.

He left her sitting in the darkness. As he made his rounds, he wondered why the hell Dana Markham's trust *mattered* so much.

"Hey baby," Donovan crooned into the phone, soothing the ruffled feathers of his latest conquest. "Don't worry, I'll find a way to see you. You know I want you." He laughed at the sly proposition she offered. "Oh, yeah, baby. That's *why* I want you, baby. You know how to please me, like no one else. Mmmmm hmmmm," he murmured. He did enjoy her. She was so desperate for attention. She didn't care

what he did to her—or with her—as long as he told her
she was beautiful and the best.

Talk about easy.

"We have to be careful though, *cara*," he reminded
her, using the Italian endearment to soften her further.
He was thinking about how to deal with her. She was beginning to get on his nerves. She was also a dangerous
toy, since she knew his true identity. Then again, he was
using her for so many things, the least of which was sex.

*"You have someone on the inside, a plant. I overheard the plan
for catching you. Be careful, darling."*

Her words snapped his attention back from the
mental list he was drafting.

"What do you mean I have a fucking plant?" Crap,
he'd yelled at her. She usually pouted when that happened, and it was impossible to deal with her. "I'm sorry,
baby," he said, struggling to sound soft and contrite. "I
was thinking about that last time . . . yeah. Then you lay
that on me. Didn't mean to yell, no. Of course not." He
rolled his eyes. The bitch didn't put out *that* well. He
wasn't going to be able to tolerate her too much longer.
He'd have to wait though, until she could find out who
in his organization was the plant.

God dammit. That was why he had failed to get Dana.
Now it was clear. His *wife* had nearly unholy luck, but his
plan had been flawless. Now he saw that if it had failed,
it was because of the plant. His plan would have worked.
It had been fucking *genius* and well executed. Fuck the
FBI. Fuck the Goddamn US Government and their Goddamn undercover agents.

He let none of his rage spill over into his words. No
hint of it escaped to warn the woman on the other end
of the line. After all, no matter how low she was in the

FBI, she still was getting him deeply buried information. No one else had managed to clue into a plant. In fact, he thought with renewed rage, his other sources had been sure his own organization was clean of any government taint.

"That's right, you luscious thing. I'm going to make you come so much," he told her, giving her a few suggestions of how and where he would fuck her. She liked the descriptions. Even if he never did it, it set her off. "Mmmm, you bet. You find out for me, you hear? Tell me who it is who's fucking up my plans, so I can deal with them, okay? Then we'll find a way. Yes, honey, a way to be together."

In her dreams, he thought. But when she mentioned Donny, Jr., he snapped back to attention. If she wanted him to listen, she'd figured out the key, he decided, actually managing to smile around the rage that threatened to choke him. Clever girl when she wasn't fuckin' talking so much.

"If you can do that, baby, I'll marry you," he declared flatly, with conviction. Her fondest wish. Hell, if she could get Donny, Jr., maybe he *would* marry her. Then, when he tired of her, she could be . . . disposed of. He was going to have to do that at some point anyway. She knew too much. He might as well enjoy her for a while first.

"Okay, baby, you call me. This number."

He brooded for hours, running endlessly through the lists of names and discarding all but a few. It had to have been someone who *knew* about the raid. Spike was dead and so was Petey. Spike wasn't smart enough to follow orders. There was no way he was smart enough to live a double life. Petey was out too, because he was mental. That left the pilot Tappen, and Pollack.

Tappen was smart but . . .

Pollack. It had to be. Why hadn't he thought of it earlier? Pollack was dangerously smart. There had always been that nearly unfathomable edge to Pollack, a darker heart than even he could penetrate.

Considering the others who had been on the team, he was the only likely candidate. Patrick was smart enough, but he hadn't gone on the raid, and he was tied to his wife and child, both of whom Donovan had given him. He wouldn't go back to the Agency. No. If it had to be either Patrick or Pollack, it was definitely Pollack. Pollack didn't do drugs and seldom took advantage of the women who congregated around the various compounds he commanded.

This changed everything.

Snatching up his phone, he scanned the numbers and dialed.

"Patrick, change of plans. Bring it back. Meet me at the house in Charleston."

He hung up and began packing. He needed to be there first, to plan and coordinate. This time, *he* would finish it. This time he would see Dana die for betraying him. And Pollack too.

Zipping the bag, he used the intercom to call one of his men. His blood was zinging with the adrenaline rush. This was it. He could feel it.

One more roll of the dice.

Chapter Nine

"All's quiet," Dana said to Caine when they switched places at two in the morning. She'd barely tapped on his door before he'd opened it, then followed her downstairs.

"Good."

She hoped he'd say more. She'd passed the hours of her watch wandering the quiet house, peering down the mountain and across the field to the side of the house, and seeking the sight or hint of movement on the driveway. Thinking.

With every step she'd grown more embarrassed about how she'd prodded him. When it came down to it, it was none of her business who he was. She'd realized she wanted to know for herself. Not because it mattered in how he protected them.

"Caine," she started, "I'm—"

"Don't say it. No apology. You're right. I know you from your dossier, from time of birth to now. You don't know me or have reason to trust me."

Okay, she hadn't expected him to capitulate. Not that easily. They stood, staring at one another for an endless, important moment.

"I have a sister," he said. "Two nieces. My dad's dead. My mom's still alive." He paused, rubbed his hands over his face. He stepped away, but only to get room so he could start stretching and bending to loosen his muscles.

It was obviously a long-held habit, but it was driving her crazy. How could she be annoyed when he was giving her what she wanted? How irritating that he'd given in and told her. If he hadn't, she could put him aside and dislike him to get some distance. How could she do that now?

Watching him move, so lithe and powerful, made her want to run her hands over his awesome ass. God, she needed sleep.

"I grew up in Iowa," he added, breaking the silence.

"A Hawkeye."

He grinned. "Yeah."

Oh God, that grin was devastating. Between that and sheer weariness, she staggered.

"What? What is it?"

Everything. Nothing. *Oh, hell.*

"It's okay. I'm all right. Just tired. You know how it is. You have too much time to think in the dark and the quiet," she managed. It was true, but she absolutely refused to tell him she'd been thinking about his smile. Or his ass.

"I won't let him get you, Dana," Caine said softly, misinterpreting her answer and surprising her with his intensity. It sounded like a vow. "I'll kill him first."

The quiet, powerful declaration was scary. To her horror, it was also a turn on. He walked with her into the kitchen and leaned on the island as she got a glass and filled it with water.

"You sure you want to say that to me, Caine?" she managed.

He laughed. "You gonna rat me out to Tervain? Tell Parlier I killed Walker with malice aforethought? I don't think so. Hell, they already figure I'm gunnin' for him for my own reasons."

Knowing he was right, she shifted under his piercing gaze. "No, I guess not."

"So, we'll keep each other's secrets. I won't tell Tervain you're thinking about ditching all of us." He moved in, taking the glass and sipping the water. He was standing so close. Her heartbeat skipped in irrational anticipation. But all he said was, "And if you happen to shoot Donovan first, hand me the gun. As a federal agent, I won't get rapped for it. You might."

She hadn't thought of possible repercussions. There were so many positives to Donovan's death, she decided, with macabre humor. "You're right. I hadn't considered prints or the investigation. Do you think he'll end up dead?"

"He won't surrender, not a second time. It'll go to the death, or he'll escape."

"Sounds like him. Macho idiot."

"His bullshit, yeah. He hasn't figured on being mortal," he said with his teeth gleaming once more in the shadows, but fiercely this time. "He needs reminding."

"From your mouth to God's ear," she said. Bringing them full circle, she took the glass back and sipped. He watched her, and she felt every nerve buzz.

The house creaked around them, while her blood sparked and itched. Should she touch him? Thank him?

"Well," Dana said bouncing on the balls of her feet, dispelling the disquieting thoughts and the giddy relief at sharing the load. "I should go to bed, so I'll be ready for the next watch."

"I'll wake you at five. Thanks for taking the first."

"I got some sleep last night, you didn't. You're healing, and you're on point in this venture, when it comes down to it."

He reached for the glass again and drained it. "Thanks," he said, lifting it in salute.

"You're welcome," she managed, but when he moved in, she retreated, forgetting the counter was at her back.

"Oh," she said, feeling the hard edge clip her waist. He caught her, the corded steel of his arms bracing her, his hand caressing the spot as if to smooth away the pain.

"Thanks," she murmured, embarrassed, as she realized he'd just been putting the glass in the sink. "I'm okay, really," she continued, when he didn't let loose.

"I know," his voice was warm, intimate. "You're . . . good. Really."

He leaned down, and the breath caught in her throat. Was he going to kiss her? Now?

He was.

His lips caressed hers, lightly at first, then with a firmer press when she responded instinctively to his touch. They didn't cling. It was too soon, too dangerous for that.

Instead, the kiss said everything. *I'm attracted*. And *I wish . . .*

Then, like a hurricane, they came together. Tongues meshed, bodies entwined. She wanted to touch him everywhere. She wanted to feel his hands, his arms, against her bare skin. His hands, a hot presence on her rear, pressed her closer. She could feel every inch of him, every surprising inch of his response to her.

She wrapped one leg around his, locking them together as they continued the hot battle. His mouth was so enticing, so engrossing. She felt as if every inch of her body were on fire.

"Dana . . ."

Oh, God, what was she doing? She warred with herself. She wanted to go on, never stop. Never let *him* stop. But the smoky groan of her name grounded her, brought her back to sanity.

When they broke apart, he steadied her. "Better let go," she said, huskily. "Your grabbing me is what got us in trouble in the first place."

"Interesting definition of trouble," he managed, his breathing still uneven.

"Not really," she said. "This is totally is not a good idea." *Please, let me convince myself.*

"No," he said, a fire still lurking in his gaze. "Then again, neither of us takes the easy path, do we?"

She stared beyond him into the shadows. It was as if the world was holding its breath, waiting for her answer.

The melodramatic imagery brought her back to the moment.

"No, but there's always hope that once, just once, it could be simple. This," she made a motion to indicate the two of them, the wild embrace. "Would not be simple."

"No, it wouldn't." He agreed. Suddenly, he laughed. "I don't think simple and Dana Markham should ever be used in the same sentence."

"What does that mean?" Now she was indignant, probably more so than was warranted. She was reeling from the kiss and trying to cover it. She had to find her balance. Now. Especially since he seemed so . . . unaffected.

"It's not bad," he protested. "It's that you're . . ."

"What? A pain?"

"No, complex. Fascinating." He drew a gentle finger down her cheek. "Interesting. On so many levels."

Oh, boy. Maybe not so unaffected. Enjoying the warmth of his hand on her cheek, Dana wished she could invite him into her world. But it wasn't possible. They came from different places, were going different places.

If they made it through the next few days alive.

"No smart remark?" he asked, cupping her cheek.

"No. But . . . thank you, I guess."

"You're welcome. And now," he said, as he pressed another, less powerful kiss to her lips, then shot her a quirky smile. "I bid you good night, fair princess."

"Interesting words, from a dragon."

"Remind me to roar for you tomorrow," he said lightly, giving her room, but taking the warmth with him.

"That'll be impressive."

"You bet."

She stopped on the stairs and looked back. He was an inky silhouette in the gloom as they silently appraised one another. Neither spoke.

Turning away, she heard the thud of Shadow's weight as he left the bed to monitor her progress up to her room. It was the only marker that anyone else existed in the house.

Her feelings tumbled over one another. Regret? She didn't regret kissing him.

Despair? Tomorrow was another day. They would make it or they wouldn't. In fact, they might even have the day to themselves, in peace. Who could predict? That would be a miracle, but miracles did happen. She had to believe that, or she'd go mad.

A star winked in the night sky beyond the bedroom window, and she wished on it.

Please, please, for just one day, I want peace.

She stripped off her jeans and dropped them by the bed, crawling under the covers in her shirt and underwear. The bed was still faintly warm from Caine's body. It smelled of soap and man. She breathed in the scent, her face pressed into the pillow. The whole day passed as a blur behind her tired eyelids. Had she only known him two days? Had she really kissed him in the kitchen? *Holy shit.*

Her wilder, younger side complained that it had only been a kiss. Big deal. They were human and healthy. It wasn't as if she was going to jump into bed with him. Hell, she'd kissed people more deeply and revealingly on a first date.

Caine's lips had been hot, firm. His mouth . . . inventive. She wondered what it would be like to explore, delve deeper. She felt her body flush, felt the tingling of need within her. A woman's need, not a girl's. If she focused much more on Caine's lips, or his ass, she was going to be seriously uncomfortable. Or she'd do something stupid.

The mature Dana reminded her she wasn't alone and wasn't free. The young, carefree Dana had had the ersatz security of youth and stupidity, allowing her to bestow kisses where she chose. Now, she was older and the sole guardian of a beautiful, wonderful boy who was sleeping a room away.

And everything in their lives hung on setting a trap for Donovan.

Directing her thoughts firmly away from the dangerous ground Caine represented, Dana focused on her house; planned how she would rebuild. She wondered if Parlier was alive.

With all the disparate ideas and questions rolling

around and popping up in her mind, she worried she'd have trouble sleeping. She didn't. The next thing she knew, daylight streamed in the windows and the cry of "Coooooool" rang out from somewhere downstairs, as a cabinet door slammed.

Xavier was awake, and she'd obviously slept into the next watch. She hoped Caine was prepared to deal with a sugar-charged boy, if he was doing what she guessed he was. One of the cereals loaded on the shelves was a forbidden favorite.

"His problem," she said aloud, crossing to the bathroom. Her backpack, with her toiletries inside, leaned on the cabinet. A small gathering of his things were set to one side. A razor, shaving cream, and the medical supplies.

Having held him, wrapped herself around him, kissed him, she felt strange showering where he'd showered. It gave her goosebumps. "Stupid," she said to the shower head. "College girl stuff."

She dressed, automatically keeping her things together, making them easy to dump into a bag in one swipe. Coming into the kitchen, she saw Xavier hovering over a bowl of floating pink and yellow blobs.

"Hey Mom," he pointed at the bowl. "Fruity-Os. Isn't it great?"

"If you want straight sugar for breakfast."

"Coffee. That's what I want," Caine said, closing the door on a cupboard. "Did you see any yesterday in your searches?"

"Yes, it's in the freezer."

"The freezer?" Man and boy chorused at the same time. "Why?"

She laughed at them. "It keeps it fresh. Let's hope its

ground, because I didn't see a grinder." It was, and soon the heavenly scent filled the air.

"How come you drink that stuff?" Xavy asked. She started to answer, then realized it was Caine to whom he addressed the question, not her.

"It's an acquired taste." Caine leaned on the island. "Like that cereal. I smell the sugar from here. I could appreciate Fruity-Os, if I was starving in the desert. Same goes for you and java." The two guys grinned at each other, both seemingly pleased at the explanation.

"Now your mom and I, we drink coffee. I'm about to ask her if she likes eggs."

"I can tell you," Xavier answered, bouncing in his seat. "She eats 'em scrambled, with toast."

Caine glanced her way. She smiled and nodded.

"What about bacon? Does she eat bacon?"

Xavier frowned, "Don't know. Mom, do you like bacon?"

Coming around to hug him, she addressed her answer to Caine. "I like bacon. You fixing breakfast this morning?"

"Yep. We'll split KP. That means you do dishes, Fruity-O-face boy."

Xavy grinned around a mouthful. "Just like at home."

"Don't talk with you mouth full," Dana said automatically.

Caine returned Xavy's grin, but said, "Your mom's up on us by two meals. We have to quit slackin' off."

She started to protest that it had been grilled cheese, some spaghetti, easy stuff; but checked the impulse. If he wanted to cook her breakfast, who was she to complain? After all, it had been a damn long time since someone had done it. Soggy cereal and a card on her birthday notwithstanding, Xavier wasn't yet ready for serious kitchen activity.

"Thank you. I'll top off my cup and sit here next to the cereal-eating machine. No," she put a hand on Xavy's arm before he could refill the bowl. "That's enough. You'll be wired for hours as it is."

It was more pleasant than she'd have guessed to simply sit, tease Xavy and take in the view of a man cooking breakfast.

Let's face it, girl, she snickered to herself, *that is one fine-looking short order cook.*

"I can make toast," the boy said, hopping off the stool and carrying the now-empty cereal bowl to the sink. "You want me to do the toast?" he said, looking at Caine.

"Wash the bowl and slap it in the dishwasher. Then you're on toast patrol."

"All right," Xavier cheered, hurrying to the sink.

Delighted at the interplay, Dana made a quick security sweep and returned to watch the show. Xavy and Caine jostled and bumped hips, knocking each other off balance whenever possible. Xavy knew to stop when Caine was at the stove, but otherwise, the two picked at each other, as boys and men will do, throughout the preparations.

"All right, shrimp," Caine growled. "Grab a stool." He assumed a French accent and twirled an imaginary mustache before bowing in Dana's direction. "For zee lay dee, zee eggs, scrambled to perfection," he made a slurpy-smoochy sound with his fingers at his mouth. "Zee toast, lightly browned—not too much. Bien, breakfast, she is served."

"Merci, Monsieur," Dana returned the bow, then leaned over and noisily kissed her son on the cheek. "And thank you to the cook's helper."

"M-o-m," Xavy drawled out the syllables, rolling his eyes. "You don't kiss the cook's helper."

"No, I guess you don't. You kiss the cook. C'mere," she beckoned to Caine, pressed a smacking kiss to his cheek. "There, Monsieur Cook, a reward for your labors. Merci, merci, one and all. Now," she turned to Xavy. "What do I gotta do to get a fork around here?"

"Oops." He jumped down with a clatter, grabbing utensils.

"Better. Thanks. Seriously," she said to Caine, catching the twinkle in his eye.

"Welcome. Seriously."

They did dishes while Dana, mug in hand, made another sweep, checking the view from all the vantage points.

The property was even more beautiful in the morning light, though it still seemed wintry at this altitude. Spring was coming though. She spotted the first haze of green leaves coloring the trees, a glow of vibrant life, silhouetted against the blue of the sky.

"Hey Mom, Shadow's got to go out."

"I'll take him," she said, motioning for the dog to join her. To Caine, she said, "I checked perimeter. Everything's quiet from every view."

"I'll watch from here," he said, at the kitchen window.

She nodded, opened the door, and let the dog go first. The deer must have scattered, smelling the dog, because Shadow bounded off the porch and into the grass, rushing in happy circles before making his way to some low bushes.

She eased out the door, scanning the hillside, but saw nothing except the glory of nature all around her. Something about the scene, the call of a hawk overhead, and the crisp breeze that smelled of earth and new growth, lifted her heart. All of a sudden, happiness radiated through her.

Testing the sensation, as one would probe a sore tooth, she took a deep breath. She laughed as Shadow bounded after a blowing leaf, snapping at the airborne plaything.

"Xavy," she called through the door. "Bring me a ball for Shadow." She heard the stomp of the boy's feet, and within minutes he handed her a grubby tennis ball.

"Shadow, fetch," she called, as she cocked her arm and let the ball fly.

"Good one, Mom," Xavier praised as the missile soared, then bounced down slope with Shadow in hot pursuit. The dog raced to them, deposited the ball, and barked for it to be thrown again.

"You do it," she said, handing over the ball.

"All right." The boy scanned the area before leaping off the porch into the yard with the excited dog. She stood, watching as they played catch for well over an hour.

The scrape of a footstep behind her had her whirling. Caine stood behind her, two steaming cups in hand.

"Just me," he said, a wry smile lighting his features. He handed her coffee. "How're they doing?"

"Dog's up by three," she indicated the catch and fetch game. "But the kid's on a comeback."

"See anything?"

"A hawk."

"Want to take a walk?"

She looked at him in surprise. It was a good bet she, Xavy, and Caine were supposed to stay in the house at all times. She'd thought he was coming to order that very thing. "Is that wise?"

"No, but we've all got cabin fever."

"You too?"

"Yeah."

Mugs in hand, they sauntered into the yard. Xavier halted at the sight of them, mouth hanging open. Shadow took immediate advantage of his inattention, snatching the ball from his slack fingers. "Hey, aren't you supposed to stay inside?"

"Yeah," Caine said, coming up next to the boy. "Dog's skunking you. Oh, he's prancing now. He knows it too."

"Oh, man, you distracted me," Xavy half-complained. Dana knew he was too intrigued by their presence to be concerned with the game.

"Don't let our arrival distract you," Dana motioned to the dog, as Shadow rolled the now slimy ball to her feet. "Ugh, that's disgusting." She picked it up with the tips of her fingers and flung it, laughing when the dog spun in hot pursuit.

A ridge of rocks poked through the earth twenty yards away.

"Can I go climb on that, Mom?" Xavier asked, his face awash with pleading. She hated to say no.

"Sure." It was Caine who answered. "If your mom says it's okay. We'll be able to see you from here."

Dana hoped her shock didn't show as she agreed. "Go for it."

The "thanks, Mom," that floated to them was an afterthought. Shadow abandoned the ball and met the boy at the craggy pile. They could be seen but not heard as they explored.

"Why?" Dana asked as she drank her coffee to ease her dry throat.

"He's sequestered enough. You said it yourself. If

you tie him down too much, he'll rebel. This is better, more controllable."

The two of them stood, silent watchers as Xavier leapt and climbed.

"We need to go down there."

"One of us has to keep watch, so you go. I'll stay."

It was hard to sacrifice playing with her son. She so seldom got to play with him. But, the vision of Caine and Xavy racing through the house playing dragon and boy was vivid.

"No, go be dragon, I'll do guard duty."

"No," Caine said, and she heard the regret. "It's my job."

"I'll relieve you, momentarily. Go." When he hesitated, she said, more firmly. "It's a request, but I hope you'll do it. He needs this." They locked gazes, and he seemed to be searching for something in her eyes, some permission or acknowledgement. Whatever it was, he found it.

"What the hell," he said with a boyish grin, handing her his cup. The shrieks of laughter and the war whoops that ensued over the next forty-five minutes would have done ten boys proud, much less one boy and one man. She scanned everything repeatedly, hyperaware that she was on duty, but the silent vigil let her think. The only problem was all she could think about was Caine and their kiss the night before. How good he was with her son . . .

When he strode over a few minutes later, cheeks flushed by the cool wind, she was picturing him naked.

"Oh, God," she muttered. "Stop it. Don't even think it." She continued to silently chant the words as he paused, laughter dancing in his eyes.

"Well, Queen Dana, your turn. Ninja boy's done this dragon in." They smiled foolishly at one another and

Dana's heart turned. *Why?* Her heart wailed. *Why couldn't this kind of man have been Xavier's father?*

"Dana?" Caine took her arm, as if to shake her. "Are you okay? What is it?"

"Oh, thinking again, sorry," she stumbled over the words, mortified that he'd caught her daydreaming and mooning over him. "Here," she shoved the mug into his hands. "Nothing's stirring."

A concerned frown darkened Caine's brow and he looked at the tree line, down the meadow. "Only a few minutes. We've been out too long."

"Yes." She turned away and went to assume her queen of the rocks role. The whole time they played, dashing in, out, and over the stones, with Shadow pacing them or darting around to tug at their clothing in fun, Dana reran the image of Caine, smiling and walking toward her. Part of her mind was engaged in playing with her son, but the deeper part, the lonely, scared part, wished Caine could be with them, be with her; that this idyllic time would go on forever.

Without seeming to halt the game, Dana drew Xavier to the porch. It was sheltered from the wind, and they picnicked there for lunch. Xavy cheered as Caine launched the ball for Shadow. His ooohs and ahhhs were a testament to Caine's strength. Between the morning's activity and Caine's impressive throws. Shadow was slowing.

"Did ya ever play ball, Mr. Caine?" Xavy asked after one spectacular toss.

"Yeah. College football. Quarterback, second string."

"Did ya get to start any? Play any good games?"

"Yeah, started in the second half of a Sugar Bowl game. Helped my team win."

"Oh, man. I bet that was fun."

"It was. I enjoyed it." Dana heard a wealth of meaning in the simple reply and raised an eyebrow in inquiry when Caine turned her way. He shook his head. Not a story for Xavier's ears, she guessed. Odd how quickly and smoothly they'd managed this nonverbal communication. It was almost telepathic.

All too easily the idea brought her full circle to wishing for things she had no business thinking about.

Caine.

Sex.

Them as a family.

Sex.

How much Xavier liked him.

Sex.

Chapter Ten

Oh, for Pete's sake, she thought. *Get your brain out of the gutter.* Once more she cursed her hotly awakened libido. It had been quiet for years. Why *now*?

The answer stood at the edge of the porch, making sure no one lurked in the woods down the hill from the cabin.

"It's getting cold. We should go in," she said reluctantly, breaking the silence. In spite of her internal exasperation, she didn't want the day to end. It had been idyllic.

Later, after an early meal of hamburgers and chips, they sat together in the sitting room. With frequent breaks for security sweeps, they passed the time with card games and a lot of laughter. She extended Xavy's bedtime, delighted with the experiences they boy was enjoying, and reveling in the sight of Caine and Xavy together. Another factor in her allowing Xavy more games was that given her earlier thoughts, and God help her, her flagrant response to Caine's kisses, she wasn't sure how she would react to being alone again with him again.

The last thing she wanted was to be—or come across as—some desperate, helpless Federal protectee.

Knowing she was dragging it out, she finally took Xavy

upstairs. He climbed into bed, snuggling under the covers as she tucked him in. "I wish we could stay here with Mr. Caine for a while," he said softly.

"Why?"

"I like him," he said simply. "He treats me like a guy, not as if I'm some punk kid. And you like him, I can tell."

Before she said anything negative or positive about the statement, Xavier continued. "Shadow likes him. He knows people. And he thinks Mr. Caine's okay too."

They had often joked about Shadow's extra sense of things. Somehow the dog always knew which kid or adult was unsound, no matter what showed to the world.

"It is fun, and I'm very glad you and Shadow both like him. And I don't know about you, but in spite of how scary he sounded on the phone call yesterday, I feel safer having him with us."

"Yeah, and he's got three guns."

"How do you know that," she asked, concerned.

"Chill, Mom. He didn't, you know, whip 'em out or anything. I saw 'em when we were outside. One in a holster on his leg, one under his arm, and one on his back, by the waistband, you know?"

"I know." She'd encountered that one last night, when she'd held onto him, trying to keep her balance as he kissed her. *Don't go there.* She quickly curbed the thought.

"Aw, don't be mad, Mom."

Surprised, she said, "I'm not, why would you think I am?"

"Your face got red for a minute, the way it does when you're mad."

"Sorry, must have had a hot flash or something," she lied.

"Must be 'cause you're hanging out with a dragon, a ninja, and a big, bad wolf," he said, eyes shining.

"That must be it. And I'm not mad, really."

"Okay. You gonna turn out the lights?"

"Yeah, but we'll be downstairs, then one or the other of us will be sleeping next door if you need us, okay?

"'Kay, good night."

"Night, honey."

Going down, she saw Caine had turned out the lights, as they had the night before. Her heart rate picked up, and her body tingled as she remembered the feel of his hands.

He stood by the window, watching the stars.

"Anything moving?"

"The space station," he commented. She hurried over. Standing close to the glass, she looked where he directed, seeing the glowing spark racing across the sky, much too high to be a plane.

"Neat. Xavy would love to see that. I'll have to let him stay up tomorrow, if we're still here."

"Yeah," Caine said, his voice a darker tone in the gray evening. "He'd like that."

He rested his hands on the curve of her neck, letting them sit, waiting, she presumed, until he saw if they were welcome or not. Giving in the tiniest bit to temptation, she relaxed, inviting his hands to warm her skin.

Kneading gently, he soothed the taut muscles, encouraging her to lean on him. It felt good.

"That's amazing. Too good, in fact," she protested, but she didn't move from under his ministering hands.

"We can't get involved," Caine whispered. Although the words were harsh, his voice was velvet. "But I don't care about rules when I'm touching you, Dana. That's not good. But I don't care."

It was a bald statement of desire. Unexpected clarity from such a mysterious man. With the anonymity of night to cover them she didn't have to be a witness, a target, a hunted woman. He didn't have to be an agent, a dark knight.

Instead, they were just . . . people.

She didn't answer. What could she say? Ditto? Instead, she let herself rest in his arms. Let herself stay. They stood for a long time, watching the stars, leaning on one another.

"I need to sit," he finally broke the silence. "My leg is aching."

"Oh, I'm sorry," she was immediately contrite. "I kept you standing there—"

"Hush. I enjoyed it. Now I want to sit. Come here." Once again, they didn't converse. They merely sat, enclosed in the darkness and each other's company. His arm was a solid weight around her shoulders, warming her to her core. For the moment, it was enough.

She couldn't pinpoint when it happened, but she plummeted into sleep so deeply, so securely, that she slept better than she had in weeks. Maybe, years.

She woke when she felt him rise. Fear leapt to life when she saw him tense and crouch by the window. There was no lightening of the sky beyond the ridges, and the valley beneath the cabin was still pitch black.

"What is it?" she whispered. Checking her watch, she realized she'd slept several hours in his arms.

They'd talk about that later. For now, she sensed trouble in his silence, his tension.

"I don't know. A bad feeling."

"I'll trust that. I'll get Xavy and Shadow."

"It may be a false alarm."

She checked her own senses, that extra, deep knowing she relied upon to warn her of trouble coming. It blazed to life, full force and hollered at her to run.

"No, I get it too. I'll snag our stuff, get Xavy."

She rolled off the couch and onto the floor. Scuttling into the kitchen, she hurried upstairs. Stuffing the few odd things left out into her pack, she slung it, Caine's bag, and their other things over her arm and ran for Xavier. Shadow leapt forward at her entry, whining.

Xavier woke with one shake.

"What?" he whispered.

"Trouble, we're not sure what."

"You got a call?"

"No, the other kind of warning."

He was used to her hunches and didn't scoff or complain. He was into his jeans in a flash. A sweatshirt tugged over his head completed his dressing, and within minutes he had backpack, duffel, and Shadow's leash. He was ready to go.

"We're going to get to the bottom of the stairs and wait for Mr. Caine's signal, okay?"

"Got it."

When they reached the landing, Caine was there, pressing a weapon into Dana's hand and handing her a duffel. He had the other two pieces of luggage, as well as the car keys.

"Let's go. I saw something move on the road, then down on the logging path. Stupid of them to come in from below."

"May not be the only direction. Should I make the dash to the car first?"

"No, I'll go. If they shoot from uphill, I'll give you covering fire before you run with the boy, okay?"

"Right."

They all made it to the car before the first shot rang out. He revved the engine on the Cadillac, and two more bullets buried themselves in the garage, barely missing the front windshield.

"Lousy shots," he muttered.

"Don't complain. Bad angle anyway," she said, checking that Xavy was down on the floorboards.

"Get down and hang on, both of you."

Caine spun the wheel hard. The SUV bucked as he slid off the road and punched the engine to take them onto the gravel again. Dodging and weaving his way down the long mountain way, he was outrunning the bullets, but he wasn't sure it would do any good if he didn't keep the car on the road.

God dammit. He'd let down his guard. Someone had managed to get too close. He'd nearly fucked up. Again.

Not surprisingly, the gate stood open.

Finally, they were to the end of the drive and he hit the gas, slinging the heavy car onto the paved road and gunning the engine. The tires squealed as he tore through a tiny intersection, whipping around a bend to climb a long rise. On the other side, he slowed fractionally so Dana and Xavier could get onto their seats and into their seatbelts.

"Sorry," he said, glancing at Dana. "Rough ride."

"No apologies necessary. Did you see them?"

"I saw one," he said. It puzzled the shit out of him, even as he was castigating himself for not being more vigilant. He was sure there had to be more of them, with the number of shots fired, but he'd spotted only one figure racing for a car. The car had been cammo-ed, he hadn't managed a make and model.

Nothing. Fuck.

"You only saw one?"

"Yeah. Had to be more. Walker never sends anyone solo, or even in twos. He favors fives."

"Yes, I know. It's his favorite number." She leaned with the turns, bracing herself on the downward passages. "His birthday."

"Figures. Stupid narcissist," Caine said, gritting his teeth as he fought to hold the wheel as he opposed the outward thrust of the turns.

At the bottom of the hill, the small state route fed back into a larger, four-lane road. Caine cut across it, staying on the state route.

"Where's this go?"

"Joins with sixty-four a few miles from here. We can head east to Charlottesville."

"Sounds good. Does it stay this winding?"

"Yeah. You and Shadow okay, Xavy?"

"I'm okay. It's a wild ride. Shadow's staying on the floor."

"Smart dog."

It was ten minutes of gut-twisting turns, a real-life roller coaster, before the road leveled out and ran smooth for the last mile.

"Great, now it straightens out," Dana said. "I think I left my stomach in one of those turns about three miles ago.

"Murphy's Law."

"It's operating in full force."

"Reach over here in my pocket and get my cell phone."

She did, muttering, "Is that a gun in your pocket or are you happy to see me?"

"Both, actually," he managed, appreciating her attempt at levity. Taking one hand off the wheel to grab the phone from her hand, he pointed at the gun on the seat. "I didn't have time to holster it. Safety's on, but it would be better if it wasn't bouncing around on the seat." She cradled the weapon in her palm, then managed to holster it when he lifted his arm for her to do so. Even that little contact heated his blood.

The woman had something that got to him. Something powerful.

And dammit, this was not the time to be thinking about some on-the-run woman in that way. Or any woman, for that matter, he reminded himself.

Still, he couldn't help but smile at her when he looked over and caught the faint, relieved look she sent his way.

"Glad we all made it out in one piece."

"Yeah." Forcing his mind to business, he dialed by feel, glad the ramp onto sixty-four was a straightaway.

"Tervain, you better answer your phone, dammit," he said when he got the senior agent's voice mail. "We're in deep shit, here. We broke an ambush at the mountain place. Call me. Now, dammit."

"That's seventy-five cents for Xavier's piggy bank from you, mister," Dana said, taking the phone and setting it in the console's cup-holder.

Caine met Xavy's grinning gaze in the rearview mirror, but spoke to Dana. "Yeah, yeah. I'll pay when you do, girl."

"She already did," Xavy piped up. "The night we got to the house."

"You carry your piggy bank with you?"

"Yeah, best way to keep it, you know?"

Caine nodded, turning his attention to the road. His heart was heavy at the realization that the boy carried his piggy bank with him, for fear that he'd have to leave it behind forever.

"Where the he . . . heck is Tervain?" he groused, hiding the worry behind gruff talk. He glanced at Dana.

"I called his cell. Short of being in church or a firefight, he's supposed to answer it."

"He's a desk agent, isn't he?"

"Hmmmmm. Yeah, but it doesn't mean he isn't a target on this one. He's a good shot and a he—heck of an agent. I'd have him along on any op, even if he's a paper pusher now. It's not like him to let it go unanswered."

"I hope he's okay," Dana murmured, her hands clenching and unclenching in her lap. Caine was glad Xavy couldn't see the obvious signs of worry. In the next moment, he was angry with himself for getting too close, for letting his concern for these two color his judgment.

What if he'd gotten them killed? He could stand anything but that.

"I do too," he managed to respond. "I'll try again in ten minutes, remind me."

"Will do. Do we have a tail?"

"Don't know yet. I'm going off in three miles, we'll sit for thirty, then go to the exit for State Route 6. That runs over to Charlottesville a different way. If we have a tail, it'll be obvious on that road."

In fifteen minutes, he tried Tervain again. He waited twenty minutes more before letting it ring out. When the voice mail finally answered, the annoying mechanical voice said it was full.

Something was terribly wrong.

He was about to tell Dana that they were screwed, then stopped, surprised at himself for being willing—even eager—to share the burden.

Before he could commit such a heresy, his phone rang.

The two adults shared a meaningful look. Dana put a finger to her lips, motioning to Xavy to keep Shadow quiet.

"Yeah?" Caine answered it carefully, gruffly, in persona.

There had been no number or name on the caller ID. As a government issue, it had special features that let it tap databases, showing caller identities that even a landline wouldn't provide.

"It's Sears," came the voice through the phone. "I'm on a secure wire at headquarters. It's bad, Caine. We got hit, and hit hard. Tervain's down. Booth is missing, presumed dead. Parlier's still critical, expected to pull through, though. We don't know if it was Walker or the inside man."

Hearing the strain in the other agent's voice, Caine asked, "What about you?"

"Got a through-and-through at the collarbone. Two inches lower and bye-bye Thomas."

"No vest again?" Caine asked. Sears was notorious for hating the Kevlar protective gear. Not that he blamed the guy, but . . .

"Hell, no, not on this case. I know what we're dealing with. I wasn't taking no chances. Good damn thing. It got me at the weak point, took the edge of the vest, turned the bullet."

"Tervain?"

"Concussion. Blunt force to the head. Just one whack, or he'd be playing a harp in heaven."

"Ambush?"

"At home. No forced entry. Wife and kids were in bed, never heard a thing. Wife woke up, got worried, found him at his desk."

"Damn."

"Yeah, she nine-one-one'd it and called it in to us." He paused, slurped something. "I got a hold of his cell at the hospital. Wife got it to me."

"What's the story with Booth?"

"Her apartment was hit, major struggle, resistance. Shots fired. Bunch of broken crap. Tables, lamps. One of the halogens was about to ignite when we got there. Not much blood, but a duct tape roll, some rope, that kind of thing. Crime scene's all over it, we're hoping for a lead."

"Great. Wonderful." Inside he was cursing a blue streak. If Xavier hadn't been listening to every word, counting the money, he would have been doing it out loud. "Crap."

That would have to suffice, for the moment.

"Pretty mild, Bradley," the other agent commented wryly. "Of course, I've been doing nothing but cussin' so I've probably done my share and yours too."

"Yeah, tender ears, you know?"

"Oh, yeah, Walker's kid. Better tell him to keep his head down. Daddy's gunning for him, for sure."

"Thanks, I'm sure I'm going to say that," Caine forced himself not to look at Xavier. No need to let the boy know he was being talked about.

"Wait," Sears' voice notched up in concern. "You sound like you're mobile. Why are you headed out?"

"Yeah, we're on the go. We got ambushed at the mountain place, 'bout an hour ago."

"Fuck, you're kidding?" There was shocked silence in the background as Sears relayed the information. "Hell, *no one* knows about that place. How'd Walker find out?"

"No telling, but it's blown. I don't know what condition they left it, we got out before they got in."

"Fuck, I liked that place. Can't use it if it's compromised."

"Yeah. Something wasn't square about the ambush," Caine said. He still had the nagging sense the whole thing was off, somehow. "We saw one, maybe two shooters. Vehicle was in deep cover, or on the road. Gate was open."

"The gate? Fuck. We'll check it out. Shit."

"Any plan? Who's point?"

"Guess that's me," Sears managed, still cursing. "Um, hell, keep driving for now. Do a vehicle transfer at the exchange in Cheverly. Or Balto. There's another in Leesburg. You have the codes, right?"

"Yeah."

"I don't want to know where you are or where you're going. Our leak's a big fuckin' hole, now, especially with Booth missing. With the big guys out of commission, I'm screwed if I get anyone else killed."

"You the leak, Sears?" Caine said it seriously. "Cause if you are, you better tell me now and start running."

There was a long silence on the other end and Caine pulled the phone from his ear to see if he'd lost signal.

"Sears?"

"Yeah, I'm here. I heard you, loud and clear, amigo. I'm not it, but . . . I wonder . . ."

"You got any ideas, spill."

"No, not from here. Call me at this number, later," he began to recite.

"Wait." Covering the phone, he said to Dana, "Grab a pen. I need you to write a number."

When she'd taken it down, he clicked off.

"What's up?" Dana asked quietly.

"We weren't the only ones hit," Caine managed. The rage at the attack pricked his nerves, roiled his gut. Parlier out, Tervain out, Booth presumed dead, Sears injured, three agents killed at the decoy house. It made him wish he'd found a way to kill Walker before he'd left the organization. Fuck the law.

They drove for another hour with the radio on to keep Dana company. Caine was occupied with dangerous plans. He would play by the rules for now, but if anything, *anything* else went wrong, any one else died at Walker's hands, he was going to stash Dana and Xavy and go hunting.

Doubling back onto the route for Charlottesville, Caine managed to pull back from the abyss of his murderous thoughts enough to puzzle over the ambush.

He had to stay cool, keep it together, for now.

Why only two people? Was Walker spreading it thin to cover more ground? If the inside man had known for sure that they were at the mountain house, Walker would have come in full force. And what about Tervain? Dammit, they needed Tervain in the game. He was the only one who knew who and where all the players were.

"Everything okay, Caine?" Dana asked softly. Caine glanced at her, then into the mirror, catching sight of Xavier asleep on the comfortable seat.

"Not really. Tervain's hurt, Parlier's out. They knew *all* the players and where the chess pieces were on the board. Booth is currently presumed dead or captured. Sears is injured, but in charge. We're running short on help."

"Booth? That's the woman, right? She's dead?"

"They think so. Her place was torn all to hell, a lot of blood . . ." he trailed off. Why was he telling her all this?

Because he trusted her.

The realization was a hammer blow. He trusted her the way he would a partner, an equal. She wasn't his protectee, she was his . . .

"I should lie, tell you we're fine, but we're not. We're in deep trouble here, Dana," he managed the words through a tight throat.

Her next question disrupted his chain of thought and

he was grateful. He'd been about to tread on boggy mental ground.

"What's next? We need to change cars, right? You mentioned an exchange point or something?"

"We'll go to Charlottesville first. We need gas. And breakfast." He made the turn onto twenty-nine north as he said it, which would take them to the west side of Charlottesville, Virginia.

"Why would Donovan go after those other agents?"

"He didn't. The inside man did. And I think the ambush at the mountain house was a feint to flush us out. A quarry on the run is easier to get, more likely to make a mistake, than one in a hole."

"But if Donovan had already set us to meet in Richmond tomorrow, why hit us now?"

He turned briefly toward her, then kept his eyes on the road. "Because he knows or suspects I'm an agent. And, if he's right and can get rid of me, he'll have a clear shot at you and the boy. Either way he wins. If he gets rid of me, gets you and Xavy, he doesn't have to pay me. If I'm an agent, same goes."

When they pulled into Charlottesville, a handy diner was on the left. While they had breakfast, Caine outlined his plan to them both. If Dana trusted Xavy, he would too.

"We'll go north and west to Leesburg, pick out a new car, new identities. We'll go to one of the warehouse stores, the outlets if we have to, and get some things we need." He looked from Dana to the boy and back. "From there, to Baltimore to a location only Tervain knows. If we're found *there*, Tervain's our leak."

"Agent Tervain?" This from a bewildered Xavier. "But . . . Isn't he in charge?"

Caine wasn't sure what to say. A huge bubble of relief

rose within him when Dana slipped her arm around Xavier and explained.

"We don't think Agent Tervain is against us, nor do we think he's the leak. But, the things going wrong are things he and only a handful of others knew about. We don't want to suspect him, but we have to rule him out. Does that make sense?"

Xavier turned to him for confirmation, and Caine nodded. "I think we *will* rule him out, but we have to be sure."

The boy seemed satisfied and, once in the car again, snuggled up with Shadow and his iPod.

"Does he always listen to music?" Caine asked, watching Xavy nod in time with an unheard beat.

"No, he's got several audio books downloaded to it too. We were reading *Harry Potter*, and I managed to bring that with us, but he gets carsick if he tries to read."

"Ah. Well, since he's not listening, I'll tell you what we else we need to do. We'll need to pose as husband and wife. Xavier will be our son—"

"Married?" she interrupted.

"Better than brother and sister." He couldn't help but look at her. "I don't think I could pull that off."

She blushed, an attractive flush that lit her features. He felt himself respond, even to such a little thing. No. No way he could pretend to be her brother.

She managed to pull herself out of whatever embarrassing thoughts she was having enough to say, "Better say he's my son from a previous marriage, or we'll attract attention. He doesn't favor either of us."

"Yeah, he's all Walker, poor kid."

"He hates it."

"I'll bet."

They talked a bit more, making plans, but until they got to the change point there wasn't much to discuss. Both Dana and Xavier dozed as Caine drove toward Leesburg, and he was left alone with his uncomfortable visions of Dana. He was going to have to treat her as a wife for their cover. Could he keep himself from going too far?

He'd kissed her the other night, sort of a test to himself. He'd wanted to prove that she wasn't really as luscious as he'd thought when he first saw her, glaring down at him, a gun pointed at his head. He'd wanted to prove it was just the moment, the intensity of life and death, that made him want her.

He'd been wrong. He wanted to kiss her again. And do more than kiss her, he admitted. He wanted to explore that fine figure, see what made her tremble.

He excised that chain of thought, knowing it would get him too riled up to focus, to be sharp. Instead, he thought about the afternoon they'd spent outside. He realized he wanted to erase the haunted, hunted look from her eyes, to see her laugh as she had when the three of them had played all afternoon with the dog.

Dana awoke as they swung into Leesburg proper.

"Pretty busy for the middle of the morning, even on a weekday."

"It's popular with tourists," he said, braking gently as an obvious visitor, as well as two locals, pulled in and out of narrow parking spaces, and darted across the narrow street.

"Where are we going?"

"To get married."

Chapter Eleven

"What?" Dana's reply was shocked, and immediate.

"We'll change identities when we change cars," Caine said as he made two turns which brought them alongside a serviceable brick building. The window glass was dark, the openings barred. Although well-kept, the building was obviously deserted. Power company signs informed passersby that high voltages were in use and to beware. "Which means, we'll be husband and wife."

Turning into the alley, Caine stopped at a roll-up door. A keypad gave them access, and he pulled the Cadillac into the cavernous space. Automatic lights flickered on, revealing rows of vehicles along the walls. As the door rolled down, closing them in, she spotted a small office area and rows of lockers.

Pulling the Caddy into an empty space, Caine switched the engine off.

"Now what?" Dana asked.

"Unload. I'll see which car's best for what we need and get the paperwork."

To Dana's relief, Caine was treating her as an equal. She knew from his body language and constant checks of

the rearview mirror that he was concerned. The proverbial black cloud hovered over him, an echo of the angry
pain he'd evidenced in their talk at the mountain house.

She was worried, scared. But something about *his* pain
went deeper, blacker than concerns about being on the
run. While she wondered about that, she also recognized
that his assessment of the ambush at the house in the
mountains was dead on. They'd been flushed like quail.

She watched him go from car to car, opening the
glove compartment in each as she piled the bags on the
tail gate of the Caddy, ready for transfer.

"This one," he called. "It's got his and hers ID, credit
cards, etc. Let's load it up."

With Xavier's help, they got everything shifted with a
minimum of fuss. It was another SUV, a Suburban. As
large as the Cadillac, it wasn't as luxurious. Dana was
sorry to close the door on the Caddy, locking the keys
within it, as Caine had instructed.

"Dana, I need you in here," he said, walking into the
office. Xavier was poking around in the other cars, including an ancient-looking, rusty, old pick-up truck.

In the office, he'd opened one of the lockers. "What
size ring do you wear?"

"A six, why?"

"You have three choices of engagement ring, and we
have to decide how long we've been married."

"Hmmm," she hummed the sound, perusing the
sparkling gems. "Are they real?"

"I have no idea. Probably."

She picked a square cut diamond with a wide band and
two sapphires. A narrower diamond and sapphire eter-
nity ring was paired with it as a wedding band. Slipping

them on, she took a moment to admire them, then felt guilty for doing so.

"Pretty," he said as he slipped a simple gold band on his left hand. "Your husband has good taste. Why not that one?" He pointed to a two-plus carat emerald cut diamond with a diamond studded band.

"It's too big for my hand."

He laughed and, suddenly, hugged her. Her heart leaped at the easy gesture. "I agree. The princess cut suits you."

"What else is in there?" she said, peering into the locker. She didn't want to think about that hug, the spontaneity of it, the heat.

"Passports," he said, handing her one, along with a wad of bills. "Put that in your purse. It's two grand. We'll distribute it to the other bags. Hide your regular ID and put wallet and license in the glove box in your purse."

"We aren't going to stand up to a serious search."

"We won't have to, I'm not planning to leave the US. We'll hit another depot if we have to go cross-border."

Dana took the money and passports. At the car, she helped Xavier rearrange things and distribute some of the money, stuffing a wad into her duffel, another into Caine's black jump bag, and a roll into Xavier's backpack as well. She had her wallet in hand when he climbed into the car.

"Let's move out, keep it low risk."

"People come here?"

"It's checked every few days. If there's one in and one out, they take the car coming in and service it. Log the miles."

"Jeez, our tax dollars at work."

"Yeah, top security clearance just to drive cars and detail them, no questions asked."

"What's it pay?" she asked.

"No idea. Over a hundred; it's top clearance," he added when she gasped in shock.

"I was joking before, but now I'm serious. I can't believe my tax dollars do that."

"It's saving our as . . . behinds, at the moment."

"You have a point."

They merged into traffic, and Dana stared out the window, thinking about the next steps. The diamonds sparkling on her left finger felt strange. Donovan had showered her with jewelry, and she'd learned to judge quality. These were real diamonds. Good ones.

She seldom wore jewelry any more, though she'd kept some of it. Most was in a lock box, in a small North Carolina college town. She'd paid for the box for ten years and had the secondary key with her will, at her lawyer's office in D.C.

"Where are we off to?"

"We'll go north, toward Frederick, Maryland. We'll get supplies at the Costco there. Head to Baltimore on I-70."

"And then?"

"Go to Fells Point. There's a bed and breakfast there. It's secure," he glanced at her from the corner of his eye. "We'll need to shop, change our personas. Clothes for all of us, change your hair. We'll get high-end watches, jewelry, that sort of thing at the warehouse store."

"We need snacks, things we can have so we don't have to go out."

"Good idea."

"So what's with this B and B? Why doesn't anyone but Tervain know about it?"

"They don't advertise. They just . . . serve."

"Not the best attributes if you want to build a business."

"The right guests find them. It's what *we* need," he said with emphasis. "I'll have to talk to them about the dog, but it won't be a problem."

"We don't go where Shadow can't," she said, standing firm. Turned in the seat as she was, she'd seen the mutinous look on Xavier's face from the corner of her eye. She knew she'd better say something before his outburst.

"Got it. I agree. We'll work it out."

"So then what?"

"What?"

"After we get there, check in. Then what?"

She saw him smile, but was taken by surprise when he reached over and took her hand, her left hand, where it lay in her lap. He interlaced their fingers, and the rings clicked together.

When she tried to shake him off, he tightened his grip. "Better get used to it, Mrs. Peterson," he said, referring to the driver's licenses, credit cards and so forth they had under the name Peterson. "When we get there, we go shopping, of course."

Xavier joined the conversation at this point. "Is that my name too? Peterson?"

"No, I think we'll make you Michael Clark, Sara Clark Peterson's son by a first marriage," Caine informed him. "We can call you Mike."

"What do I call you?"

"Charlie. Charles Peterson, to be exact, but you'll call me Charlie. You'll obviously still call your mom, Mom, so that's no problem."

"We didn't decide how long we've been married, what our story is." She was trying to distract him; distract herself from the way the warm clasp of his hand arrowed a pang of need straight to her heart. And her belly. She wasn't going to think about that, she lectured herself. No getting involved.

"No, we didn't. What do you think? Two years? Three?"

"I know, I know," Xavy was practically bouncing in his seat with excitement. "It's like Kenny's parents, the De-Marcos. They've been married for maybe, I don't know, four years? Anyway, they met on a cruise. You could say you left me with your mom, Gramma whaddayacallit . . ."

"Clark," Caine supplied.

"Yeah, Gramma Clark, and went on a cruise with your girlfriends. That's what happened with Kenny's mom. He," Xavy pointed at Caine. "He could be like Mr. De-Marco. He was on the cruise with some of his friends, and that's how you met."

Dana checked Caine's reaction. A twinkle sparkled in his eyes, but his face remained serious.

"That sounds good. You okay with that, Sara?"

"Fine with me, Charlie."

"No, Mom, you have to call him honey. That's what the DeMarcos do. She calls him honey, and he calls her sugar pie."

Caine laughed out loud at this one.

"You call me sugar pie, *Charlie*," Dana warned, "and I'll be supremely pis—irritated."

"How about dear?"

"Fine, but no sugar pie." She knew it was petulant, but having him calling her sugar pie was too . . . icky. She'd met the DeMarcos, and they did hang all over one another as if they'd gotten out of bed ten minutes before and wanted to go back.

Thinking about marriage and bed was a bad thing to

do around Caine. Dana's hand was nearly on fire from holding his. Once again, she tried to slip free, but he rubbed the back of her hand with his thumb. The blaze spread to her belly.

"Got it," he said, never acknowledging her attempt to pull away. "I'll respond to Charlie or honey, either one," Caine said, shooting her a wicked smile. He glanced at Xavier. "Anything else you can think of?"

"You have to hold hands. A lot. They do that too. Kenny says his Grandad calls it billing and cooing. What does that mean, exactly?" Xavier asked her.

"If you want a literal definition, it means to act the way lovebirds and pigeons do. They make a lot of noise when they're courting. But for people, it means holding hands a lot. Hugging. Sitting close together, that sort of thing."

"Yeah, yeah, that's it. You have to do that," he grinned at them. "It'll be cool."

"Cool?" Dana repeated, not sure she was ready for Caine to bill and coo. She was concerned about spontaneous combustion, especially if he was going to keep caressing her hand . . . or anything else. *Don't go there,* she reprimanded herself. "Hmmm," she managed. "We'll certainly try it, see how we do."

"We'll be fine," Caine assured, continuing to stroke her hand. How was it possible for him to turn her on with the merest breath of a touch?

To reroute her brain and her wayward emotions, she asked questions.

"What do we do after we check in?"

"Why, honey," he said, his voice saccharin sweet. "There are lots of things I'd like to do when we check in."

When she glared at him, at the double entendre, he laughed.

"We'll check in, do some shopping," he replied, more seriously. "Then I'll take my darling wife and our son to the Baltimore aquarium. Won't that be nice?"

"Super," she muttered as Xavier went into raptures over the possibility of the aquarium. Even the prospect of shopping could be endured if he could see whales and dolphins.

The entrance to Chessie's, the B and B in Fells Point, reminded Dana of the pub in the *Harry Potter* books, the one leading to the wonders and dangers of the magical world. The door was nondescript, with iron grating and an old-fashioned and very dilapidated mailbox hanging on the wall next to it.

"You sure this place is okay?" she asked Caine as they parked in front of the building and he pointed to the door. Crammed as it was between two larger storefronts, one of which seemed abandoned, the door promised very little in the way of luxury. It put her more in mind of bed-bugs and rats the size of the motorcycles parked nearby.

"Don't judge a book by its cover. Not on this, anyway. Trust me."

"It's worked so far," she said, still dubious. "You going in first, or do we all troop in and scare them to death?"

"I'll go. Lock the doors."

"No worries, there," she said as he got out, glancing again at the line of Harley and Yamaha cycles. The door had barely closed when she engaged the locks. She saw him smile. He gave her a thumbs-up and disappeared through the shabby entrance.

"What is this place, Mom?"

"A hotel. A bed and breakfast."

"Yeah, I heard you say that before. What's it mean?"

"You get breakfast with the price of your stay."

"Like at the Hampton Inn or Comfort Inn or something?"

"Yeah, but usually, B&B's are small, family run. They're often in old gorgeous houses or mansions. They usually have only a few rooms and lots of antiques and stuff." She frowned at the peeling paint on the building's facade. She wasn't expecting antiques in this B&B, that was for sure.

"Uh, Mom?"

"Yeah?" Hearing the worry in his voice, Dana stopped watching the street and shifted to face him.

"You think it's, uh, okay? You don't think it's, you know, a trap or anything, do you?"

"I don't think so, sweetheart." She'd had no bad vibe about the place, other than thinking it was run down. Was Xavy getting something she wasn't?

"Do you have a bad feeling about it, honey? In your gut?"

"Huh?"

"A hunch, a feeling?"

"Oh. No, but it's spooky. One door in, no doors out. That kind of thing. Weird."

She relaxed, marginally. Xavier had shown no sign of having her ability to get feelings about things, but he was ten and a half. She hadn't really had much of a way with it until she was twelve or thirteen.

His assessment of the place was dead on, however. The more she considered it, the more worried she became. If Caine hadn't chosen that moment to return, she might have gone after him; an incredibly stupid idea. What was wrong with her?

Caine scoped the area as he strode to the car. Had she

not been watching for it, she would have missed that entirely. Damn, he was good.

He got to the car and waited for her to unlock it. Climbing into the driver's seat, he started the engine.

"They have room. I got a suite. One bed, a pull out sofa for you and the dog, big guy," he said to Xavy. To her, he said, "Don't worry, I'll sleep on the floor."

"I can sleep with Xavy. Shadow can sleep on the floor."

"We'll work it out, inside. We'll drive around to the loading dock. I'll let you, Xavy, and the dog out, unload, then park. They've got a space waiting."

"You know these people? Trust them?"

"With my life," he said calmly. "They're former operatives. They know the drill."

As he rounded the corner, an industrial garage door rolled open half a block down. It was in a modest brick building with windows that shone in the early afternoon sun. The sleek, steel-framed panes were obvious replacements, a modern contrast to the mellow, nineteenth century brick. The curtains were perfectly aligned in every window, and fountaining out of wire hayrack planters underneath the spotless glass, a riot of pansies and a variegated vines tangled in a cheerful artistry of green and purple.

They passed into the garage which was clean and brightly lit but small. There was barely enough room for Caine to reverse the truck, easing into a loading area.

They all piled out, Shadow with a ringing bark. Dana called the dog to heel, digging out his leash and handing it to Xavier.

"Hook him up," she said as he took the leather lead. "I want to check this out."

She climbed the steps to the loading dock as two men

came through the door. They were both tall, but one was stocky, a front-lineman build, the other a rangy, lean basketball player type.

"Mrs. Peterson, so happy to have you with us. Mr. Peterson gave us very few details about your situation, which is how it should be," the rangy one said, shaking her hand, before going to operate a lift which brought their luggage from the floor of the garage to the top of the dock. "Less for us to tell, you know."

The other man shook her hand as well. "We love to have guests," he beamed, then added, "but knowing who they are and what's going on is absolutely none of our business."

Their matter of fact attitude, almost a comical opposite to any true, inquisitive innkeeper took her totally off guard.

"Now, Mrs. Peterson, if you and your son, Mike, will follow me? Yes, son, bring Rover right along with you." He led them into a wide, industrial-white corridor. It too was sparklingly clean.

"His name's—"

"Rover, for now. Just as you'll be Mike for right now. We don't need to know any differently, do we, Chaz?"

"No, no, not in the contract, m'dears," the big guy seconded, pushing a heavy cart with their luggage piled on top. "All we ask is that you keep Rover quiet if you can. We don't really allow dogs. Well, service dogs of course, like yours, Mike."

"O-o-okay," Xavier said, glancing at her for direction in this strange, *Alice-in-Wonderland* situation.

"So, Mrs. Peterson, knowing something about your husband," he said, pausing when she visibly jumped. "I'm referring to Mr. Peterson, of course."

"Of course."

"Yes, well. I've put your family on a side hallway that can quickly lead to this area and the garage. If you need to come down in haste, there's a special stairway, which I'll show you upstairs. The stairs come out right here."

He pointed to a beautiful wardrobe, not far from the freight elevators. It was no less than nine feet tall and ornately carved in a style from nearly two centuries before. In front of it and the elevators, there was a huge, gorgeous Oushak rug.

"We don't use it often, but TJ," he indicated his partner, "gave it a test run when Mr. Peterson went to fetch you. Everything works, no creaking on the doors, even." He tapped a steel dumbwaiter door, about three by three feet square, next to the elevators. "This would bring your luggage down for you quite speedily as well, if you have time for it."

"Are you anticipating any . . ." she hesitated. What the hell do you call trouble to a pair of Cheshire Cat innkeepers? Suddenly, the name of the place made sense. "Trouble in the rabbit hole?" she hazarded the phrase.

Chaz looked sharply at her, but TJ threw back his head and laughed. "Oh, Chaz, Mr. Peterson's done well for himself. Chosen quite the wife. Good job, ma'am, good job. You've done that puzzle faster than anyone we've met, including your very luscious and quite brilliant spouse. Mr. Peterson, that is," he amended, making sure she knew to whom he referred.

Xavier turned from one to the other in total confusion. Dana smiled at him. "It's okay, honey." At least she hoped it was.

"It's very okay, young man. Never fear. Part of our service here at Chessie's is to preserve any fiction you walk in carrying, whether that's a wedding ring," he reached out and tapped the gold and diamond band she wore, "or the name of your impressive dog, Rover."

"Rin-tin-tin might have been more appropriate, Teej," Chaz commented, pulling the doors closed on the spacious elevator. It might once have been a freight hauler, but it was now brightly painted, with an elegant faux finish and nail head trim.

"Yes, I considered it, but it's such a mouthful. And the short version," he shuddered. "Tinny? What an awful moniker to hang on such a gorgeous animal."

Dana felt like Alice. The banter was amusing, and they were obviously getting somewhere, but she wasn't sure where somewhere was. The luggage was with them, but Caine was absent.

It was the innkeepers' fault, she decided, trying not to glare at them. They were so . . . so . . . incongruous. They didn't look gay or have any physical mannerisms that would make one think they were a couple, yet they talked as if they were.

The simple ease with which TJ pulled the luggage cart and the bulging muscles in his arms were impressive, as well as intimidating. And Chaz was no less well-built, though he moved with a more cat-like grace than his counterpart.

Then there was the décor along the twisting way to . . . wherever. It was stunning. Old Masters paintings, or outstanding reproductions, highlighted beautiful faux marble walls. The walls were interspersed with mural scenes of gardens and distant castles, which belied the lack of windows along their path.

"Here we are, The Mushroom Suite. You'll be quite comfortable, I know. Go on in, make yourselves at home." TJ rolled the luggage cart in, parked it at a bumper ten feet inside the door.

Dana couldn't believe her eyes. The suite was a loft space, with high ceilings, hardwood floors, and a view of the harbor. The huge, tinted windows were framed by elegant drapes which hung from iron rods. A long wooden pole hung down as well, and Chaz jogged over and took hold of it.

"Isn't this fabric yummy? Irresistible texture to it. But I needed a ton of it. It took me forever to get these things mounted, too. Anyway, when you're ready to block out all that water, tug on this," he grasped the pole and demonstrated. The drapes, their iron rings jingling, easily closed.

"The bedroom's in here," TJ added, pointing to a walled off area with double doors where an enormous bed floated on a sea of gorgeous red Persian carpet. "Bath's over there," he waved to a second set of double French doors which stood open.

"And for you, young Master Mike, the couch here pulls out into a very nice sofa bed. Far more comfortable than what you're thinking, believe me. TJ and I have slept on every bed in our establishment. There are no uncomfortable beds here, m'boy." He shook Xavier's hand, then headed for the door.

"You ring us if you need anything, you hear? Dinner's at seven. Oh," he turned as he almost reached the door. "And don't take handsome Rover there outside. We have a most magnificent courtyard where he can, uh, make use of the facilities, shall we say. The plants won't mind, and neither will we."

"I'll clean up after him," Xavy said, immediately, eager to be sure his beloved Shadow wasn't considered a nuisance.

"But of course. We'll find some bags for you, have them handy. All right?"

"Yes, and thank you," Dana began, resting her hand on Xavy's shoulder.

She saw both men suddenly tense, and to her shock, each produced a weapon. "Get behind the wall there, with the boy, Mrs. Peterson," TJ said, his voice no longer languid and somewhat vapid. Now it was brisk, businesslike. "It's steel."

Chaz had moved with equal alacrity to flatten himself on the wall by the entrance.

Now she heard what they had. The sound of footfalls on the polished wooden floor of the hallway.

Chapter Twelve

"It's me, Ca . . . Mr. Peterson," she heard the caution in Caine's voice.

"Ah, dear boy," Chaz said, holstering the weapon he'd been brandishing seconds before and swinging wide the door. "Welcome, welcome. We've been showing your lovely bride the suite. Such a handsome son you have. Smart as a whip. Bring them down for a bite before you go out. The dog can have a romp in the atrium and stay with us while you shop."

"Thanks, guys."

Chaz gave him a comradely buffet, and Caine staggered under the impact. TJ smiled, rubbing the same spot as he passed, as if to say, "Sorry for the hit, old man." Then he too disappeared, pulling the three-inch-thick wood and steel door closed behind him.

"Hey, Mr. Caine," Xavy said excitedly. "They showed us an escape route and everything. And there's this chute, for laundry and stuff? But they said if we had to break and run, we dump our luggage down it so it comes out downstairs. Cool, huh?"

"They think of everything. Good men, Chaz and TJ."

"Chessie cats," Dana said, still puzzling over it.

"Damn. You figured it out. Took me three years."

"Have you ever read the books?"

"No."

"That's the answer, then. It would be hard if you hadn't read them. Xavy has, but he likes *Harry Potter* better."

"So do I," Caine said, giving Xavy a conspiratorial wink.

"Yeah, my teacher said that *Alice in Wonderland* guy was smoking something," Xavy giggled the words and Caine responded with a snort of laughter. As the two of them joked, Dana checked out the amenities.

The bathroom was worthy of a five-star spa. The tub was a small pond, and the counters gleamed with granite. Soaps, towels, perfumed bath oils, and candles abounded. The spacious cabinet held more luxury items side by side with bandages and packaged, sterilized instruments. There were drugs, and even a splint, all neatly packaged and labeled.

In a carved trunk under the bedroom window, its ornate design reflected in the glass, she found an emergency ladder, a purse, a wallet, and a loaded gun, holstered with the safety on, extra magazines in the purse. She shut the trunk, wondering once again who their hosts really were. That undetected escape, or a spare weapon, was an amenity, the way a spare toothbrush or a razor from the front desk would be anywhere else.

"Find anything interesting?" Caine asked, coming out of the bathroom in clean jeans and one of the new shirts they'd picked up at Costco.

"An escape ladder and an extra weapon, if we need it."

"We might."

"Hey Mom, check this," Xavier ran in, brandishing three game boxes he'd found in the TV armoire. "The new *Badger Man* game and a couple others I haven't even seen, ever. Can I try them?"

She glanced at Caine to see if he thought Chaz and TJ would mind. He seemed to read her mind, flipping her a thumbs up.

"They're okay," she handed them back. "Take a look while I get a shower. You can play them all later." Xavier gave a whoop and plowed into the plastic packaging.

"Are you going to check in with Sears?" she asked Caine.

"Not yet. I'll call from the aquarium. I can use a scrambler on a public phone. I want to avoid the cell."

"A pay phone? Are there any left?"

"You can use my cell, Mr. Caine, if you need to," Xavy said, as he came back in for help with one of the cartons. He pulled a sporty yellow and black cell phone from his sweatshirt pocket. "I charged it last night."

"Thanks. I may need to. And don't forget, I'm Charlie now." When Xavy nodded, he continued, directing his comments to both of them. "I don't want to click into the FBI network from a cell. There's a chance it's how we were traced."

They game-planned a bit more, and scouted a route for their shopping trip. Xavier was ecstatic to get time to play. Caine joined him on the floor as Dana took her bags into the amazing bathroom.

She felt instantly better when she stepped into the luxurious stall. Who wouldn't, with all the jets and cascades, not to mention the lotions and potions available in the cavernous shower? It was meant for two, with dual controls and a long, wide bench seat. The images the set-up conjured in her mind would have boiled water all by themselves. Shower sex with Caine, steamy and amazing, was her first and foremost thought.

Wrapped in a thick terry cloth robe, her body still a-tingle from the erotic images, Dana dried her hair. She struggled to push the sensual feelings away, lock them down. She had more immediate concerns than making love with an awesome, hard-bodied, sexy . . .

She flicked the dryer off, leaned on the counter. "Stop it, right now, Dana. He's not your friend, he's not your lover, and he's not your husband. He's an *agent*, you're a tool to get Walker. Nothing more, nothing less."

Faced with her reflection, she forced herself to make a long, hard assessment. She was in her thirties, a mother. No sex kitten, la-dee-dah girl to attract a man of Caine's experience. She scrutinized the circles under her eyes, the fine lines at their corners. But, her traitorous mind prompted, her legs were long and her body and breasts firm, in spite of having a child. She wasn't gorgeous, but she wasn't a hag either.

Dammit. She wasn't in the market, nor was he. They had a job to do.

"Keep that in your mind, Dana," she told herself. "It's all about the job. This is no time for a crisis of femininity or hormones."

With a soft knock, Caine opened the door. "You okay?"

Strengthening her resolve, she gave a curt nod. "I'm fine. Just talking to myself."

He started to say something, but hesitated. She realized he was staring. "Well, ah, let me know if you need anything."

Where was the confident Agent Bradley?

"Okay, but I'm fine." Crap, now she sounded unsure. She needed to be firm. Competent. Ah, hell.

"Dana . . ."

"Caine?"

He met her gaze. The moment seemed to draw out forever. His eyes were searching, for what, she didn't know. She wanted to fling herself into his arms and have him tell her it would be okay. Even if it was a lie, she needed to hear it. He must have seen something of what she was thinking in her face.

"If you need—"

"It's all right," she lied, striving for a brisk demeanor. "I sometimes get tired of it all. The running. The hiding." She congratulated herself on being so matter of fact. Who cared if he thought she was being weak or female? As long as he didn't guess what she was *really* warning herself about. "It gets harder and harder."

"Tell me about it," he said, coming in.

"Caine, you shouldn't be in here," she gripped the robe, sure that if he didn't leave immediately, she might forget her resolve and drag him to the floor.

"Okay. But, Dana?" He stepped back, closing the door, half shielded by its bulk.

"What?" she peered around the wood, wondering what he was hiding.

"You should know something."

"What?" she clutched at the robe, concern making a cold knot in her belly, where only heat had been before.

He glanced back, eyes shooting to her hands, then flicking to the juncture of the robe where it parted over her thighs. His fiery gaze returned to hers. Everything in her responded.

Holy shit. "What? What is it?" she demanded, unable to stand the tension, the sexual fire between them any longer.

"I want you." He closed the door and was gone.

"Oh, my God."

Dana made her way to the toilet and sat with a thud. "That's supposed to help?" she nearly wailed the words. "All this craziness, and he hits me with that?"

Resting her head in her hands, she let her damp hair shield her from the omnipresent mirrors. The strange thing was that when she took internal inventory, his words, the revelation of such stark desire, *did* help.

Ephemeral as it was, in her changeable world, it was a solid, palpable thing to hang on to. She began to laugh.

When she walked into the main room, Caine and Xavier were storming the walls of an alien castle. She broke up the fun and wrestled Xavier into clean clothes. He made a token protest, but all three of them were hungry, so it was mild.

Within minutes they had found their hosts in an elegant drawing room.

"Ah, TJ, dear," Chaz drawled. "Here are the Petersons and steadfast Rover come down for a late lunch. You look refreshed, my dear," TJ said, holding a seat for Dana. She took it and he offered her a napkin and a basket of fresh rolls. The others sat, and Chaz began piling food on the table. Pot pie with a flaky crust joined fresh fruit and a crisp salad. Everything tasted divine.

"There now, that will satisfy the body for a bit," TJ indicated their empty plates. "To satisfy the soul, you should go play." He pointed toward Shadow, who was chasing butterflies in the atrium. "The pup has the right idea."

Chaz chuckled along with them at the sight, before saying, "Now, Macy's and the boutiques are too far to walk. Best get a cab. The aquarium is three or four blocks on foot." he winked at Caine. "It's a good time to go, midweek, midday. There may be a school group or two at the aquarium."

"Walking on this foot," Dana indicated the one she'd cut, "is probably not a good idea. Same for you, Caine. Better to save your strength."

"Good thinking, Mrs. Peterson. You ready to go, Mike?"

Xavy was taken aback by the name, but quickly caught on. "Yessir, Mr. TJ."

"Good lad," TJ praised. "I'll have a cab here in a flash."

They rode to Macy's in the comfort of a yellow cab. The driver didn't look at them when they got in and hardly spoke. He accepted cash with a nod, then drove off.

"So what are we looking for at Macy's?" Dana asked.

"High-tone casual. Think CEO and his wife on vacation. We got top accessories at Costco. We need the threads too."

"Got it."

"You have a credit card, Mrs. Peterson. Use it. Don't stint. We need to look the part," he said quietly. Speaking in a normal tone, he put a hand on Xavy's shoulder. "C'mon, Mike, let's get those shoes for you. I know your mom wants to shop without us in the way." He smiled warmly, giving her a peck on the cheek. "Have fun, honey. We'll meet you in the men's department in . . . what?" he looked at his watch. "An hour? Is that enough time?"

"Plenty," she said, then nearly choked. That probably wasn't in character. She wasn't a shopper, and it had been a long time since she needed dress clothes. Crap. "Well, maybe not plenty," she amended sweetly, and saw the approval in Caine's smile. "So why don't you two come find me?"

Xavy rolled his eyes, and they both laughed. "Okay, hon. See you in a bit." Caine used the scene to press another kiss to her cheek. "Good save," he murmured, for her ears only.

"Thanks."

* * *

They dropped five shopping bags at Chessie's before making their way to the aquarium.

"How come we need all that stuff?" Xavy said as the cabbie pulled into traffic, seeking another fare.

"Character, Mike. It's all about character," Caine pontificated. More quietly he said, "Dress like Mike, you feel like Mike. You act it. Harder to see Xavy, if he's acting like Mike."

"Got it," the boy managed, losing interest in the discussion as the passed a group of street singers practicing on a park bench.

"They're pretty good," he said, taking the hand Caine held out to him. It made Dana's heart clench to see how quickly and easily Xavy had accepted Caine as a father figure.

He wanted her. He liked her son. The knowledge alternatively delighted her and pissed her off. Why couldn't anything just be normal?

The Baltimore aquarium was minimally attended. They strolled through, and Xavy "oohed" and "ahhed" over the sea creatures. At the show, they sat close enough to get splashed, and Dana stayed with their things while Xavy and Caine went poolside for a picture with the killer whale after the show.

Caine was the perfect attentive father, making Xavier laugh and chucking him on the shoulder when he burped and didn't say excuse me right away. And toward her, Caine was full of warm glances and light touches.

It was *killing* her. Her attraction was real, and so intense, that every touch, every glance was piling fuel on the fire. She *knew* better, she told herself. It *wasn't real.* But it felt so damn good.

"That was great," Xavy enthused as they left the enclosure. "Wow, I've never seen anything that big. And did you see me feed it, Mom?"

"Oh, yeah. I even took pictures."

"Really? Real ones? That we can keep?" The stolen facets of her boy's childhood were never more poignant than when he asked these kinds of questions. So hopeful, so unexpecting of something every other kid took for granted. Normal kids got pictures taken all the time. Copies for grandma and grandpa and aunts, uncles, and cousins.

Instead, Xavier avoided cameras. God forbid, if his picture appeared in a newspaper or newsletter, someone might send it to Donovan. That could get them killed.

"Yeah. Maybe we can put some on your cell phone and iPod."

Pressed against Caine's side, she felt him stiffen, though his face revealed nothing amiss. He looked down at her and smiled, but his words were a warning.

"Someone's watching us," Caine said, linking their fingers. "One of the aquarium staffers, the woman."

"Xa—Mike," she said, and the tone of her voice was enough to wipe the delight from his face, turn him from a happy child into the serious, mini-adult she'd come to love and hate. He was instantly wary, on alert.

"Afternoon, folks. Could I have a word with you?"

"So, Patrick, you know what to do?"

"I'm ready, boss."

"There are other things in the works," Donovan said,

with a dark smile, thinking of the chaos he'd instigated inside the FBI. "So stay loose. Flexible. I may need your team to move on a moment's notice."

"What about the warehouse?"

"Use it as base, for now. But be ready to meet me for cover. I won't talk about it on the wire, but we're close."

"Great news, boss." Patrick's excitement was genuine, Donovan thought with amusement. He was so transparent.

"Yes, I'm optimistic." His assistant waved to him from the doorway. A business call was coming in. "I'll be in touch."

"Yes, Paulina?" His cousin, as homely as she was smart, was devoted to his interests. The penalties were too high for her not to be, of course.

"It's the Spaniard."

"Hold everything else."

"Sí."

"Señor," he said, engaging the line. "You call at a good time."

"You have your . . . package?"

"Soon. Today, I hope. Tomorrow, perhaps. But if my people don't complete the entire transaction, I'll want you available to eliminate the remaining contenders for that package."

"I understand. The usual fee?"

"Yes. Paulina will call."

"Until next time, then, amigo."

Donovan's lip curled. He hated that term, it smacked of those who tried too hard to be his friend.

But, all he said was, "Sí, until next time."

"Paulina," he called in irritation, as he hung up. "You have everything ready for him?"

"Sí, Donovan. And the tickets, the passports, they are

prepared," she said, slipping into the room, closing the
door behind her. "Señor Daniels is here. He is pacing."

"Let him. He can't charge for pacing, the blood-
sucker." While he ruthlessly used lawyers to confuse and
obstruct his trail and hide his varied businesses, Donovan despised most of them.

He knew more about corporate law than three-quar-
ters of them and had certainly taught most of his own
lawyers everything they knew about profit innovation.
The more he taught them, the more they charged him,
and, he was sure, their other clients. His only satisfaction
was that they could no more sell him out to the Feds
than a priest. They were too enmeshed in his work, and
their own, to go to the authorities.

Donovan checked a note he needed in his PDA, then
with a wicked smile, he ushered Daniels into his office.
To his credit, the man only huffed a bit about the wait as
he strode in and began pulling folders and files from his
polished leather briefcase.

"I have a number of updates as well as the files we discussed. In addition, I have the materials you requested
this morning."

"Excellent. I have some useful information for you
as well."

When Daniels looked up in surprise and a bit of confusion, Donovan just smiled. Let him stew on that while
they worked to make Donovan, Jr., even more a part of
the family businesses. He also needed to be sure that all
the properties in his wife's name would devolve to
Donny on her death, since that was imminent.

It was nice to be able to plan these things.

"Let's get to work, then, um, Mr. Walker."

"Please, please," Donovan said, shedding his neatly

tailored jacket before he sat at the desk. "Have we not worked together long enough to leave formality behind?"

"Well, um, yes, Donovan, I believe we have," the lawyer said, smiling in his pleasure.

If people only realized how easily they were manipulated. Of course, if they did, life would be so much less amusing.

"Come then, Trent, let us wrap this up so I may tell you about the new business venture I've discovered for that Armenian client of yours."

He ignored the man's start of surprise, opened the first folder, and began to read, his gold fountain pen poised to sign or make notes.

When Trent left several hours later, Donovan was satisfied that the property matters he'd specified were handled. His will and trusts had been amended to his satisfaction, and the matter of Donny's guardianship when Dana died was well managed.

As an added benefit, Trent was his new "best friend." The information he'd provided to the lawyer on the Armenian was worth a considerable amount and Trent knew it. He could tell the man was mentally spending the money before he even left the building.

"Paulina, I'll be dressing."

"Yes, Donovan."

He was halfway into the change to his street persona, when Paulina knocked on the door to the spacious dressing room.

"What?" She wouldn't disturb him unless it was urgent.

"It's that woman."

Ah. His insider. Very good. "I'll be right out."

"Sí." Paulina's voice was stiff with disapproval. He still

called Donny's mother his wife, and since his church-loving cousin didn't believe in divorce, she didn't like Donovan's other women. Of course, she also saw this particular one as a double danger, given her FBI status.

"Hey baby," Donovan crooned, curbing his impatience. "What are you wearing?" As much as he wanted to demand why she was calling, what news she had of Donny, it had to be about her first. Otherwise, she might decide Donny was worth too much and use him as leverage.

She giggled. God, he hated that giggle.

"More than you'd like me to, I'm sure," she gushed. "But we'll have to talk about that later. I've gone under, honey. No one knows that I'm not where I'm supposed to be, so it's safe to talk, at least. I got some information for you. Oh," she added, as if in afterthought. "I nearly caught up to Pollack and your son last night."

"Nearly?" he snapped. The idiot woman had gone rogue. Stupid bitch. Why couldn't anyone *think*? He needed her inside, not chasing—

He cut the thought off. She had done it. There was no going back.

"They're in the wind, but I've got the tracking, so I'm on it," she said, sounding stung by his sharp retort. "They're in Baltimore. They're still planning for the meet, you know. So either way, baby, you've got them."

"That's good news, sugar," he forced the endearment through stiff lips. "Are you coming to me, now?"

"Oh, I wish I could, lover, but I have one more option to get you the prize and I'm going to try for it."

"Be careful, baby. Don't risk yourself." *Please*, he thought, *risk yourself.*

He heard her girlish sigh and rolled his eyes. Was everyone working for the FBI this stupid? He should be thankful. It was why he was free, but it provided so little *challenge*.

"There's no risk, really," she gushed and started to tell him how clever she was. Thankfully, Paulina interrupted once more.

"That sounds really good, sweetie. I hate to do it, but I have to go. Business, yeah. You too." She made kissy noises into the phone, but he cut the call, folding the cell into his pocket.

"Something you need?" he said to Paulina, as he slid his arms into a leather jacket.

"The documents are notarized. I will send them to Señor Daniels. I have the items for the lock box. I was going to put them there now. Unless there is something else?"

"Of course, it is fine to do that errand now. I am going out. Well done, Paulina. What would I do without you?"

She smiled shyly, "You lead my family. You take good care of Maman, and my sisters have all made good marriages, thanks to your care. I seek only to repay that kindness."

"You have money? Everything you need? I may not be back tonight, and may have to leave quickly. Do you need me to give you money?"

"Oh," she said, flustered. "Oh, well—"

Her very hesitation told her she was in need. Paulina was the only one of all his relatives who never asked for money, even when she needed it. It was both irritating and a relief at the same time.

"I have told you, you must ask for what you need. I'm here to provide for you." He peeled fifteen bills off the roll in his pocket, handed them to her. He unlocked the desk, produced a corporate checkbook, and wrote her six checks, each for several thousand dollars. "You know how to handle this. Different banks, deposit it in small doses so you don't attract the IRS track."

"Yes, Donovan. I know. Thank you." She bowed over the checks he handed her, averting her eyes. He heard her sniffle.

"Now, now, Paulina. Don't let things get desperate. You do excellent work for me. I wish to reward you for your loyalty, your service."

"Yes, Donovan. Thank you." The phone rang in the outer office, and she pulled herself together and hurried to answer it. He heard her pleasant greeting as he secreted weapons and another untraceable cell phone in his jacket.

"It is Patrick," she said from the doorway. "It is urgent, he says."

Chapter Thirteen

To Dana's relief, the staffer was the marketing director for the aquarium. She'd seen Xavier feeding the killer whale and noted his fearlessness.

"He's a handsome boy, and we're searching for, uh, multicultural youngsters for our advertising campaign. Do you live in Maryland?"

"Yes," Caine lied smoothly. "We're from Cumberland. The Deep Creek Lake area."

"Oh, that's a beautiful area," the woman started to ask about particular sights, but both her phone and her pager went off at the same time. She glanced at the pager, rolled her eyes, and excused herself to take the call. "I'm with someone at the moment, but I'll call you as soon as I get free," she told the caller. Ending it, she got right to her point. "I'm sorry, as I was saying, we have plenty of girls, all ethnicities, and two boys, but they are uh, too, uh, homogeneous, if you know what I mean. Would you consider letting him be a part of the group? He'd get free membership to the Aquarium Club for a year, a small fee for participating, and a chance to spend two days feeding the dolphins."

"That's quite an offer," Caine said, smiling at the woman. "Can we take your card, think it over? We're on vacation, and we'd have to look at our schedules. How about we call you when we get home?"

"That would be great. Mike," the young woman turned to Xavier, handing him a card as well. "We'd love to have you visit again, even if you don't help us with the commercials. Give me a call before you come. I'll get you a special tour, okay?"

"Wow, thanks."

They left the woman's office, exchanging glances. Dana's was relieved, she was sure, and Caine's revealed his amusement.

"The good news," Caine said quietly, directing them to the gift shop, "is that we're being taken for a family, we're presenting the right look," he added, with a wink to Xavier.

To Xavy's delight, they emerged with books, a stuffed snake, a stuffed whale, and a toy for Shadow.

"There's a restaurant over there," Caine slid on sunglasses, then pointed to the old power plant renovated into a combination bookstore and bar. "We can get a snack, and I can use the phone. They have twenties vintage phone booths in the restaurant according to the guard in the aquarium."

He took Dana's hand and strolled to a bridge they'd need to cross to reach the restaurant. Music poured out, and Xavier spotted a sign saying the restaurant had milkshakes.

"Cool, can I have a milkshake, Mom, while we wait for Mr.—" at her sharp look, he amended the request. "While we wait for Dad?"

"You bet," she said, bending down so her face was at his

level. She hoped her smile eased the sting of that visual reprimand. "But there's a kiss toll to cross this bridge. You don't pay it, you go over the side and into the briny deep."

He giggled and tried to dance past her, but she grabbed him, swung him around, and tickled him until he paid the toll.

"Now Mist—Charlie, he has to pay the toll too."

"Oh, yeah," Caine said, laughing. She looked at him, at a loss for what to do. "I'm *liking* kiss tolls. Good suggestion, Mrs. Peterson."

"Mr. Peterson," she tried to make her voice stern, in the face of Xavier's giggles and Caine's exaggerated swagger. "We are in a public place. I don't think . . ."

"No, you think too much, Sara," he said softly as he slid an arm around her waist. "Just kiss me, dear. I'll pay the toll."

She tried for a peck on the cheek, but he turned at the last minute and their lips met. Clung. Parted, to return for more of the sweet pleasure of tasting one another.

"Wow, some toll," Xavier said on a whistle. "What'd you do, uh . . . Charlie? I only have to kiss her twice when I've scr—messed up."

"I take it s-c-r-e-w is on the money list?" Caine said, looking down into Dana's face. He was smiling, but she saw a puzzlement in his eyes.

"Yes, unless we're referring to the use of hardware and the application of force thereto," she answered his question even as she wondered about the sea of emotion. "I get some of my quarters back if he lets fly with a curse word."

"Ah, I'll try to remember that." He used his arm to turn her and grabbed Xavier too, throwing an arm around the boy's neck. "As it happens, Mike, since I'm about twice your weight, I needed to pay a bigger toll.

You keep growing the way you are, and you're gonna have to kiss her twice too, you know."

"Awwwww, man, really?"

"You bet. Bigger load, bigger kisses."

"Jeez Mom, you sure you can stand it?"

The laugh caught in her throat as Caine's grin flashed and he said, "Yeah, honey, think you can deal?"

"Oh, I think I might be able to manage."

"Does this mean I get a milkshake?"

Dana laughed, and for one moment, one precious moment, allowed herself the fairy tale. Within a few short days, she'd managed to create a dream of a man for her to love and for her son to enjoy, freely. It might be fleeting, it might be all playacting, but God, it felt good.

"Sure. I'll get one too. What about you . . . honey."

"Yeah, chocolate for me, and a burger and fries. Man needs a snack, you know," he claimed when she made a surprised noise.

"Snack?" she said, reading the menu pasted on the wall. Pictures of the plates, heaped with French fries were prominently figured. "If the pictures are any indication, the fries are a meal, not a snack. And you guys just ate."

He bussed her cheek and let her go. "That was hours ago. We shopped, we daringly faced our fears and fed killer whales. We need fries, right, son?" he ruffled Xavy's dark hair, and the boy grinned happily. As if by coincidence, he turned to see the phone booths.

"Hey, check out those cool old phone booths," he nodded toward them as the hostess pulled out some menus and turned to indicate a table. "You get a seat, honey. I need to call to the office. I won't be long, I promise," he added when she started to protest, trying to stay in character. "Really. We're on vacation. I told you I wouldn't do much work." He kissed her again, surprising her and drawing a smile from the young hostess.

"I'll just check in with my assistant since I couldn't get my cell to go through; honest, it'll be fast. Go ahead and order for me, I'll be right there."

Their bases covered, they went their separate ways; Caine to the phones, Dana and Xavy to the table. The hostess rattled off some specials and left them with the menus. The food had just arrived when Caine slid in the booth next to her.

"Interesting info on the call. We'll talk about it in the room," he murmured.

"Okay."

They spent an hour in the restaurant, eating and laughing, then played some of the games and let Xavier try a motorcycle ride. They even wandered through the bookstore for a while. No trace of the professional agent leaked out through Caine's *I'm a dad* persona. It was easy for Dana, she was Xavy's mom, but to see him take so easily to the role . . .

Dana was disappointed when they prepared to troop out, find a cab.

"Hey, Dad!" Xavy called, surprising both Dana and Caine with the moniker. He was hanging over the bridge walkway. "Look at the boat."

They watched the boat and several others in the harbor for a few minutes, but the breeze was cool and before long, they returned to Chessie's.

In the room, Xavy returned to saving the video universe while Caine and Dana sat in front of the gas fireplace. Shadow was happily asleep in front of the hearth.

When Dana would have taken a chair across from him, Caine patted the seat at his side.

"Snuggle down in here with me, Mrs. Peterson, and let's talk."

"It isn't necessary to—"

"Ah, but it is. You're not comfortable with it in public, and that may get us all killed." He said it conversationally, but that simply heightened the impact.

Heart heavy, she sat, leaning into him when he pulled her to his side. It was the game, after all.

"That's better. There's another thing too, Sara," he added, his tone still easy, light.

"What's that?" she pulled away enough to look at him.

"I want to hold you." Something hot and wild smoldered in his eyes and set fire to the needs coursing within her. "Very much."

She was overwhelmed with a sudden desire to rip his shirt open, drag him to the floor, and make love like there was no tomorrow. The vision was a bucket of cold water. There might not be a tomorrow.

"What?" Caine asked.

"Tomorrow is not promised to us," she whispered, averting her gaze.

"No, but we'll do what we can. Now get comfortable. Kick off your shoes." She did as he bid, even as every nerve ending flared to full alert where she was pressed into him. "That's better."

He let her settle as much as she could before he dropped the verbal bomb.

"The meet at the warehouse tomorrow is a go."

"What?" Dana cried, leaping out of the seat.

"Ssssh," he urged, glancing at Xavy.

"We're to meet Sears in Richmond in the morning, make the switch for Xavier."

"Oh, God. Caine, what if something goes wrong? I don't like this, it doesn't feel right."

"Sears and I agree with you. We both want it aborted, which may still happen. But the higher ups want it finished. They think the meet will accomplish that."

"Then, we're going?"

"We'll see," he prevaricated. "It's under discussion."

"Discussion?" Indignant, she flung herself back into the comfortable seat, bumping into him.

"Yes," he ooofed, shifting his arm back around her. "Relax. I'm betting the idea will be killed before midnight."

"Oh, I hope so." She tried to relax, she really did, but relaxing meant instant, sizzling contact with his magnificent body. There was only so much a woman could take.

To distract herself, she asked about Chaz and TJ.

"They were with a different branch. CIA, counterterrorism stuff. They retired. Government frowns on male to male fraternization, so they bagged their jobs and opened this place."

"What happened to *Don't Ask, Don't Tell*?"

"That's the military. This is Spookville. Whole different level, if you get my drift. They frown on gushing over drapery material."

Dana could see that. Then again, when the man doing the gushing walked and talked like a Green Bay Packer, it would be hard to assume he was gay. "It's still hard to tell, for sure, that they're gay."

"Yeah, they keep the habit of not being obvious. Then again, since most of their guests don't want to be seen, or heard of, word doesn't travel."

"What about taxes and all that?" She couldn't help it, the idea of an all cash business, run by former operatives made her think more about mobsters and money laundering than above-board operations.

"You think the IRS is going to question them?" He snorted. "Right. Then again, they assure me that they keep meticulous records. Mr. and Mrs. Peterson will be duly registered and marked paid in full. They'll report the income."

"How much?"

"Two thousand a night."

She whistled, shocked. "That much? The shower wasn't *that* great."

"Anonymity doesn't come cheap. Nor does the kind of cover they offer. No need to stand watch tonight."

"Hey Mom," Xavy called from across the room. "I'm hungry."

"Already?"

He came and slouched into the chair opposite them. He seemed unaffected by how closely Caine was holding her, but she'd seen him catalogue the whole scene. Not exactly subtle, but then again, he was ten.

"Yeah," he yawned the word. "Tired too. It was really early when we took off."

"Yeah, long day for us all," she agreed.

"What about pizza?" Caine asked, eyes half closed. "A place around the corner delivers. Good crust, fresh toppings." She sat up, but Caine didn't disengage his arm nor let her pull away.

"Oh, boy," Xavy enthused, even as he yawned again. "That'd be great. Can we get ham and pineapple or beef and mushroom?"

"One of each, I think" Caine said, reaching for a cordless phone which lay on the table. Lowering his voice to a sepulchral level, he added, "The Dragon is hu-u-u-n-ngry too."

Xavy giggled and turned to her as Caine talked with their hosts and placed the order. "Hey Mom, I got high score. Not a big brag with a new game, but it was hard and really great. I hope I can play some more tomorrow before we leave. It's a really cool game."

"I hope you can too, then," she replied, truly hoping he could. "Let's get your bed made so you can get in it as soon as you've eaten." To her surprise, he nodded and got up to help her pull out the bed. He must be tired to do that.

"You gonna sleep in here with me?" he asked as they made the bed.

"Do you want me to?" His face told her he didn't want her to, but he didn't know how to say it. "It's okay if you'd rather sleep by yourself, honey. Mr. Caine can have the bed and I'll sleep on the chaise over there."

"Vice versa," Caine joined the conversation. "You take the bed. I need to prop my leg, relieve the muscles. It'll be easier in the chaise." They argued the point, but in the end agreed to Caine's way. That handled, he left to get the pizzas from wherever TJ and Chaz laired at night.

When he came in bearing the fragrantly steaming boxes, she knew something was wrong. He gave a slight, warning shake of his head. They'd talk about it when Xavier was in bed.

How parental.

"Good thing Luciano's makes an extra-large pizza. Dragon and boy were starving," Caine observed when they were done, stacking the plates and nestling them in a basket tagged for that purpose.

Xavier was ordered to the showers before bedtime,

and once ensconced on the sofa bed, was allowed to watch a movie. Within ten minutes, he was asleep.

Sitting by the fire once more, Dana was nestled into Caine's warmth. The insidious arousal that had plagued her earlier was back, lurking in her belly, urging her to do things, to take risks. *At least kiss the man,* her libidinous psyche yelled.

She was about to give into it when he spoke.

"Chaz got an alert. Someone's searching for us, within the organization." The words were a rush of cold reality, erasing every lascivious image and chilling her heart. "They have sources I'm not privy to. They checked for me."

"Can I say for the record, that the idea of that scares the shit out of me?" Dana tried to keep her voice level, but didn't succeed.

Caine's arm tightened around her, and she didn't resist the urge to rest her head on his chest. The hollow ache of despair crept over her. How could she ever escape Donovan?

"I'm going out. I need to make a call but not from here. I'm calling in a favor. I have a friend, outside the organization. I want to disconnect the GPS tracking on the truck. It's modified, so I can't do it without setting off telltales. It's one of the few things left. I have to know how we're being traced."

He sighed and rested his chin on her hair. The warmth of his breath on her cheek, the steady thrum of his heart was somehow more reassuring than any words he might have said. In fact, the total lack of platitudes or despair from him bolstered her spirits. He hadn't given up. She shouldn't either.

"Okay. How long do you think you'll be gone?"

"Don't know. I'll need to find another landline phone, get some distance. Catching my contact may take longer than that. Getting the data may take a while too. Go on to bed." He kissed her forehead. "Rest while you can, it's safe."

"No such thing."

"Yeah," he said, "but this is the closest you'll find while Donovan's alive."

"There's a sad thought."

"No, just a true one, for now."

She pulled away from him. "Why not sad?"

"Irritating. Sad says you think you can't do anything else to help yourself."

There was a look on his face she wasn't sure she wanted to decipher but couldn't leave be. "What do you mean?"

"Xavier asked me if I was going to kill Donovan."

"Oh my God."

"Don't get wigged. It was an appropriate question at the time."

"Appropriate . . ." she began, then shook her head. "Nevermind. Go on."

"Anything can happen, Dana. We go to the meet, and shots will be fired. I won't lie to you, even if I would to anyone else," he said bluntly. "If I have a viable target, he's going down."

"You know he'll shoot, he won't give you an option otherwise."

"Yeah," he gave her a bleak smile. "You or me, it'll be self-defense or line-of-duty, straight up."

"What about the law? A trial? You told us, Tervain told us, Donovan has a lot to answer for."

"I'd rather he answered to St. Peter." His direct gaze challenged her to agree, to be honest.

Searching her feelings she realized he was right, and she nodded. He smiled and squeezed her hand where she'd braced it on his chest. "We can't hesitate, if the situation arises."

"I know. It's just . . ." she trailed off.

"Do you still love him?"

"Hell, no," she barked, pulling away, shocked he'd even ask. "I'm not sure I loved him in the first place. I told you, I was young, pregnant, and scared, so I married him and stayed with him. You know all that."

"I do, but it doesn't change that he's Xavy's father. That makes anyone think, especially about killing."

He stood and stretched, getting ready to leave on his errand. The now familiar movements sent another zing of need nipping along her nerves as the cloth of his shirt stretched over his chest and shoulders.

He continued to talk as he moved. "'This is my son's father,' you might think. 'How can I kill the father of my child?' No matter how bad he is, it can be the thing that stops you from pulling the trigger in that split-second, critical moment." He knelt down, a black knight in a black shirt and dark jeans. As he took her hands, his eyes bored into hers. "If you get the shot, take it, Dana. Don't hesitate. He wouldn't, if the positions were reversed. Remember that."

"I will."

His eyes searched hers, looking, she presumed, for surety that she meant what she said, that her hand would be steady on the trigger. He must have found it, because he nodded, a grim smile turning up the corners of his mouth.

"If I'm not at the door in five hours, contact Chaz on the house phone. Don't leave the room. He'll help you get out of here and over the border."

She nodded, appreciating that he didn't patronize her by suggesting she contact the organization if he were taken out. At this point, if they got him, she'd never be safe going to the FBI.

Standing, he pulled her to her feet, wrapping her in his arms. "I'll be back. We'll get through this."

"See that you do come back," she tried for a smile. "I have uses for you, Agent Bradley."

The gleam returned to his eye in an instant and she realized how her words sounded. Appalled at her obviousness, unintentional as it was, she started to stammer a disclaimer.

"No," he put a finger to her lips. "Don't spoil it. It was too much fun to think you might have meant it."

He pressed a hard, but all too brief kiss to her lips and let her go. Taking his jacket and the weapon he'd laid on the table by the door, he was about to leave. The door was swinging shut when she spoke.

"Caine?"

"Yeah?" he pushed it back open, darkly handsome, his mind obviously already out the door, on the track of the information he sought.

"For better or worse, I did mean it."

There was a moment's hesitation, then his smile, hungry and triumphant, shone in the darkened entryway. "Hold onto that, Dana Markham. I'll be back before daylight."

Chapter Fourteen

Striding down the sidewalk in a less-than-desirable part of Baltimore, Caine surreptitiously scanned the streets for trouble. He was worried, and, for only the second time in his career, deeply concerned that his emotions were screwing with him.

What the hell was he going to do about Dana?

He'd laughed at hapless agents falling for their protectees. He'd never once, in all his years, had even a stirring of attraction for a witness or a mark.

Only the accident in Tijuana, and his partner's death virtually at his hands, had broken his nerve, involved his emotions at a deeper, more dangerous level. It couldn't happen again, ever. That experience had left him so damaged, so wounded, it had taken him a year to even be fit for duty, much less sound.

The department wondered about that soundness, even now.

"It's a job, Bradley," he muttered to himself as he slouched into a bar. Even on a weeknight, the crowd was solid. No one noticed him push through the throng and head beyond the taps and high-tops to the phone in the back.

Somehow, Dana and Xavier were more than just an assignment. They meant too much. He wanted her too much. Not just for sex; though if he stayed with her too much longer playing the devoted husband with no connubial perks, he was going to go mad.

He'd realized, as they sat together by the fire, or joked with Xavier, that she fit him. She made sense to him. She was smart, savvy, and self-aware. She was a great mom, a sharp companion, and one hell of a sexy woman.

Visions of Dana had the blood pounding in his loins, and he took a deep breath, redirecting his mind to the task at hand. He dialed the number, concentrating on the deal. He had to quit thinking about Dana that way.

Had to.

With a long series of whirs and beeps, a number connected and began to ring.

"Madre," a gruff voice answered.

"de Dios," Caine replied, giving the code answer. The man asked three more questions, all of which Caine answered.

"Uno momento," the voice said. Luck was with him because within ten minutes, the line connected again.

"Hey bro," another, lighter baritone, came on the line, immediately recognizable by inflection. Caine only knew the man by his voice.

"Hey. Wazzup?"

"Nada. Hear there's trouble at the factory. Bunch of your people off duty for a while."

"Yeah, one permanently."

"Perm? Didn't catch that. Who?"

"Booth, presumed."

"Crap. Hate it when that happens."

"It's a bitch."

"Truth. Whatcha need."

Caine told him. Baritone hemmed a little, seemed worried. It made Caine twitchy.

"Crap, man. That's bad. Like, its sooo classified. I'm gonna do it. 'Cause I know you, know the sitch, you get it? But you forget, okay? Get it done, then you put it right outta your mind. Deal?"

"Right." He never forgot anything. Part of his problem was that he didn't. If it was bad, it haunted his nights. If it was good, it paled in comparison to the bad.

Baritone walked him through disabling the GPS tracking on the company vehicle and how to avoid any screening as they passed through toll booths, tunnels, or other security laden features.

"Hey, man," he concluded. "Don't get dead."

"Do my best, dude."

They rang off with no goodbye, each to their own worries.

It was after one in the morning when Caine let himself into the room. Dana was asleep on the couch. He was surprised that she had slept through his return, given the state of vigilance she seemed to maintain.

"Dana," he whispered, checking to be sure he wasn't waking Xavier. "Let's get you to bed."

"Hmmmm," she murmured as he lifted the blanket and eased his arm behind her. With the stitches in his leg, he wasn't sure he should lift her, but he wanted to, wanted the weight of her in his arms, even for a brief moment.

Her arm snaked around his neck and before he knew

it, her mouth was pressed to his, warm and inviting. Taken by surprise, he gently returned the kiss.

She wasn't having anything to do with gentle. Her grip tightened, and she pulled him closer. He went.

Mouth to mouth, fused to one another, they battled with the passion roaring between them. Tongues tangled, and he barely suppressed a moan as her hands found the tail of his shirt, skirted the weapon, and dived beneath to dance a trail up his spine.

"The bed," she said, between the hot, melting meeting of their mouths. "I want you in the bed."

"Dana—" he started to object, only God knew why.

"Don't argue with me, Caine, unless you don't want this." Her eyes were huge in the still-dancing firelight. The honest desire burning there convinced him the way nothing else would.

"C'mon," he offered her a hand, and they raced for the bedroom. "Should we check on Xavier?"

"I already did, right before you got in."

He closed the doors, locked them, even as he peeled off his shirt, toed off his shoes. "I thought you were asleep."

"Dozing," she answered, then dove at him, her mouth and hands busy as she undid his belt buckle. "God, you're gorgeous."

"Same goes," he bit his lip on a moan as she took him into her hands, caressing his shaft with her long, clever fingers. He tugged her shirt and bra away with her able assistance. She ceased her teasing and touching for two seconds, long enough to toss her jeans to the floor and climb onto the bed.

The guys had talked about the bed earlier, when they arrived, but Caine hadn't taken it in. He hadn't believed he'd be sleeping in it, so he hadn't listened. When it gave under his weight and the smooth nap of the comforter slid silkily under his skin, he appreciated it. But only for a moment, then Dana demanded all of his attention.

Hair streaming down, she pushed him to his back, straddled him, rocking up and down along the length of his cock until he nearly exploded.

"We need . . . Oh, man . . ."

"Protection. Jesus. Check the drawer, TJ and Chaz thought of everything else," she said, a frantic hunger in her voice.

Sure enough, there was a box of condoms in the bedside drawer. Donning one, he reached for her, letting his hands talk for him, tell her of her beauty.

He touched her everywhere, reveling in her gasps and quiet moans. She arched up, a graceful curve of womanly delight as his fingers caressed the curls at the juncture of her thighs. The thrust of her breasts drew him, and he suckled the nipples, to her obvious pleasure. As he worked his way down her torso with his mouth, she writhed in his hands, her wet heat driving them both to further heights.

"Caine," she wailed softly. "I need . . . I need . . ."

"I know, darling," he muttered, rising above her, poised to enter her enticing body. "Are you sure?"

"God, don't ask me that. Just make love to me."

"Dana—" he hesitated, but she didn't.

Her strong hands gripped him from behind, pulling him forward, burying him to the hilt in her welcoming warmth. The sheer strength of her, the rhythm she had already begun blanked his mind to any doubt.

"Ahhhhhh," she cried as she flashed to a climax within seconds and nearly took him with her. Gritting his teeth, he held on while she rode it out, then began to rock, setting his own pace, bringing her to the brink again, then slowing down, taking her right to the edge again.

When she came the second time, he couldn't stand it. Her agile body bowed, and everything about her, her beauty, her sexy body, her wicked mews of fulfillment overwhelmed him, and he soared into the oblivion of passion with her name on his lips.

Later, as they lay spooned together, the suite quiet around them, the doors open once more, he heard her sigh.

"You okay?" he asked quietly.

"Marvelous. No regrets, Caine. I wanted this."

"I did too, Dana."

She rolled within his arms and kissed him, a sweet, lingering, loverly connection. "I want to do it again, but we have to get some rest. I'm so relaxed," she said it on a yawn. "I could sleep till next week."

To his surprise, they did sleep. He was amazed at how deeply he went under. He couldn't even remember dreaming. It was just after dawn when his internal alarm roused him.

Waking next to Dana, Caine realized he'd slept the night through. To have even four solid hours, with no sudden awakenings was miraculous. To sleep without dreams? Restfully? Almost unprecedented.

Bracing himself on his elbow, he took time to enjoy the sight of her. She was deeply asleep, her hair fanning over the pillow in a lush wave. She was smiling, a satisfied expression.

Had they really made love? It seemed like a dream; a beautiful, wonderful dream. His body stirred, responding to her nearness, her scent.

He was about to wake her with a caress, see if she would consider a repeat, when a cry from Xavier had him leaping from the bed. He was into his jeans in seconds, and heading toward the boy, gun in hand.

Behind him, Dana had flung the covers aside and was throwing on clothes as she ran.

He reached the room first to find Shadow standing on the bed and Xavier thrashing in his sleep, crying out, "No, no, you can't."

"Hey, big guy, wake up," Caine urged, shaking Xavy. It hurt him to see the utter panic etched on the boy's features. "C'mon, we're here."

"You have to pick him up, sometimes," Dana said, coming to kneel on the bed. "I almost can't do it anymore, he's getting so big. Xavier," she called, trying to rouse him from the nightmare. "Wake up, honey."

The sound of her voice, sharp and clear, must have broken through the dream because the boy's eyes flew open and he turned frantically from one to the other.

To Caine's utter surprise and immense delight, Xavier leapt into his arms, sobbing about sharks, and the dangers of the nightmare world. Maintaining his hold on the crying boy, he reached out, found Dana's hand, pressed the weapon he still held into it.

"I got this," he said over Xavy's head, which was tucked under his chin. "Go on back to bed."

She looked momentarily lost, as if she didn't know how to act when her son didn't need her comfort. "You're sure?"

"Yeah, I know you could do it, but this time," he indicated the boy's quieting demeanor. "I think the guys can handle it."

She padded back the way they had come, stopping

twice to look at him. Each time, he nodded and waved her on, the other arm wrapped firmly around the now-hiccoughing boy.

"Man, that was a wild one, big guy," Caine said, conversationally as he soothed the boy. "I've had a few of those. Got a whopper one time after I saw the second in the *Alien* series." And he really had. "Fell out of the bed, I was so scared."

"Get out," Xavier managed, through the hiccups. "You did not. You have to pay a dollar if you tell a story. An untruth."

Caine closed his eyes, resting his chin on the top of Xavy's sweaty hair. "Wow, steep price. But I won't have to pay 'cause I'm not lying. I did have a nightmare and fall out of bed."

"Cross your heart?"

"You bet," he said, making the gesture on his chest.

"I didn't fall out of bed."

"No, got me on that one. You want to tell me about it?"

"Yeah, Mom says it helps, and she's usually right."

"Moms often are. Here, scoot up, lean on the pillows."

They got comfortable and Caine slipped his arm around the boy, who, given tacit permission, burrowed into his side like a young bear.

"Comfy? Good. Now spill, it's got to be a good story."

They sat for a long time, with Xavy detailing the dream, then segueing into stories about his school and his friends.

"I'm afraid I won't ever see 'em again."

"Your mom's pretty set on it, and she's one of the most determined people I've ever met."

"I know. She's never told me a lie, she calls it an untruth," he said primly. "But I think this might be one of

those times when circumstances change, don't you?"
There was such despair in the young voice, that Caine's
heart clenched, aching to make it better, knowing he
had no right.

He could hear Dana saying those very words, in that
very way, to appease a sorrowful boy.

"It may be, but she's stubborn. If she says you're going
home, I wouldn't count it out."

"Really?" the boy was getting sleepy now, his words
slurring as he struggled to stay awake and talk. "Will you
come and visit sometime?"

Caine wasn't sure if Xavy heard his answer or not.
When the boy began to snore, he decided it was just as
well. For a long time, he sat holding the sleeping child.
Reviewing the years, the blood and mistakes, he compared them to what it might mean to raise a child. Holding Xavier, Caine wondered if his existence had any
meaning whatsoever.

Wasn't this the ultimate meaning? Calming the fears
of a child you loved? Helping him to grow and learn
right from wrong?

The concept of loving Xavier made him ease his arm
away, slide out of the bed. He tucked the covers around
the sleeper, and called Shadow up to watch over his
young master.

The impulse to pull the curtains, stare out at the water,
and seek his answers in the restless flow of the harbor's
pulse was almost overwhelming. Ever cautious, he didn't
go near the precious drapes. Instead, he went in to bed.

Dana was propped on the fat pillows, but her eyes
were closed in sleep. It appeared as if she had been waiting to ask him about the nightmare, quiz him about the

boy's reaction. Or worse, ask him why he'd bothered, when he would be gone so soon from their lives.

His body was loose, easy, from their lovemaking. His heart, that powerful organ, was aching, demanding he take this woman, this child, in and make them his. To renew his own life, change it, with them. For them.

Those were forbidden dreams, he decided, as he sat on the edge of the bed, his head in his hands. He tried in vain to shove them aside. They couldn't be a family. There was too much evil in him. He was too besmirched by the worlds he frequented, even in the name of justice.

Dana was too tired of running, vulnerable. It would be unfair to come into her life when everything was uncertain and mess it up any further.

And yet. And yet . . .

And nothing, he concluded in despair. He was a shadow among the shadows.

Even as the thoughts played in his mind, he got in beside her, drew her down with him. She didn't wake, but like her son, burrowed into his embrace.

A fierce need for her, like a wild, demanding, protective beast, rose within him, nearly choking him with its intensity. He admitted she was a match for him, but now, having made love to her, he had her taste, her scent. He knew her now, the way a wolf knew its life-mate, on every sensory level.

He never wanted to let her go.

A colder, saner part of his mind kept screaming that he had to pull back, to detach. He damned it to Hell. With her close in the circle of his arms, he willed it all away, along with the specter of Donovan Walker.

The subtle beep of his cell woke him less than an hour

later. He managed to get to it, silence it before it woke Dana.

"Yeah?"

"New info and more," his baritone friend said. "This Web site. Twenty-four hours, no more." The standard www was followed by a string of letters, which he committed to memory.

"Got it."

"Later."

Still in bed, he listened for Xavier, but the boy was quiet. He let an another hour pass before he woke Dana. It was a sensual treat to see her surface to consciousness, her lips curving under his as she returned his kiss in full measure.

"Good morning," she said, her sexy voice deeper and more siren-like than before.

"Morning. I hate to say it, but we have to go."

Her eyes cleared in seconds, sharpening into laser focus. She quickly rose, pulling her hair off of her face and into a ponytail.

"Xavy?"

"Sleeping. I got a call from my contact. He's got info for me. I need to get to a library computer. They're less traceable."

"Okay, do we pack? Are we coming back here?"

"Someday, I hope, but not tonight."

She looked around the room, as if seeing it for the first time. She avoided his eyes for a moment. He could tell that she was struggling with something. His heart, that silent menace, clenched in pain.

"I don't regret last night, Caine." Her voice was firm, her gaze level.

"I don't either."

"Good. But whatever this is . . . was . . . is, we can't let it get in the way of the . . . mission . . . protecting Xavier. But it was right . . ." She was twisting the covers in her hands. Whatever she was saying, she didn't believe it.

Her body language shouted regret. His soul iced over. He could see her pull away. He knew the reason. It was his darkness. His inability to give her what she seemed to want.

"I know."

"It's . . . difficult," she dropped her gaze, finally. "I don't do this, but . . . emotions, sex . . ." Her words were jumbled, scattered. When she finally met his eyes, he saw pain there. "I won't put anything before Xavier."

It had been the moment then. For her.

He knew better, dammit. He knew better than to let people in, give them the room, the ability, to hurt him. He walked to the bathroom doors. He had to go, get distance. Now. And he hoped the shower would wash away . . . something. Everything. He doubted it would. He doubted anything would wash away the feelings she brought him.

"I can't put anything before Xavy." The safe harbor he thought he'd found disappeared in the wash of words.

"I understand." In the mirror beyond him, he saw the reflection of her bewilderment. He had no idea why she was puzzled. He didn't care.

He shut the door, and her, behind him and tried to drown his pain.

They left Chessie's before nine. TJ and Chaz loaded the truck and bid them goodbye. They hugged Xavy, and TJ slipped him something, she wasn't sure what.

Dana's heart ached. Caine had been . . . different after

their talk in the bedroom. Something she'd done or said had changed him, hurt him. She searched her mind, even as she was hugging TJ, saying her farewells.

That too confused her. She realized how much she trusted and admired her hosts. Her gratitude was waved away, but how could she begin to express that she'd felt normal . . . free, for the first time in years, under their roof?

Loving Caine had been magnificent. She still felt his hands on her skin, her breasts; felt the ache of her inner muscles, liberated from their long hiatus.

It made her smile. Her sexuality had never been in question, but her boy always came first. Caine understood that. He put Xavy first too. How could she not love that?

But what had she said?

"Penny for your thoughts," he said tersely, driving onto the ramp for I-95 South.

"I'm not sure they're worth the copper."

"Let me be the judge," he said. Anger colored his voice, puzzling the hell out of her. Why was he mad? "Spill."

The wheels beat a steady rhythm on the road as they drove. And she pondered how much to reveal.

"It's been a while for me. You know that."

"I guessed."

"It would be tempting to believe any emotions that arise are a result of . . . you know," she prevaricated, embarrassed. "They could be a false positive, if you will."

She was talking in code, as was he, dancing around the subject for Xavy's sake. From the corner of her eye, she saw her son rocking along to the beat of the music in his earphones, evidently paying no attention to the adult conversation.

She knew better than to trust that completely. He'd been known to eavesdrop a time or two, learning far more than she would have wanted for him to know.

"On the feeling front? You think it's fake?" There was a strange note to the statement. A coldness, and more of the fierce anger, the source of which she couldn't identify.

"No," she said patiently. "Just the opposite, in fact. I'm saying it might be false, due to the circumstances. Tension, being chased, lives at stake kind of stuff. And Xavy—"

He cut her off. "I get it."

Chapter Fifteen

When Dana started to ask just what it was he got, he glared at her, turned on the radio.

At the split to the 495, Caine took the western route toward Bethesda.

"Are we going to Bethesda?"

"No, Rockville. One of the library branches is right off the highway, easy access, clear exits. I can check the info and get out quickly."

"Ah." Now that he was talking again, she wanted to get back to what was bothering him. Maybe it wasn't her at all, she decided. Maybe it was this information.

"Maybe Xavier and I could take Shadow to a park or something. He and Shadow are getting antsy. Yesterday was good for Xavy, but he's used to being outside more."

"The way we did at the mountain house?" he said it with pain in his voice.

"Exactly, where we had so much—"

He cut her off again. It was pissing her off.

"I'll get the data. I'll find the nearest park, and we let the guys blow off steam. Ten minutes tops, though. Deal?" He didn't even look at her.

"Deal," she agreed bleakly.

"Hey, that sounds great," Xavier exclaimed, leaning over the seat. Proof, as usual, that she could never take the mother-guard off her tongue. "Can we find a place with some room to throw the ball for Shadow?"

"Yeah, you bet," Caine managed, a gruff note in his voice.

While Caine went in to the library, Dana filled Xavy in on the game plan.

"Can we get McDonald's?" he wanted to know. "I'm starving."

"Sure," she said, watching for Caine's distinctive, tall form. She scanned all the exits, knowing he wouldn't come out the one he'd gone in.

The set of his jaw told her that something dire had happened, but he said nothing.

"Got a line on burgers and directions to a park," he remarked as they pulled out of the lot and into traffic.

"Excellent," Xavier rubbed his hands together. "I could eat a horse."

"Dragon like horse," Caine rumbled, making Xavy laugh with delight. His strange attitude toward her didn't seem to be reflected in his feelings for Xavy. They played the "dragon like" game until they hit the McDonald's.

"What about Brussels sprouts? Do dragons eat those?"

"Bleeech, dragons do *not* eat Brussels sprouts. They want meat, young boy."

"Horse, perhaps?" Xavy giggled as they sat down. Unwrapping his cheeseburger, he waved it at Caine. "Looks like horse to me."

"Don't laugh. They serve it in the McDonald's in Paris."

"Grooosssss," Xavy commented, hastily swallowing a mouthful. "You're joking, right?"

"Nope. Frog legs too. And snails."

"Wow, France is gross."

Caine laughed with her at that, but when their eyes met, he turned away.

The park was large, with a play set and huge open playing fields. They took Shadow to the nearest soccer area and began to throw the ball. To Dana's dismay, they were joined by another couple and their dog, a border collie.

"Hey Mom, check out Shadow, he's playing!" Xavier yelled, waving toward the romping dogs.

"I see."

"Watch this," the other father called to them. "Cul, go out." The black and white dog froze, then tore out on an intercept trajectory with the fluorescent green Frisbee the man flung his way.

Shadow, two seconds behind, but with a longer stride, nearly got there first. The boys clapped and laughed, Xavier playing with the other boy as naturally as if he'd known him for years. They tossed the disc, managing to keep it away from the dogs a scant four or five times out of ten. The dogs would chase each other until one of the boys took the Frisbee to start all over again.

Dana, her heart aching, watched from the edge of the field. Her resolve, already firm, hardened to adamantine. If Donovan had to die to give her boy this, she wouldn't hesitate to pull the trigger.

Caine and the other man joined the game, wrestling with boys and dogs in a whirling, barking mass of energy.

"Your husband really gets into it," the other woman remarked, smiling indulgently at the scene. "It's nice to see someone else do that too. Eb, that's my husband, he says you have to be an old-fart papa the way he is to know how short the time is that they even want to play with you."

"I agree." What the hell else was she going to say?

The woman held out her hand. "I'm Claire, by the way. Claire Upman. My husband's Eb—short for Ebbit—and our son, Tommy. He had a doctor's appointment today. Shots."

"Ugh," Dana commiserated, shaking the woman's hand. "I hate those days. I'm Sara. Sara Peterson."

"Good to meet you. I haven't see you around here. We're here a lot," she explained, laughing at the boys' antics. "This is just a quick trip as a treat before taking him in to school. But we're usually here every Saturday too. What about you? Playing hooky?"

"No, we're from Cumberland," she fumbled for the details. Dammit, she hadn't committed them to memory. She'd been too wrapped up in Caine. "We took a few days off for some travel. Family stuff," she improvised. "We're on our way home, but had to stop, let the boys get some energy out."

"I know that routine." She suddenly pointed, "Oh, wow, look at them go." The boys were chasing the dogs now. "Man, it's too bad you don't live around here. My Tommy doesn't usually jump in so readily. He's eleven but short and a little shy, so the older boys don't treat him like a peer, you know?"

"Yeah, but I'll bet he'll get a growth spurt before too long, show 'em all," Dana said reassuringly. It always amazed her how quickly women talked of personal things when meeting over children. She knew quite a lot of embarrassing information about Xavier's friends and their families, both from the kids themselves and from girl-chatter at PTA meetings or class functions.

"Oh, do you think so? I'm hoping he'll take after Eb. Your boy is . . ."

"Tall for his age, yeah. He's ten, but everyone thinks he's twelve."

"He doesn't have his father's big build," the woman observed, squinting and shading her eyes to get a better view. "He's got more of a basketball player's leanness."

"Oh, Charlie's his stepfather. But they have the best time together," the lie flowed easily, thank God. "We've only been married a short time." Crap, she couldn't remember how long they were supposed to have been married.

"Well, that explains the newlywed googoo eyes he keeps shooting you," the woman smirked. "Lucky you. Eb and I've been married for fifteen years, and I'd give a pile of money to have that pre-kid time again, at least for a few hours. Or days," she slanted Dana a knowing look.

Not liking the turn of the conversation, Dana made a noncommittal noise, then said, "Oh look, it's a major chase now."

Eb had the Frisbee, and boys and dogs were in a dead run after him. Caine was laughing at them, but not in the midst of it. He scanned the area before closing in on the action. He favored his injured leg, but covered it so well, she'd have missed it if she didn't know.

"Go long, Charlie," Eb called and Caine trotted their way, arm snaking out to catch the flying disc seconds before Shadow's teeth clamped onto it.

Grinning at the other woman, he paused long enough to give Dana a kiss and mutter, "Kiss toll," as if everything were normal between them. He turned and flipped the missile into the fray.

Claire sighed. "As I said, lucky you. It's nice you have such a spark. And with such a guy."

The words arrowed into Dana's brain. A spark. That was so pale a word to describe . . .

"Oh no," the woman teased. "That brought a blush. Sorry."

But she didn't sound the least bit contrite.

It hit Dana with the impact of a freight train. That was no spark, it was a freakin' forest fire.

Dammit, dammit, dammit. She did *not* want to be in love with Caine Bradley; especially now, when he was treating her as if she were a leper. But a wall within her gave way, and emotion fired in the pit of her stomach.

It was a conflagration.

It was staggering.

Her rational mind knew the little water bucket she had, full of reasons why it was stupid and useless, would never be enough to put it out.

Caine saw Dana go pale and stagger a bit and was instantly on alert. He ignored the other man's questions about what he did and where he was from in an effort to see what had so deeply disturbed Dana.

"Excuse me, Eb, I'll be right back." Gritting his teeth to block the pain in his leg, he jogged over to where she stood, hands rubbing her arms briskly, as if to warm them.

"Hey honey, you okay?"

"I'm fine, really. I got one of those walk-on-your-grave shivers, you know? Must be the wind."

"Oh, I get those sometimes," Eb's wife said, reaching out to pat Dana. He saw that Dana was uncomfortable with the contact, but she held her ground, giving him no notion of what was bothering her.

"Charlie, I know you met Eb; this is his wife, Claire."

Caine held out his hand and they shook. Hers was a firm grip, and she gave him a sly smile. "Your lovely wife here tells me you're practically newlyweds. You're a lucky couple, I adore it when people are so smitten. It's great to see in this divorce-me-now kind of society, don't you think?"

Oh. That gave him an inkling of where the women's conversation was directed. No wonder Dana looked off her game.

"Yeah, it is, isn't it, honey?" He leaned in and kissed her again, sensed a shimmering quiver in her skin. "You okay?" he whispered.

She returned the light peck then playfully tugged at him so he would lean closer. "I'm fine, but I have to get away from this woman."

"Hey Charlie," Eb called. "Okay if Mike goes over to the jungle gym?"

"Yeah, I'll be right with you."

"We'll all go over," Dana said. "I'll need to leash Shadow with the other children around."

"Oh, yeah," Claire said, jingling her own dog's leash. "The park patrol doesn't come around much, but they get snarky if your dog's unleashed. Then again, so do some of the parents."

"I don't blame them, especially with our dog," Caine said, whistling for Shadow. To his delight, the dog responded instantly. "He's big. I think some find him intimidating."

"I'll bet he's a pussycat, isn't he?" the woman cooed and went to one knee to pet Shadow. The dog tolerated the caresses, but was focused on Dana and Caine, who had summoned him.

"Yeah, a bed dog," Dana remarked, clipping the leash on.

"I'd better go get Cullen before he finds a deer scent. Last time it took us an hour to catch him, once we put the Frisbee away."

The woman clucked to her dog and cunning creature that he was, he headed the other way. Claire called something to her husband and pointed to the dog. He nodded and waved her on. Dana took a seat not too far from the jungle gym, Shadow at her side.

"I'll stay with Mike," Caine said, giving her a reassuring squeeze.

"Hey Charlie, check out the boys," Eb said as he walked over.

To Caine's amazement, both boys were on top of the jungle gym, hanging upside down. "Wow."

"Braver than me, I'll tell ya'."

"Yeah," Caine's answer was noncommittal. The boys' agility reminded him painfully of dangling off a cliff in Afghanistan, two members of the resistance clipped below him and hanging on with everything they had after having slipped. His heart jolted, and he wondered if it would be too obvious, too overprotective, to tell Xavy to get down.

"So, you and the family are traveling home?"

"Yeah."

"Too bad. Never seen our Tommy take to someone so quickly. Be nice if you were local." The other man sighed. "Tommy's a good boy, but introverted. Stays to himself. Your boy seems more outgoing."

"He is. His mother's been really great about getting him out, but I think it's in his nature anyway."

"Nature. Yeah. That's the problem. Tommy's more of a bookworm, ya' know? He likes the park, though."

"Yeah, I know. Hey Eb, if you've got these two for a sec, I need to talk to Sara."

"Go ahead, I'll be right here."

Knowing he could be at the jungle gym in seconds, Caine went to Dana, sat beside her and slid an arm around her, pulling her close.

Smiling at another parent walking by, Caine waited until the woman was out of earshot before he said, conversationally, "What happened with Claire? The way you looked I thought Walker was here in full riot mode."

"I'm sorry . . . honey," Dana apologized. "Claire was nattering on about us being newlyweds and acting it, and . . . I nearly freaked. I realized I didn't remember our cover, how long we were supposed to have been married, none of the details. I've never had to go to ground with anyone else. Just me and . . . Mike."

He tightened his grip. He told himself it was for support, but it was a lie. He wanted to hold her, protect her. He wanted to tell her everything would be fine. But, she'd made it clear she didn't want that. Besides, it wasn't true. They were still very much in danger.

"I get it." He glanced around, checked for listeners. "My contact says the leak isn't fixed. Walker's not counting on us walking into the trap, though he's ready if we're stupid enough for it. He's planning on running us down. My contact thinks he'll call, confirm the meet in Richmond. He also believes he's got us on radar somehow and is going to hit sooner."

"Sooner?" Dana exclaimed, struggling in his grasp. Her head whipped around as she scanned for danger.

"Stop it, Dana. We didn't come this far for you to panic."

He saw the flush of anger, the fire in her eyes. He couldn't have said why it made him want her desperately.

Here. Now.

So he did the one, socially acceptable thing that came to mind. He kissed her.

Anger flavored her response, but she did respond and he grinned. She might not want him, but God, what a woman.

"What was that for?" she hissed even as she covered her emotions with a sunny smile at a gorgeous toddler and her nanny.

"You're beautiful when you're angry," he said, whispering it in her ear.

"Clichés now, *Charlie?*" she emphasized his name.

Ah, still mad.

"Not when it's true. It's time for WitSec, *Sara*, and protective custody. Both of you. It'll buy you a couple years of peace. For that." He pointed at the boy, now balanced on a rope bridge in a pirate ship play structure, laughing like a loon. "He shouldn't wonder if you'll come home."

Under his arm, her body tensed. For several long minutes she was silent. Maybe now she would agree. He wanted her to agree. He wanted to know she and Xavy were protected.

While his head told him the program was compromised—for her, even WitSec wasn't secure—his heart wanted her safe. He knew the new identity, the security another life would bring might be false, fleeting, and dangerous. Yet somehow it seemed better than what they were doing.

"No."

"What?"

"We've been through all this, Ca . . . Charlie. Tervain's put the plans in place. We have to see it through." She was silent for a moment as they watched Xavier navigate a tire bridge, then slide along a slant beam with an audible "Wheeeeee." "It's for his sake that I have to go, end this."

"But . . ."

"Who are you?" she said suddenly, facing him. "Why are you saying this?" She must have seen something in his eyes, his face, because she turned away, a hand to her mouth. "Don't do this to me," she whispered. "I'm not strong enough."

He hesitated, then said, "Dana . . ."

"No, Caine." She said it quietly, with conviction. Her ironclad decision showed in her posture. "I'm not what you think. I'm damaged goods, too scared to trust, and this . . . this thing between us . . . who knows what that is?"

What was she saying? Was she changing her mind? "No way to find out if you get killed."

"Or you do."

"We need breathing room . . . Sara," Caine said, barely remembering to use cover.

Anger rose at the realization of his mistake. Where the hell was his professionalism? If he didn't pull it together, he was going to get them all killed. Perfect time to re-member he was a man, just in time to forget he was an agent and have them all end up good and dead because he fucked up. Again.

"If we go in, even prepared for a trap," he hissed. "We may not come out. We might never know . . ."

"Know that we're not suited? Know that it was a fleet-ing moment of attraction?" she growled, her voice low, but hard. She didn't look at him, never glanced his way, even as she leaned into him. Her attention was all for the playing children. He saw the fire in her striking eyes as he looked down at her, the dark lashes framed the elegant sweep of color on her rosy skin.

"And if I tell you it isn't momentary, for me?" He knew he risked all his emotions on her answer; a roll of the dice.

She froze, her body rigid in the circle of his arm. Shadow whined, and stood, responding to the subtle cues of distress.

"Hey Mom, look!" She waved at Xavier, pretended to laugh as the two boys raced each other around to slide down a twisting slide, competing for who could get there first.

When she finally looked at him, her gaze was sharp, and something . . . exultant shimmered over her features.

"Then all the more reason. Dammit, it's time to quit circling the wagons and go on the warpath ourselves," she declared fiercely.

It took him four full seconds to process the analogy.

Then it pissed him off. She wasn't being reasonable. He was the agent, the expert. He knew what Walker would do. He knew what would happen. Dammit. Why was she being so stubborn?

"You can't be serious," Caine snarled. He fought to maintain casual body language even though he was fighting mad. "Circle the wagons, my ass. I can't protect you."

"No one can. Not anymore. There's no guarantee, period," she told him, with equal intensity. "But if Donovan goes down, then Xavy has a chance for this," she nodded toward the boys playing once more on the jungle gym.

"And if Walker escapes, goes underground again?"

Swiveling on the seat, she gazed at him, her face

solemn. "Do you think he'll survive this? It's him or me, Caine, and he knows it. I'll kill him, or he'll kill me. It's time to make a stand. I won't run anymore. We do it Tervain's way, take the chance, or I take the car, go home to Petersburg and clean my house. I'll meet him there, on my ground, if I can't do it any other way."

"No, not that way, that's the worst possible . . . Canada—"

"No. That's out. I did a lot of thinking when you were out last night. I'm not running." She gripped his arm. "Help me. Help me do it the other way, the best way. I know the risks. Hell, breathing is risky sometimes. I have to try."

He opened his mouth to protest. Then shut it. What the hell did he know? Maybe she was right. The thought of risking her, risking Xavier, froze his heart, but the thought of them forever running, threatened to break it.

"Are we done fighting about this now?" she asked, not calmly, but softly. "Because we can't sit her like this much longer. It's too obvious."

"Yeah. We're done. For now. I'll relieve Eb, then we'll make our excuses." He rose to stretch and spotted Eb's wife.

"What?"

"Claire caught the dog. She's on her way over. Endure it, if you can," he said, hearing her sigh. "My leg's rested. We've finished arguing. I think we're done here."

His attempt at humor was met with a snort of laughter, quickly disguised as a cough when Claire strode up. With that validation, he left her to fend off the other woman.

"Whew," Claire said, plopping down on the bench. "Stubborn dog. He gave me quite the run. Then again,

I needed it." She winked at Dana, and mock-whispered, "And it gave me a few minutes to myself, you know?"

"Yeah," Dana replied, glancing at Caine and Xavy.

"Wow, look how much fun they're having."

"It's a treat to watch. I think they've tried out every piece of equipment on the playground."

"Really?" Claire sounded surprised. "That's wonderful. Tommy usually sticks to the swings. Then again, he's almost always by himself."

"Well, he's made up for it today," Dana pointed to where the boys were, setting the Frisbee on the pirate ship's deck, sliding down to grab it and toss it onto the jungle gym once more.

"I'll say. I'm amazed. Your boy's a great influence on him," Claire enthused. "Oh, Sara, I do wish you lived close by."

"It would be nice," Dana murmured as a pod of small boys came running onto the playground. They were all dressed in soccer uniforms.

"It must be first day of practice for the little guys. Half-day kindergarten around here," Claire rolled her eyes. "Thank heavens I'm past that and don't have to find entertainment for him all the time."

Kindergarten. It was so long ago. Dana wistfully remembered Xavy's first day of school as she watched the younger boys run to various pieces of favorite equipment. The noise level on the playground increased tenfold.

Where had they been for kindergarten? Cleveland? Milwaukee? No, Milwaukee had been first grade. She was trying to ferret out the city when she heard Xavier holler.

Chapter Sixteen

On her feet in a flash and running before she knew it, Dana beat Shadow to Xavier by less than a second. Caine beat them both.

"Baby, are you all right? No, don't move, but tell me—"

"I didn't hit my head, Mom," he said, struggling to sit. She pushed him down. Gently. "But my arm hurts."

"Let me see."

"Ow," the boy exclaimed, clutching at his forearm.

Caine pried his hand away. "Hang on, buddy. Let your mom see it." A reassuring presence, Caine knelt next to Xavy, while Dana peeled the jacket away. Blood ran down her hands from a cut on his arm.

"Oh, shit," Xavier said, his face going pale and green.

"Don't curse," Dana said automatically.

"Is it bad?" the boy's voice was frantic. "It's bleeding. Maaaaama, it hurts."

"Not too bad," Caine remarked calmly. "You hit it wrong, did a little damage. We'll just pop into the emergency room, have it checked out."

"Shady Grove Hospital's close by," Eb said, hovering

beyond Caine, a frightened looking Tommy clutched to his side. "Is he going to be okay? Oh, gosh," he fumbled.

"He'll be fine," Caine reassured, as he helped Xavier to his feet and herded them all toward the car. Shadow, on full alert, rumbled a growl at anyone in their path.

"Oh, Sara, I'm so sorry," Claire said, ignoring the dog's warnings long enough to give Dana a hug. "You hang tough, Mike," she hugged Xavy as well. "It's just a scratch."

Dana helped Xavy and Shadow into the car as Caine got directions from Eb. She managed a wave as the other family called their goodbyes. True to Eb's directions, they were at the emergency room within minutes.

"How are we going to handle this? It's a paper trail."

"I've dealt with this before." Caine deftly parked the car, then lifted Xavier into his arms. "If we need it, there's an insurance card in my wallet."

The ER was quiet, and they were seen quickly. "Hmmm, good long cut you got there, young man," the attending physician muttered. "On a jungle gym, you say?"

"Yes, we're on our way home to Cumberland. We were at the park, and he was restless after being in the car."

"Ah, yes. Well, a couple of stitches and you'll be right as rain. Have a scar to show off to your friends at school."

"Mom," Xavy's voice wavered between manly stoicism and tears.

"It's okay, honey. The doctor will numb your arm, then do the stitches. You don't have to watch."

"Here," Caine said, swinging a leg over the high bed and sitting behind the trembling boy. Dana didn't miss the wince as his own injury was affected by the maneuver. "Lean into me and shut your eyes. You'll feel the needle stick for the numbing stuff, that's it."

"Ouuuuuuuuuch," Xavy wailed and flinched as the doctor began numbing the area, and Dana winced with him. It hurt her to have her baby hurt. To see Caine there, solid as a rock, holding her child hurt too, in a pleasure and pain sort of way. The conflict must have shown in her face, because he reached out, held her hand tightly, mouthing, "It's okay. He's okay."

With a nod, she distracted Xavy with chatter about the dog and how much fun it had been to watch him play with Tommy.

"He was cool," Xavy muttered, eyes screwed shut to block the possible sight of a needle. He pressed so tightly into Caine's embrace that Caine's back bowed in an effort to match the force. "He's read all the *Eragon* books."

"Oh, that's unusual." Two readers. No wonder the boys had played so well together.

"We were playing castle and fortress. Then one of those little kids yelled and I looked at them and missed the next rung. . . ." his voice trailed off, and he bit his lip. "Mommmmm, it hurts," he protested. His free hand was gripping Caine's arm. Even as he called for her, Xavier hadn't let go of the man who held him so protectively.

Meeting Caine's eyes, she saw worry and the fierce need to shield and defend, far more than was explained by his duty. Her heart turned over once more. He loved her boy.

She might have been able to talk herself out of loving him, after a century or two of torment, but it was a lost cause now. That he cared for, maybe even loved, her precious son, set Caine so far into her soul, she'd never get him out.

"What? What is it?" Caine asked, and Xavier's eyes flew open too.

"Nevermind. Really. I'm okay."

"Maaaammmmmmaaaa," now Xavy did wail, because he'd seen his bloodied arm, sutured with spidery threads. Seven of them.

"Oh, baby," Dana took them both into her arms, since they were inseparable at this point. "It's okay, it's fine."

"It is indeed," the doctor said, satisfaction evident. Tools clanged into a metal basin, and he started dabbing the area clean. "Seven stitches, m'boy. A good, lucky number. Maybe it'll keep you away from any more emergency rooms."

Xavy stuttered something affirmative.

"Jacket's a total loss," the doctor said, twitching the sleeve he'd cut away. "Sorry 'bout that."

"It's okay," Dana repeated. "We'll get another."

"How long's it been since your young man . . ." he flipped the chart, checked the name. "Since Mike had a tetanus shot?"

"Shot?" Xavy protested. "Mom, no . . ."

"It's okay," she soothed. "Last year, boosters and tetanus."

"Excellent. Okay. I'm going to write you a scrip for antibiotics, a short course. Don't want an infection. I'll give you a scrip for prescription-strength Tylenol for the pain. Deal?" This time, the doctor spoke directly to Xavier, holding out his hand for a shake.

"D-d-deal," the boy managed, then huddled back in the refuge of Caine's arms.

"You did good, too, Dad," the doctor winked at Caine. "He'll be fine. A bit of rest, keep that arm clean and bandaged, some antibiotic ointment, you'll be all set."

Dana left the curtained area with the doctor while Caine helped Xavier down from the table and got their things.

"He'll be all right, really?"

"Fine. In a couple of days, he'll be itching to get the bandage off and see the stitches. Don't let him," the doctor warned. "But don't worry either. No serious damage. It's a long cut, but not too deep. Bandage might have done, but it's right on that line of the bone, and he's still growing. The stitches heal it quicker'n a butterfly."

"Okay, but . . ."

"Now, don't worry, Mrs. Peterson. Have his pediatrician call here if he—"

"She."

"Right, if she has any questions. She can take the stitches out in a week or so."

"All right," Dana mumbled, accepting the prescription forms. "Can we get these filled on premises, Dr. Moore?"

"Yep, first floor pharmacy," he called, walking to another cubicle. "Have a good trip home."

"Those the scrips?" Caine asked, leading Xavier, one arm around the boy's shoulders.

"Yes, we need to get them filled."

"Elevators are through there," a passing nurse pointed the way. At their startlement, she grinned and pointed to the papers in Dana's hand. "Saw the scrips. Go up one floor, hang a left, you'll see the pharmacy."

"Helpful, friendly staff. I hate it. Makes me suspicious," Caine muttered as they reached the elevators.

"What doesn't?"

"You, Shadow, our boy, Mike," he said, steadying Xavier. The boy was wobbling as they walked.

"Are you tired, honey?" she asked him.

"Yeah. And my arm's really starting to hurt," he said plaintively.

"We'll get some painkillers into you and get on the road. You can lean the seat all the way down and rest."

Caine handled the pharmacy the way he'd handled the ER check in. He offered his gold credit card and asked for all the forms so he could submit to insurance himself. The clerk never batted an eye, handing over the forms and bottles with alacrity.

It wasn't until they were in the car, heading south that Caine realized his hands were shaking. Sweat rolled down the back of his neck.

"Pull over," Dana said quietly.

"What?"

"Xavy's asleep already. Pull over, let it pass."

"Let what pass?"

"The shakes. I know the look and the feeling."

Taking her advice, he pulled off the road and jammed the gearshift into park. Dropping his head to the steering wheel, he let the sensation of helpless terror flow over him.

Her hand rubbed his back, a soothing pattern of circles and caresses as she might have done for Xavier.

"It's okay. He's okay."

"I know, but . . ."

"But. Yeah, that gets ya, right in the gut."

He shook all over like a wet dog and scrubbed his hands over his face. "Wow. Scary."

"Understatement of the century. It doesn't hit you when it's happening. You put one foot in front of the other, do what you need to do. It's when it's over that you have to hold onto the world. I've had that feeling a lot."

"That sums it up," Caine muttered, letting the worry and fear fall away, as hard as it was. Oh, God, he was as hooked by the kid as he was by the mom.

* * *

"You have news?" Donovan barked into the phone.

"They're in Maryland. One of the credit cards your source gave us just got used. Elam's been tracking for it."

"Where?"

"Rockville."

"And?" He'd heard a hesitation from Patrick. There was something else.

"It was at a hospital. For the boy."

"What?" Donovan's rage erupted, spewing through the phone line. "Find out what she's done to my son. Find out."

"Yes, sir. I'll call as soon as I know. But I didn't want to wait . . ."

"Find out." Donovan hung up the call. He was glad Paulina had left for the bank. She was too tempting a target for his rage. He wanted her to fear him but not that way. He wanted to kill someone, break something. Burn something. He wanted Dana at his feet, begging for her life. He wanted to watch the life leave her beautiful eyes, know she wouldn't thwart him, haunt him any longer.

"Aaaaaargh!" he hurled the statue from the corner of his desk. It flew across the room, gouging a dramatic hole in the elegant paneling. The mark, a crackle of broken splinters on the walnut finish was like a shattered window. As he watched, the whole panel cracked with a sound like a gunshot.

It was so satisfying, so invigorating, he wanted to do it again. He found himself searching for something, anything, heavy enough to throw.

The sheer idiocy of the action brought him back to himself. Thank God no one had seen him scurrying around hefting things, testing their weight in anticipation of their impact.

"*Loco,*" he hissed. "I must control this. I *will.* Control. This." He spaced the words out, drawing in great gasps of air to level his racing heart. "She drives me to this, demon that she is. Witch that she is, to have stolen my son."

He paced the floors, still striving for calm. "No, I must focus on Donny. On my son. On his return to me." He stopped, closed his eyes, and felt his system balance. "Yes, that is it."

What would Sun Tzu do? With this as the battlefield, how would the greatest of generals have played for a win?

He began to smile. Yes. That was it. He opened his phone and dialed.

"Pollack," he barked, still smiling. "Where are you? How soon will you be in Richmond?" *You false son of a bitch,* he thought, cursing Pollack for a traitor in his mind.

"Tomorrow," came the flat, irritated reply. "And yeah, I know it's changing the plan. The kid got hurt. I had to take him to the emergency room."

Donovan frowned. Why would Pollack tell him the truth with no evidence of fear or surprise. Was he being played from both sides?

"What happened?"

"Kid tried to make a break for it."

"You hurt my son?" Icy fury suffused him. No one hurt his son.

"No. He cut his arm on purpose so we'd have to go to the ER, so he could try to escape." Now he could hear the wrath in Pollack's voice, the deep desire to hurt something or someone. Here was that darkness Donovan had sensed, felt a kinship with.

"Clever."

"Fuckin'-A. No offense, but I can't wait to dump these two on you, man."

"No offense taken, my friend," Donovan managed a laugh. "I had doubted you, Pollack," he said, pacing with different energy now. He felt the rush of things coming together, of the fates playing into his hands. He knew he was going to win. "But not now. Bring them to me. I'll be waiting."

It was late when they talked to Sears, told him about the call. No doubt now, that Richmond was a trap. They stopped at a hotel for few hours. Sears had urged them to go to ground, let him run some scenarios.

Dana toyed with the sparkling ring on her finger, watching it flash in the fading light, sliding it around and around. She realized that she wanted the engagement ring to really mean something. She wanted the chance, the emotional room, for it to be possible.

She'd chased the options around and around. Even as she'd denied the possibility, maybe it was time to disappear. Her way. She'd let Caine know where they were. Only Caine.

"I know how," she whispered to the black of the ceiling. "It's not that hard." And she did know how, the same way Donovan did. Her impromptu strategizing came together, and she saw the pattern, the logical sequence in which it would work.

Caine came out of the bathroom. "You're thinking so hard, I can hear it over here," he said. "Tell me what you're so busy planning."

With remarkable calm, she told him. "I do know what to do. I can make it work."

"Everything would have to go perfectly. Are you sure you'd make it? That Xavy would?" His was the voice of reason.

"I know there are risks," she said, snapping with impatience.

"You've come too far, Dana, to chance Xavy now. This plan risks him. If it goes sour, you do Walker's work for him. He gets Xavy. And, God forbid, what if Xavy's hurt or killed? Then all the sacrifices are in vain."

It was harsh, impossible in fact. She hated that he was right, hated that she had no option.

"We'll figure it out, Dana. Together."

She was about to question the words, the meaning. Everything. But his phone rang once more. She was beginning to hate the sound of Caine's cell phone. It always interrupted something important between them, and it always brought bad news.

Minutes later, the hotel phone rang, and she picked it up.

"Mrs. Markham?"

"Tervain?" she looked at Caine, who nodded. "Are you all right? They told us . . ." she listened intently. "Yes, I'll put it on speaker."

Oblivious, Xavier slept on the other bed, Shadow's head propped on his hip.

"Hey, old man. Still alive?" Caine said, by way of a greeting when the speaker was engaged.

"For now," Tervain replied with apparent cheer. "Takin' it day by day, ya' know?"

Dana shot a look Caine's way, and got a shrug in reply. Tervain sounded . . . different. It worried the hell out of her.

With terse phrasing, Caine explained the arrangements that needed to be made. "Are you sure about this course of action, Mrs. Markham?" Tervain asked. His voice was eager as it flowed through the connection, even as he questioned her judgment.

"I will not run any more, Tervain. Donovan will never stop. Not while he's alive and free. If we confront him, using the decoy, we stand a chance of ending this, one way or the other," she added.

"You could be hurt. You know it."

"My affairs are in order. You have the details," she reminded him. "You introduced me to the lawyer, remember?"

"I remember. I had hoped it wouldn't come to this."

"We don't get everything we want, do we?"

"Not even for Christmas," Tervain said, irreverently. "I'm duty bound to remind you, you can go witness protection again. We'll cover you. You know that."

"I know. But sooner or later, I have to make a stand. I choose here and now."

There was a sigh from the other end, but he didn't sound defeated. It sounded more like he was mentally changing gears. "Okay then, hang on. People," he said, "We're a go." There was rustling in the background, the sound of a door closing, and Tervain was back. "The meet's tomorrow, in Richmond, right, Caine?"

"That's what's set. Walker's up to something, more than what we guessed. He was too pleased."

"I hope not. We don't have much time as it is. Head for Smith Mountain Lake, Caine, you know the place."

"Got it."

"Excellent. Dana, we're in your debt. This time—"

Dana cut him off. "Let's just get on with it, okay?" She couldn't stand it if he spouted clichés about justice. She no longer gave a damn about justice. If her attitude guaranteed a one way ticket to hell, so be it.

Tervain had a last warning.

"If you get to the lake house and there aren't lights, get the hell out. If the lights don't flash the right sequence, get out. If anything doesn't jibe, haul ass. Our decoy is already there, as are the three veteran agents to guard the boy. You know them all, Caine," and he rattled off names and events which were gibberish to Dana.

"Top choices."

"I'll be there before you leave for Richmond."

"Why not Sears?" They heard a sigh on the other end and exchanged glances. "What? What's with Sears?"

"The bullet wound went sour. He's in the hospital with a one-hundred-plus degree fever getting IV antibiotics."

Relief coursed through her. An infection. Not dead. Thank God. "Give him our regards, Tervain," she said, meaning every word. "He held it together until you got back."

"He did," Tervain responded. "And I will. Now get going."

When they'd hung up, Caine sat across from her, took her hands. "Dana, are you sure? There's still WitSec."

She shook her head. "No, I'm not sure. I'm scared to death. I'm scared I'll die, I'm scared I'll kill Donovan." She pulled her hands free, paced to the door, and returned. "Hell, I'm scared I *won't* kill Donovan, and this will never end."

He reached for her, and she backed away. "No, not now. I won't argue with you." Her voice broke and she took a hiccoughing breath. "Damn. I don't want to wake Xavy."

"The bathroom."

She glanced at the exterior door. Double locked with a chair propped under the knob.

"Shadow, guard," she ordered in German. The dog didn't move, but his whole posture changed.

With Caine's hand on her waist, she preceded him into the small room, braced her hands on the sink as he closed the door behind them.

"C'mere."

His arms were open, and she walked into the haven they offered. Whatever he was angry about, whatever lay unsaid between them, she didn't care. When he enveloped her in his embrace, she let down the steel with which she leashed her emotions, let the tears of anguish escape.

"Let it go," he murmured, resting his chin on her hair, rubbing a hand down her spine. "Let fly, love. You've been bottling that in for too long. Shhhhh-shhhhh," he soothed, rocking her where they stood.

It seemed forever before the storm of weeping subsided. He held tissues out to her, continuing to cradle her as she calmed.

"How long's it been since you did that?"

"Cried?" she managed, rubbing at her gritty eyes. How long had it been? "Like that? I can't remember."

"Too long, then." He caressed her cheek, framed her face with his powerful hands. "You're due a break. You've paid in to the plan, it's time the plan paid off for you."

"From your mouth to God's ear," she managed through the residual sobs catching in her chest. "He's the only one who can give me an ending, at this point."

"Yeah. Maybe, for once, The Man is on our side."

She nodded. "It seems to be all I do. Pray, that is. Pray we don't draw attention to ourselves. Pray Donovan doesn't find us. Pray that somebody shoots him before he can get his hands on Xavy."

He stilled. "You really pray that?"

"So sue me." The rumbling sound of his laughter lightened her heavy heart.

"You're a rare one," he said, easing her away to kiss her once more. It started off as a benison, a simple, easy meeting of the lips.

It didn't stay that way.

Chapter Seventeen

Before she knew it, she was struggling out of her shirt, working the buttons on his.

"Oh, God, Dana, I need . . ."

"Yes, me too," she tore her mouth away from his long enough to pull her shirt off.

Mouths fused, they let the wide sink carry their weight as they grappled with the firestorm of needs overtaking them both.

"Here, let me . . ."

"No, like . . ."

"Ahhhhhh," she couldn't suppress the moan as he found her full, turgid nipple, suckled it, and kissed his way to the other. Every touch of his skin to hers sent currents of need flowing through her body, energizing her, and driving her nearly frantic with excitement.

She arched into him, and he groaned as she connected with his rock-hard erection. He was magnificent. His body was hard and strong. Scars, like battle flags, crisscrossed his chest. She used her tongue to soothe them, to kiss away the reminders of darker times.

She wanted time.

There was only now.

They were locked together, their hands frantically caressing and seeking. Within Dana, passion and desperation warred for the upper hand.

With deft command of her body and his own, he bowed her onto the counter, delighting her with hot, wild, nipping kisses down her belly and thighs.

"Oh, God, Caine," she cried, feeling herself melt into a sensory creature. "Yes, touch me . . . yes, like . . . ooooooh." She moaned as he teased her with his tongue, driving her to the brink of orgasm. Her body was slick with a sheen of sweat and the desperate craving for fulfillment.

"Dana, let me," he said, slipping his hands under her hips.

"No, I want *you*," she managed, desperate for the feel of him within her. Someday there would be time, but . . . "Inside me. Now."

Pulling him forward, she wrapped her legs around his hips, and welcomed him, drawing every bit of him within her. In spite of her determination, he took his time. Every inch was an unholy torture of pleasure.

"Dear God," he gasped as they moved together, each rocking to the other's rhythm. "What you do to me."

"Feeling's mutual," she barely managed the reply, pressing her breasts to the firm planes of his chest, drawing his mouth to hers.

His hands braced them both, balanced them while his body rocked them toward completion. In the opposing mirror, she saw his muscular rear, saw her own hands gripping him, pulling him deeper.

The image, the picture of the two of them intertwined in lovemaking, was intense. Seeing it as she felt it was such an erotic image, coupled with the intense pleasure of his mouth on hers, that her orgasm rose with lightning speed.

"Oh-oh-oh," she gasped, closing her eyes to the sensory overload.

"Touch me, Dana."

She did, sliding her hands frantically over his back, but she returned again and again to feel the thrust of his hips, give their rushing joy that much more power.

"Now, Caine, now."

"No," he demanded on a rasping breath. "Look at me, Dana, I want to see it, see you fly free."

Her eyes flew open, meeting the fiery emotion in his. His groan echoed on the tiles, his eyes were firebrands, boring into hers. She rose, arching and sliding to meet his thrusts, shuddering with the power of their joining.

He covered her mouth with his own, a wild passion of mating tongues. He caught her near-scream of exultation as she vaulted over the edge. With a last deep, powerful thrust, he let her intense writhing send him over as well.

A sense of time and space returned to her slowly.

She couldn't say she'd returned to normal. Oh, no. It was much better than that. Sweet Lord.

"Oh my," was all she managed as the breath tore in and out of her lungs. She was wrung out, both from crying and from the storm of their lovemaking.

"Understatement," he muttered, his panting breath a warm caress on her mussed hair. "You're the master of understatement."

"Hmmmmm. How about one word?"

"Go for it."

"Magnificent?"

"Good word. Call you, and raise you."

"What word?"

"Mind-shattering."

"That's two, but I feel too spectacular—there's another useful adjective—to complain."

"Yeah."

They were still joined, still breathing in unison, and Dana wondered if her heart, or her body, would ever be the same.

"We should check on Xavy," he finally managed. "But I don't want to move."

"Mmmmmm. You're right on both counts," she murmured, amazed that it was he, not she, who first thought of Xavier. "I have another word."

"Hmmmm?"

"Shower," she managed.

He groaned. "Torture me with visions of you, wet and naked. Go ahead."

"I'm naked now."

"Yeah," he ran a caressing hand to her breast. "You are."

"We should move."

"Mmmmmm." They rested in one another's arms for a few more minutes. For Dana, it was a desperately needed eddy in the blinding current of the events shaping her days.

Reality, in the form of a muscle spasm in her thigh, made sure she didn't stay in the calm water for too long. "Muscle cramp."

He lifted her easily, and it thrilled her that he was so strong. She never considered herself small, or weak, but the gesture made her feel positively doll-like and petite. In a queer sort of way, although he'd said nothing, it made her feel cherished.

In a good way.

Given those thoughts, his next words surprised her.

"We'll get through this, beautiful Dana. Together." He held her away a bit, tapping her chin to get her to meet his eyes. "You hear me?"

Nodding, she managed a smile. "Yeah. It sounds good. I know there's a lot unsaid between us, Caine. A lot undone. But together? That sounds . . . good."

"Yeah." He patted her on the butt, a gentle, playful swat. "Hit the showers, girl. You smell like sex."

The abrupt change to humor threw her off, but she recovered. "And you don't?"

"Not as much," he grinned at her, pulling on his pants and throwing on his shirt. "I'll sit with Xavy, then I'll shower. Then we'd better get on the road."

"Deal."

Xavier was stirring when she came out, her hair drying rapidly in the warm room. He rolled and bumped his arm, leaping into full wakefulness from the pain.

"Owwwww," he complained.

"Hey, buddy, that had to hurt," she said, coming to sit next to him. She brushed his hair from his eyes. "Let's get you some more Tylenol and a shower. You'll feel better in clean clothes, then we'll get some chow, okay?"

"What time is it?" he muttered, rubbing his eyes.

"Almost ten. You slept a long time."

"My mouth is sticky. And my hip hurts too."

"Probably where you landed. Here, have some water."

Like a creaky old man, Xavy stood, and Dana called Caine out of the bathroom to help. They wrapped plastic over the dressing and stood, one on either side of the partially closed door, as he managed a shower.

"He's doing great."

She looked at Caine, surprised at the strain in his voice. "Actually he is. Considering how much he's hurting, he's calmer than he's been before when we've had to move this fast." She managed a smile. "Must be your good influence, dragon."

"He matters to me, Dana. More than I believed possible." He rubbed at his face, met her gaze. "So do you."

"Caine, I . . ."

"Mom?"

With a look of unvoiced apology to Caine, she answered her son. "Yes, honey?"

Caine nodded. How easily he understood her. The thought stayed with her as she helped Xavier dress.

With the car loaded, they retraced their first drive, merging from Interstate 66, to Highway 29, heading for Smith Mountain Lake.

Caine filled her in on the agents and the security arrangements. "There'll be an agent with him at all times, and two on watch. Two sleeping. They'll switch off every four hours until they're relieved. Tervain's taking no chances with him, Dana. If I thought he was, I wouldn't agree."

"I . . . see," her heart skipped again, to the thought of loving him, of him loving Xavier. "Maybe we should talk about . . . other stuff. About after."

"After?"

"If we make it."

His face changed from its intense focus on the road, to a darker, more somber look. "We shouldn't look that far ahead. We need to focus on the now."

So, it had been sex and the comfort of the moment for him, she decided sadly. Could she have expected any more than that, really? She had no doubt that he cared, more than he wanted too, but it ended there. When he said nothing more, she felt her heart sink.

Closing her eyes, she blocked out the sight of the endless white line down the middle of the road; the emptiness of the night. When she felt her head loll to the side, she jerked upright.

"Sorry, I dozed off there. I'll try to stay awake."

"No need."

"We're making good time," Dana commented sleepily.

"Yeah—"

"What's that?" She sat up, abruptly, ignoring his hiss of alarm as they both saw the cluster of cars ahead of them. Three men stood in the road, waving them down.

"Do we try to run through them? What if they're Donovan's men?"

"Mom?"

"Get down, Xavy," they ordered, in unison.

Before Caine could slow down, or blast through the now-frantically waving people, there was a pop-pop-pop and the SUV slewed violently sideways.

Xavier screamed.

It was no consolation that Caine worked to change the tire in the cursing company of half a dozen other motorists, all fellow victims of a box of nails. When he finished, it was after midnight.

Exhaustion dogged her thoughts and was imprinted in the set of Caine's shoulders. Even switching drivers hadn't helped. Worried, Dana finally spoke up.

Xavier's injured arm had taken a beating when the car's tire blew, and they'd skidded to the side of the road. Thanks to the drugs, he was sleeping, albeit rest-lessly, in the back seat.

"We have to stop. Unless someone's on our tail right this minute, no one could track us here. If there's a leak inside, they may know about Smith Mountain too. Staying here until morning, when we can navigate makes sense."

Without a word, Caine slowed, turning in at a roadside motel. The Mountain Inn appeared to be clean, if basic. They discussed options, but Caine reluctantly agreed.

"Impeccable logic," Caine finally said. "But I don't have to like it."

"I know. I'd rather be where we're supposed to be," she said, a touch of aspersion in her voice. "But it's going to take us at least two more hours to do all the doubling around and hunting for the house, especially in the dark."

"I know. That's why I'm stopping," he said, losing a bit of patience. "You win, okay? I'll get the room."

Caine headed into the motel office, his limp more pronounced than earlier in the day. Dana wondered if the tire change had opened the wound. He had such animal grace, it was hard to remember he was hurt. The wound must be aching for him to be so brusque. Either that, or he was worried.

Then again, they were all on edge.

"Are you fighting with Mist . . . Charlie, Mom?" Xavier asked, tentatively from the darkness.

"Not really, honey," she soothed, annoyed with herself for letting Caine's attitude get under her skin. "He agrees with me, but he doesn't want to. It's making him cranky."

Shadow began to whine in earnest as they sat waiting.

"Mom, I think Shadow really has to go," Xavy said. "You want me to take him out?"

"No, stay put. I'll get him."

Digging out her jacket, Dana pulled it on and got Shadow out of the SUV. He bounded forward on the lead, making a beeline for an arrangement of azaleas. In a few minutes, she was able to take the dog back to the car.

Caine's face was tight and closed as he returned. She easily recognized smoldering anger.

"We have to leave."

"What? Why?"

"They don't allow dogs. If you hadn't had him walking, we'd have slipped him in, but the manager saw him."

"Damn," she said, cursing the luck, his irritation, and the situation in general. "I'm sorry."

"Forget it," he said, curtly. "Not your fault."

She was about to argue the point, when she saw a man waving frantically at them from the doorway of the office.

"What's that hotel guy want?" Xavier asked, pointing to the man who was now hurrying toward them.

Since the man had planted himself in the driveway, still waving and blocking their exit, Caine put the car in park and got out. Chances were slim that it was a trap, but she saw him loosen the gun at his waistband, his hand ready on it if the situation warranted force.

"Sir, my wife pinned my ears to my head, if you get me." Dana heard the man call. Even at a distance, Caine's blank incomprehension of the colloquialism was obvious. "You know, read me the riot act for turning ya'll away. I tell ya' what. If ya' leave the dog in the car, I'll let ya' have the room. You okay with that? I kin put ya' in the lower down rooms, away from the road, so even if he barks some it won't wake nobody."

"Hang on," Caine replied, returning to the car. "You okay with that? Leaving Shadow in the car?"

"I hate it, but it's one night. We'll be at the safehouse in the morning. I really don't think we have a choice."

"I'm really tired of being in the car, Mom. I'm really sleepy." His voice was so mournful, and he sounded so young that Dana reached a comforting hand to him, squeezed. "I don't want to leave Shadow in the car, though."

Caine nodded. "I know. We'll sneak him in later, after the first watch."

Ten minutes later, they were opening the door to a plain, slightly stale-smelling room with two double beds. A big TV sat on a low dresser, and a tent sign advertised all the cable channels, even the premiums.

"That's cool," Xavy managed, sleepily as he lay down. "They have HBO, too."

"Yeah," Dana agreed, knowing he'd be asleep in seconds. Nestled in the bed with Xavier, taking the first watch, Dana began to surf the channels.

"How about staying more than three seconds on a station," Caine complained into the darkness.

"There's five hundred. It's a waste of time if I know right away it's something stupid."

"Good point," he paused, then went on. "You're thinking out loud again. Quit doubting. We're committed. I'm with you," he said, propping up on one elbow to look at her. "For whatever it means, we're in it together."

She scanned his serious face, the flicking light from the television highlighting the planes and valleys of his features.

She was about to speak when his phone rang, a trill of sound in the quiet room.

"Crap," he muttered, fumbling for the device. "It's

Tervain. He's gonna be pissed." He glanced at Xavier. "I don't want to wake him. I'll take it outside."

He answered the call as he eased through the door. She heard the first part of his explanation as he pulled the door closed behind him.

Fighting her fatigue, Dana was determined to stand her watch. She sipped cold water and wiggled her feet, trying to keep her blood moving without waking Xavier.

She automatically froze when the door opened, then relaxed when she recognized Caine.

"I walked Shadow," Caine whispered as he returned. "But the night guard's out there. I put the dog back in the car, for now." Sitting down on the side of the bed, he looked at her, a wry smile playing around his full mouth. "Tervain's fired up; that's no surprise. But he agreed with our decision."

"Not that we needed his approval, but it's good to know," she managed. He was looking at her, *that* way. Her blood heated and her belly tightened. He took the remote from her hand. "I'm awake now. I'll take first watch."

With a soft kiss on her temple, that did nothing to cool her memories of their earlier encounter, he turned off the television. She heard the rustle of the curtains, and saw the lights from the parking lot reflect on the barrel of his weapon, as he opened the door a mere crack to check the lot.

She'd called him a black knight. It was so apt in so many ways. He was as distant from her as if he was encased in steel. Perhaps that was it, he'd walled off everything, and everyone, shutting himself inside his dark armor.

The thought was so sad, so depressing, she couldn't stand it. Life was so full, even when it was full of danger.

Rolling to one side, she pulled the blanket over her legs, made sure Xavier was well tucked in. Freedom was so precious, so real. There were so many things . . .

Sleep claimed her so quickly she didn't have time to wonder about the strange, sweet smell of cologne drifting in on the breeze.

Chapter Eighteen

Dana woke with a gun to her head. The barrel was cool, and smooth. The firm pressure on her brow let her know the person on the trigger end meant business. The sharp tang of a snapped ammonia capsule stung her nose, explaining why she was so suddenly, and shockingly, alert.

"Get up," a voice whispered. "Tie Bradley's hands."

Rope landed in her lap as she struggled to rise. The weapon stayed tightly pressed to her temple.

"No tricks. You don't matter to me. Nor does he. I want the boy. You cooperate, you stay alive. Try anything and you both get dead. Either way, I get the boy."

"Who are you? Why are you doing this?" Dana asked as she tied Caine's hands. He'd fallen, or been rolled, onto the floor at the foot of his bed. When she tried, surreptitiously to rouse him with a shake, a hand snapped out of the darkness, to cuff her.

"Quit stalling. Pull it tighter. Don't try and leave them loose, Mrs. Markham. I'll hurt you for it."

She pulled the rope constricting Caine's wrists. The voice was familiar. Low, but female. In the darkened room, the other woman was a bulky shadow, even with the glimmer of light silvering the room from the now partially drawn drapes.

"You get down on the floor between the beds and put your hands behind you. I've got more rope for you."

Something about the words, the voice, clicked into place. "Agent Booth."

"Yeah."

"Everyone thinks you're dead."

"I know. Walker taught me well."

Dana gasped. Booth was the leak, the insider.

"But, but, you've been missing for days, how did you—"

"Tapped Tervain's private cell, Sears's too, and inserted my own double scrambler. Once you contacted Tervain, you were easy to track. I knew it would just be a matter of time. You made it tough, staying here. I was already at the house. I'm behind schedule. Fucking flat tire."

Booth jerked the rope, the smooth nap of the bindings cut into Dana's wrists.

"Why?" She couldn't figure it out.

"Why, what? Why am I leaving you alive?"

"That, too."

"Caine saved my life a few years ago. I didn't know he was the plant in Donovan's organization, and didn't care once his cover was blown. I'd never been to Donovan's house, so I never saw him, never knew. Donovan and I met other places," Booth's voice turned caressing and feminine when she said Donovan's name, giving Dana all the information she needed as to why a veteran agent would turn. "He's amazing."

"He's a killer," Dana stated flatly. "Listen to me, Agent Booth. You're not over the edge yet. Nobody's dead at your hand. Don't let him turn you into a killer too."

"He isn't turning me into anything I've not already fully grown into on my own." There was derision in her voice now. "I'm doing this as much for me as for him. He won't stop raving about his son. Hell, he doesn't know how much trouble the rugrats are. You've done all the hard work after all, up till now. My sister's raised a boy on her own, I know what a job it is. He gets the boy, he'll quit obsessing over him. I'll get all his attention."

"Then why—"

"That sympathy only means I don't kill you, Mrs. Markham. My life's just starting. With him. I'm taking his son to him. It's all he wants, his truest desire. He enjoys the money, the power, but he craves Donovan, Jr., dreams of him. Pines for him, if you can believe it. When I bring the boy, I'll have him, have his heart. I'll be his woman, or as close to it as anyone can get," she said with reasonable humor and insight. "I know what he is. I know who he is."

Dana remembered Caine's theory that Donovan's obsession was with her, Dana; a twisted love that would never die unless he did. A possessive, evil thing which sought her death rather than let anyone else have her. Booth, it seemed, knew all that and wanted Donovan anyway.

With a last jerk of the rope, Booth came around to face Dana, bending low to look her in the eye.

"The difference between you and me is, I may be in love with him, but I'm not stupid, naïve, or blind. I know him, flaws, arrogance, and all, and I want him, regardless. He's everything I've ever craved in a man, in bed and out."

"You've signed your death warrant."

Booth laughed, and there was a bit of hysteria behind the mirth. "I'm already dead, remember?"

"Not from us, Booth. You can still salvage something from this. It's Walker who's the threat. The minute he has Xavier, he'll kill you. It's his version of shooting the messenger, Booth. Don't do this."

"It's you he wants dead, not me."

"Are you going to kill me for him? Do his murder for him?"

"Oh, no," Booth said, checking Caine's binding with a brutal jerk of the ropes. She smiled at Dana, and even in the gloom, Dana saw the despair underneath the bravado. "He's sane because you're alive, you know that, right? He walks the edge. You die? He'll lose it. He thinks he wants you dead, but he doesn't. Not really."

Booth pushed at Caine's body with her foot. He struggled for a moment, but never seemed to fully reach consciousness. It must have satisfied her, because she turned to the sleeping child. Carefully, Booth began gently tying Xavier's hands in front of him.

"He's hurt, Booth. A cut on his forearm. Please, be careful."

"What happened?"

"An accident, he cut it on the playground. He needs the antibiotics, bandages."

"Donovan's not going to like that," the woman muttered, being even more careful of how she moved the boy. He'd fallen asleep fully dressed, making her task easier than if he'd been in pajamas. As Dana surreptitiously tried her bonds, Booth rummaged through the few bags on the floor, finding Xavier's, throwing his shoes in, and slinging it over her shoulder.

Dana was watching Xavier, willing him to wake up. She

nearly jumped out of her skin when Booth materialized at her side.

"Open your mouth," Booth was leaning over her, nudging her.

"Wha—" a gag was slipped in to choke her words and was tied firmly behind her head.

Silenced and bound she watched, shrieking inside as Booth carefully lifted Xavier, grunting a bit with his weight. Kicking the door open, she struggled into the darkness, the sleeping child in her arms.

Dana wept, sobbing harder when she heard Shadow barking frantically into the darkness as his master was carried away. Despair threatened to overwhelm her as the distant sound of an engine starting floated to her over Shadow's furor. It faded, leaving the silence of a country night to be punctuated by random barks and the hoot of an owl.

Sagging to the floor, Dana prayed for oblivion. How had this happened? Her boy, her child . . .

She heard a hissing sigh. Caine. Oh, Lord, was he dead? What if he was allergic to the gas Booth had used? What if he was ill? Choking? If he was dead, and Xavier taken, she would go mad. Stark, raving mad.

Struggling with the ropes, Dana worked at the knots until her fingers and wrists were raw, her hands and arms aching with the pressure. Caine stirred once, but no matter how hard she tried, the noise she was making was too faint to rouse him.

Booth had efficiently tied her ankles as well, but using her elbows, Dana finally rolled to the edge of the bed and worked her way upright. Wiggling along the mattress, she came to the end, squinting in the bare bit of light to see if Caine was still breathing.

He was. Thank God. Struggling to stand, she leaned into the television, fumbling along its lower rim, pushing every tiny button she felt, hoping to turn it on, get some light.

Color flooded the room as a poker tournament blazed onto the screen, but in silence. She'd managed to mute the thing as well as turn it on, but at least she had light. The faux glitz and glamour shone in stark contrast to the difficult conditions it illuminated.

Caine was down, unconscious, bound, and also gagged. She was bound and gagged but conscious. Not much better.

She scanned the room for anything that would cut the ropes. Booth had jerked the phone jack out of the wall, disabling it in one quick pull. She didn't know where her purse was, didn't see its black leather in the flickering light. She had a survival knife, but it was in the car, with the bulk of their luggage.

Survival knife. Hadn't Caine strapped one to his leg yesterday, when he'd dressed after his shower?

Sinking carefully to her knees, Dana took tiny, shuffling "knee steps," as full as the hobbling ropes on her ankles would allow. It took forever, but she got to where Caine lay. The power of his body warmed her, gave her strength to keep going. Inching her way along his prone form, she felt him stir.

"Mmmmmpf, Caaaahhhhnnnn," she fought to get the words out, make him hear. He gave a feeble twitch, but his eyes stayed closed. She continued to make noises, trying to rouse him as she inched down his long legs. At his feet, she turned so she could get her hands placed at the hem of his jeans. The pants were new, stiff with sizing and rough under her swelling hands.

"Kah'maahhn, Caaahhhnnnn, weech oaup," she cried around the gag.

"Ah," she crowed in triumph as her searching fingers found the leather sheath and inched down the heavy sock to fumble with the buckle. Doing it backwards, with no way to see what she was touching, was maddening.

"Shaz's it, D'na," she encouraged herself. "Kape hrying." Her throat rasped with dryness from the gag and from trying to speak. Frustrated tears blinded her, and emotion slowed her fingers to a fumbling mass of painful twigs, pawing at a futile task.

"Mmmmmmffffff," Caine's exclamation was akin to a shout in the quiet room. She redoubled her efforts, using her hips to jostle him awake.

"Kaaahhhnnn," she called, bumping him hard. "Weeeech oaup!"

He coughed and she heard the sound of retching. Booth must have muzzled him tightly, activating his gag-reflex.

"Kaaaahhhnnn."

"Mffcksgingon?"

She guessed he was saying "what the fuck is going on?" Yeah, she wanted to know that too.

She bumped him harder. "Ouu ah weeeeek?"

When he didn't answer, she swiveled around. He had the gag clenched in his teeth and was pulling into the fabric with all the strength in his neck. She heard the unmistakable screech of tearing cloth, and with a bit more effort, he spat the pieces of black cloth to the floor.

"You okay?" he managed after taking in deep lungfuls of air, his head resting on the floor.

"Kaaaaaa."

"Xavy?"

A sob escaped her, clear even with the gag.

"Oh, God, not dead?"

"Nu-ho," she managed the word, shaking her head to emphasize the words.

"Taken?"

"Booooff."

"Booth?" he roared the name, struggling with the ropes binding his hands and feet. His flailing about unbalanced her and she tipped over onto him. "Oooof. That bitch. Crap. Unholy, fucking crap," he continued to curse in vivid, fiery detail, verbally disemboweling Booth, Walker, Tervain, the agency, the hotel manager and, last but not least, himself, for staying here instead of going on to where they would have been secure.

His cursing voice set Shadow off again, but they were so far away from the office and the front of the motel where the few other guests were staying, it was doubtful anyone would hear. Caine must have had the same thought because he made no effort to yell for help.

"At least they'll know to come looking for us when we don't show up at the lake house," he muttered, as he tested his bonds.

She wanted to tell him that the people at the lake house might be dead already. Booth said she'd gone there first. She didn't say she wasn't already a killer, all she'd said was she wasn't going to kill Dana or Caine. Not this time, anyway.

Thinking about the woman's demeanor, her conversation as she calmly bound them and stole away with another woman's child, Dana decided Booth wouldn't hesitate a second time.

"Can you reach my knife? She's tied me like a calf, and stuck the desk chair through the leg loop. I can't turn over and I can't kick my way free unless I kick the fucking desk off the wall, which I don't have enough leverage to do."

"Wiiee sill."

"Lie still?"

She nodded, managing to wiggle into position again and resume her fumbling hunt for the straps that held the knife to his calf. It was sheer luck that his pant leg wasn't snugged tight under the ropes. She'd take that small favor from the fates, and be grateful. One strap finally gave way.

"I felt it come loose. The other strap will be harder," he rasped, his panting breaths robbing him of moisture to lubricate his throat. "It's higher, the pants don't slide very easily."

"Eye kno."

"Guess you do know. Higher, yeah. Underside of my leg," he directed her through the long, frustrating process of finding the buckle and undoing it. "You got it. Can you pull it out?"

Her aching hands forgotten in the hope of getting loose, Dana painstakingly fingered the knife from its holder.

"It's damn sharp. Be careful."

Heeding his advice, she kept her brushing, searching fingers on the hilt, tugging at it until it swung free. She gripped it, blade out, working to keep the wicked edge away from her fingers.

"Okay, I'm going to twist sideways, try and see where the knife is and direct you in cutting yourself free. You with me? Good. Hold the hilt, get a firm grip. You got it?"

"Gaaaat eeet."

"On three."

It took agonizing minutes of careful cutting to sever the ties on her hands, then mere seconds to free him, once the painful return of circulation to her fingers allowed her to grip the blade once more.

Stripping the gag from her mouth, she went to the tap and drank straight from the faucet, barely pausing to breathe as the water brought blessed relief to her parched throat.

Coming out of the room, she grabbed her shoes as Caine searched for his cell phone. To her surprise, he found it under the bed.

"Wonder why she left that?"

"Didn't see it. Probably thought it was in the car when she didn't find it on the nightstand."

"And she wasn't chancing Shadow to get it."

"Right."

"She didn't search us, take your weapons or money. Why?" Dana finished with her shoes and had Shadow's leash in hand, the other on the door.

"Has weapons of her own. Doesn't think we'd get loose till late morning, much less come after her anytime soon. Also, if she takes them, she has to dispose of them. One final reason, if she's found with the boy before she gets to Donovan, she can claim she rescued him, but if our weapons are in her possession, she's screwed."

"I'd bet the last is it more than anything else," she said, flinging the door open.

He had her arm, jerking her inside before she took a step.

"What the hell do you think you're doing?"

"Getting Shadow, he can track her to where she had

her car, see if I can find anything that will tell us where she's going."

"You didn't even look before you walked out. She could have a sniper."

"Oh, for Christ's sake, Caine. If she'd wanted us dead, we'd be dead." Wrenching her arm free, Dana stomped to the car, leashed the dog and held her shirt to his nose where Booth had grabbed her.

"Find this, Shadow. Find her, find Xavier."

With that, she gave him the command to track. With a bellowing bark, he tore across the parking lot. Dana raced with him. A scant path through the brush at the edge of the property led to a picnic area, and from there to an ice cream parlor, closed until summer. At the far side of the parking lot, Shadow lost the trail.

Whining and pacing, the dog frantically cast over the gravel, nose to the ground. He crisscrossed the area, finally sitting down. The spot was centered in between two of the lot's lights, a shadowy area where a person's actions would be concealed without being in total darkness.

Using her flashlight, Dana peered at the ground, noting a deep path in the gravel. Following it toward the road, she prayed for any sign that might tell her which way Booth had turned, taking Xavier away.

"Thank you, God," she breathed, as she saw the muddy depressions where Booth had pulled in and out. The red-brown spray and mud crossed the road, through the median cross over and pointed the way south. A perfect, undisturbed trail of wet, sticky, and very distinctive mud, speckled liberally with the gravel from the lot. It had to be recent, had to be Booth. Any straight traffic on the road would have erased the traces, mussed the exact placement of the gravel, wiped away the globs of clinging soil.

Thank God for mud. For big, goopy red mud.

"She went south," Dana said, hurrying to the truck. Working quickly, she loaded Shadow into the SUV and climbed into the driver's seat. Caine climbed into the passenger seat with a groan, gave her the keys and her phone.

"What is it?" She managed. "What's wrong?"

"The gas. Just drive. I'll manage."

Peeling out of the lot, she peppered him with questions.

"Did you get Tervain? Are the other agents okay? Does he have any idea where she's going?"

"Yes. No, and no."

"Oh, Lord. Did she kill the other agents?"

"No, they were drugged, like us. When I got Tervain, he'd just arrived from DC and was rousing them and cutting them loose."

"Are they coming with us?"

"Tervain's got his hands full. All five agents were hit hard by the gas, one's critical. Another has a concussion. Also . . ."

"What?"

"We were ordered to stay put, wait for contact."

"You're kidding, right?"

"No."

"Idiots."

"He has a point, Dana," Caine managed, before a fit of coughing doubled him over. "Bloody, fucking hell, that hurts," he rasped as he sank into the seat. "I think either she kicked me in the ribs or I hit something when I fell."

"Or you're allergic to whatever she used, and your lungs are protesting."

"That too. Back to the issue," Caine said, gripping his side as he took careful breaths. "We can't be sure she's heading south. We can't be sure she isn't switching roads, hiding her trail so she can take the highway to DC. She may be going over to 77 or 81 to Knoxville or westward."

"I know, Caine. But I have to do something. Right now, we're less than two hours behind her. If we *are* on the right trail, maybe an hour. If Xavier's awake, he might be able to signal us, leave a trail, something. I want to stay as close as possible."

"Dana, he's a kid, drugged, probably scared out of his mind. You can't expect him—"

"Shut the hell up, Caine," she snarled, a fierce anger rising in her breast. "I *can* expect him to help himself. He's my boy. He's smart. He knows what this means. He and I knew Donovan might get to him. If he can, if he's awake and able, he'll do something that we can track."

"Dana, he's in pajamas, barefoot . . ."

"No, he slept in his clothes. He has his phone, it's either on him or hooked to his iPod. The iPod's in his bag, and she took that. If he can get to the phone, he can call or text message. Something. Anything. He could send pictures from the camera part of the phone to my phone. He *knows*, Caine," she pounded a fist on the steering wheel in time with her words. "He knows there's only a small chance to get to me, to us, before he's in his father's clutches for good."

"Give me your phone."

"What?"

"Your phone. Let me have it so I can monitor anything incoming."

She fumbled it into his hands, never taking her eyes off the narrowly illumined roadway. The horizon was unmarked by any shape or movement, the stars obscured by clouds. No lights shone in the windows of the few houses they passed. Businesses along the way were dark, deserted.

Miles rolled by, and despair choked her. Tears blurred the white lines dividing the lanes. He had to be alive. They had to find him.

Had to.

"Sweet, Holy Mary, Mother of God," Caine breathed the oath like a prayer.

Chapter Nineteen

Caine couldn't believe his eyes. A text message scrolled across the small screen on Dana's phone.

From Xavier.

Going east. 4 lanes. She sed S Carolina? OK. Tied. On seat w/blanket over. Big car. Blue? Will call on mute. LY, X

"He's okay. We need to get on Highway 58," Caine said, scanning the map. "He says he's heading east on a highway. That's the only thing close to here. Jesus, I can't believe he's doing it."

"Thank God," Dana sobbed, hitting the gas, taking the curves in the road with competent speed. The swirling view in the headlights made Caine's head swim, and he closed his eyes. Whatever chemical Booth had used wasn't out of his system yet. Queasiness roiled his stomach, and his head pounded in time with his pulse.

"Did he say anything else? She didn't hurt him?"

"Nothing else," Caine managed through clenched teeth. "He's in the back. Covered with a blanket. Evidently she said something about South Carolina."

"Donovan had properties there, near Myrtle, another near Charleston."

"Maybe she's headed there." He willed his system to level out, to give him a break. Anything but this sickness. He couldn't afford it. "I have to roll down the window," he managed. "See if the air can clear my head."

Her hand gripped his arm. "Are you okay? Do you need me to pull over?"

"Even if I did, I wouldn't ask it of you. I've got a bag if I need to be sick. My head's pounding like a freaking gong."

"Did you hit it?"

"Don't think so. I think it's the gas."

"Oh, of course. Do you know what it was?"

"No idea. Not my specialty."

She linked her fingers with his, not letting go until she needed both hands on the wheel. It helped. He didn't know why, but hearing the rings click, as they had in Baltimore, helped. The brisk night air whistled in the window and worked to clear his lungs. He wanted to hang his entire head out the window in hopes that the miasma of chemicals would blow away.

"I think Shadow would like to do the same thing," Dana said, managing a smile for him.

"I'll make room."

"There's water in the console here," she patted the container between the seats. "Maybe that will help."

"Yeah, thanks." He'd forgotten the bottles stashed there. He drained one and felt miraculously better within minutes. Uncapping another, he sipped it more slowly, and the headache receded. She rummaged behind the seat as he reached for a third bottle. "What do you need? I'll get it," he said.

"My purse. I have it now," she said, dragging the leather

satchel onto the seat. "In the zippered part, there're three bottles: aspirin, acetaminophen, the generic stuff, some painkillers. Take the aspirin. It's buffered and will help the headache, especially if it's from dehydration."

"I'm better."

"I can tell, you're not gripping the armrest so hard."

"You're an observant woman, love."

"Thanks."

Now that he wasn't feeling quite so wretched, he was able to notice her state. Her hands, clutching the steering wheel, were white-knuckled. Her voice was steady, but her breathing wasn't. She was on the verge, close to losing her composure.

"We'll find him, love. We will. I was wrong to doubt you, and him."

"I know I told you he would, but . . . but . . . I can't believe he actually managed it," she said, a wobble in her voice. "We've talked about what to do. We have these code words and phrases."

"Tell me," he encouraged. Talking would give her a pressure valve, relieving some of the tension.

"If Donovan ever tried to get him at school, he was to call the police first. Then me. If he was in trouble, the code phrase was 'Queen to King's level three.'"

"*Star Trek.*"

Her smile was weak, but it shone in the darkness. "We watched the old ones on *TV Land*. They were hokey, but a lot of fun."

"Yeah. *The Trouble with Tribbles*. What else?"

"If they shoved him in the trunk he was supposed to kick out the taillight, wave as hard as he could to attract attention."

"That's a good one. What else?"

"If someone besides Donovan had him, he was supposed to be polite, not antagonize, but try and leave a trail, try and get to people who would help. Anything."

"You taught him scenarios."

"Everything I thought of, we talked about. Practiced."

"How long have you been at it, that kind of scenario building?"

"Three, four years."

"Since he was six or seven."

"Yeah."

"No wonder. Kid's got guts, like his mom. He said the car was probably blue. I'm guessing the interior is, at least. Unless 'blue' is a code word."

"No, but I did tell him to give as much information as possible. The make and model of the car—he loves cars, so that's never been hard—the license plate, that sort of thing."

"You two are a hell of a team."

When she glanced over at him, tears streaked her cheeks. "I hated to do it. Hated to constantly make him feel unsafe, on alert, cautious. I hated the look in his eyes every time we'd be somewhere and I'd ask him, 'What would you do if your father came right now, here and did such and such?' Or 'That car we passed, what color was it?'"

"Did he hate it?"

The question evidently caught her off-guard, because she hesitated before answering.

"Sometimes," she said, evidently remembering moments when she'd gotten the reaction she'd mentioned. "But on the whole, no, I don't think he did." Surprise rang in her voice. She sounded lighter, more sure when she continued. "Not that much. He saw it as a game, I guess. Like the strategy things he gets into with the video games."

"Which came first, the video games or the strategy sessions?"

"Video games. Much as I hate them, I couldn't always take him out to the park or encourage him to run around outside."

"Understandable."

"My alternative solution was a Game Boy at five and successively more complex games on the computer and television console thingies as he asked for them."

"He's good."

"Really good."

"I'll bet they actually helped when you began teaching him strategy."

"I'd never considered it that way, but yeah, I guess they did."

"What do you—" he started to ask about other things they did together, continuing the distraction, but her phone was buzzing once again. "The phone. It's Xavier."

"What does he say?" she kept trying to see the screen and drive too.

"Focus on driving. I'll read it as it comes in."

"Sorry."

He waited as the text showed up, letter by letter. "She's still on 58. He saw the road number." They had turned onto 58 as well and were heading east, but they were well behind Booth and the boy. He hoped Xavier gave them more information or told them if she took a southerly turn.

"Do we call Tervain?"

"Do we dare?" he countered. "I don't want to miss anything from the boy, and I can't use my cell, its compromised."

"What about Sears?"

"You said she snagged him too. Besides, he's in the hospital."

"Crap. You're right. Who could get a message to Tervain and not alert her? TJ and Chaz? Your contact, the one who told us we were being tracked? Someone else in the agency?"

"My contacts, Tervain's team, are out of commission."

"What about Tervain's secretary?"

"His who?"

"His assistant, the woman who works with him. You know, Sophia? I have her number. It's programmed into my cell."

"You are amazing. Incredible," he praised.

"Desperate. Panicked."

"Hey, we're doing good. Don't jinx it."

"What else does Xavy say?"

"He's going to try to call at some point when he thinks she's distracted. He's going to put it on speakerphone so we can hear her."

"Oh, God."

"How do you mute your phone? We don't want her to be able to hear us, or God forbid, Shadow, so we'll have to be on mute."

"It shows as an option once the call comes in."

"Got it." He turned on the light, scanning the phone's features. "Here. Ah, another text message. He's going to call, may have to cut it off suddenly if she gets suspicious or if he thinks the battery's running down."

The phone trilled a few minutes later, and when Caine answered he immediately muted it, turning the volume as loud as it would go. It was good that he'd been quick because Shadow, heretofore silent, let out a bark that made Dana swerve in the road, she was so startled.

As she shushed him, Booth's voice came through, loud and clear.

"You awake, kid?" the woman asked. They heard a rustling noise and Xavier spoke.

"I'm awake. Who are you? Where're you takin' me?"

"My name's Booth. Don't you recognize me?"

"You're FBI. You were at the house. Why did you take me?"

"I'm taking you to your father. Shut up and listen," she said, silencing Xavier's protest. "Your dad's anxious to meet you. See you. I left your mom and Agent Bradley tied up. I owe Bradley. If you screw up and tell your dad they're alive, don't count on 'em staying that way, you get me?"

"You didn't hurt them, did you? My mom, is she—"

"I said I didn't hurt them. But they'll get dead real fast if you blab to Walker, got it?"

"Got it."

"I can't believe she's doing this," Caine commented softly. "She's going out of her way not to hurt anyone, but she's taking the kid to Walker."

"She's in love with him," Dana put in, as they listened to Booth bad-temperedly reassure Xavy that Caine and the dog were okay too. "I feel sorry for her, but if she stands between me and Xavy, I'm going through her."

"Same goes."

"Good to know." Daylight had come upon them as they drove, and he heard Dana cursing under her breath. "What?"

"Gas, we need gas."

"We're lucky she didn't slash the tires and shoot the gas tank. We can't run empty." He scanned the road. According to the map, they were running parallel to the

North Carolina line. Danville, Virginia was behind them, but they had yet to hit South Boston.

"We want an easy-off, easy-on exit. There," he pointed, seeing a road sign indicating multiple fuel stations. "You start the fueling, I'll keep listening. When we're done, I'll drive."

"Are you well enough?"

"Yeah, my head's clear."

Whipping into a Gas-n-Go, Dana took the credit card Caine held out. She set the tank to fill and bolted for the bathroom. She'd had to go for the last hour.

When she hurried over, he motioned her inside and did the same. The sounds from the phone were innocuous enough. Booth had the radio on, and Xavier was humming along with the song.

"Durham," came a whisper from Xavier. "Just passed a sign for Durham."

"What'd you say, kid?"

"I was talking to myself, lady," he sounded sulky, petulant, as if she'd interrupted something important. "That sign said Durham. That's where Duke is. Nobody can touch them when it comes to basketball. They rock. We going to Durham?

"No."

"Where're we going then?"

"None of your business."

Xavier was silent, as was Booth. Dana kept checking the phone to be sure they were still connected. She said a quick prayer that there was good cell coverage on whatever this road was.

"Can I put on my headphones? Listen to my music?" Xavier finally spoke again, disrupting the quiet that had stretched Dana's nerves to the breaking point.

"You're taking this pretty calm, kid," Booth said, sounding suspicious. Xavier must have heard that as well.

"I'm scared shitless," he said, and he made it sound as if he meant it. Dana bit her lip, her heart aching for him. Then, in a little boy voice, a bit cocky and smug, he added, "But I'm, you know, like . . . curious."

"What do you mean?"

"Uh, well, like, I, uh, don't remember my dad. My mom won't talk about him," the boy blurted the words, as if he were ashamed to say them. "For a long time, everybody told me he was dead. Now I get to meet him. I don't like it, I'm scared, but you aren't giving me much choice here, are you?"

God, he sounded so strong. So adult.

"No, I'm not."

Evidently, Xavier had struck the perfect balance between combined fear and interest, because Booth told him to put on his headphones. They heard more rustling, then the phone cut off.

"What happened?" Dana was frantic. "I need to call him, don't I? Where . . ."

"What is it?" Caine looked away from the road when she broke off, trying to see.

"Text message, bless him," she said, reading.

"Turn off 2 sv batt. LY, X"

"How long to South Boston?" Caine asked. The dashboard GPS showed them where they were, but she didn't know how to work it well enough to get an answer to that kind of question. It was easier to check the map.

"Thirty or forty miles."

"We're close. Better than I hoped. Your heading south paid off," he praised.

"Thanks." She let her head fall onto the headrest. Driving down the road, with no Xavier sitting behind her, knowing her son was in danger, was killing her. Shadow poked his nose over the seat and whined. She smoothed the fur on his long muzzle. "I know, boy. We're going to find him. Promise."

"We need more information soon. She could turn off at any of these feeder roads. Thing is, if she's heading for South Carolina, especially the coast, she'll want 95. If she does that, and we can catch her, that's good. But if she gets onto those side roads, we're screwed. Xavier'll have a lot harder time giving us clues without arousing her attention."

"Please, God," she breathed the prayer. "Let us catch up."

"We'll get to him, Dana, before Donovan does. We have to believe that." He reached out, tangled his fingers with hers.

"Thank you." Hearing him say it bolstered her courage. "What about Tervain's assistant, do we call her?"

"Yeah. You'll get a beep, if Xavy calls?"

"Yeah."

"Go for it. Once you get her, give her to me."

"With pleasure."

The phone rang a number of times before a light, feminine voice answered. "Mr. Tervain's office, Sophia speaking."

"Sophia, its Dana Markham."

"Oh, my God. Mrs. Markham, are you okay? Never-mind, hang on," Dana heard her shouting for Tervain. "He's coming. I'm praying for you, ma'am."

"Dana?" Tervain was breathless when he came on the line. "Are you there? Where are you? Are you all right?"

"I'm here. We're in southern Virginia, heading for South Boston. Xavier's been able to text us, give us a heading."

"Is Caine with you?"

"Right here. I'll let him tell you," she said, handing the phone to Caine.

"No," Caine said, after listening for a moment. "I won't. So deal. Yeah. Right. We think she's heading for South Carolina, maybe the coast. Dana says Walker had holdings in Myrtle and Charleston. Were those shut down? Confiscated? Sold? Well, find out," he snapped, then paused, glanced over at her. She put all her questions in one look and he shook his head. "Yeah. Her phone. Yours and Sears are black, that's how Booth tracked us. Yeah, split-scramble and forward. Never suspected because she was ours and presumed."

The men continued their short-hand, terse conversation for a few more minutes. When Caine clicked off, he handed the phone to Dana.

"So?"

"He's pissed, cranky, wants us to pull out of the chase and let them take it."

"Like hell," she said. She'd give no quarter to anyone on this, not with Xavier's safety on the line.

"Ditto. He'll call. They'd figured one of their cells was black—compromised."

"Took 'em long enough."

"Yeah. They're mustering, but without a fixed locale, their hands are tied. Jurisdictional crap. Tervain's heading for Raleigh-Durham and hopes to intercept."

"That's something, I guess."

"Dana?"

"Hmmm?"

"I want you to know that I'll do whatever it takes. You

know that, right?" He took his eyes off the road long enough to meet hers. "This isn't some bullshit thing. Between us. I think . . . I know I . . . love you, and Xavy, too." The words spilled out, fast, nearly desperate. "You need to know, in case."

Clenching her eyes shut to staunch the tears, she pulled their joined hands to her cheek. "Oh, God. I know you will. We've got to be in time, Caine. We have to be."

"I hope he calls soon," Caine whispered, almost as if to himself. "It helps to be connected."

It amazed her to hear her own thoughts spoken out loud.

Shadow paced restlessly as they drove, whining a bit. He would sit, then pace. It was driving her crazy, but she didn't have the heart to tell him not to do it.

The phone vibrated in her hand, and she jumped.

Her heart sank when it wasn't Xavier.

"Hello? Yes, Tervain, he's right here."

"Yeah?" The two men talked, longer this time. Caine was silent, absorbing whatever Tervain was relaying.

"Yeah, we're going through South Boston. Make sure the highway patrol knows not to stop us. It's daylight now, and we're going to be breaking a lot of speed laws."

Dana noted the conglomeration of fast food shops, gas stations, and businesses that surrounded the interchange. Traffic was heavy. Morning commuters, she presumed. But it was moving. Thank God.

"There, the sign for Durham he mentioned," she exclaimed, pointing to a road marker ramping south for 501 to Durham, North Carolina.

"Yeah," Caine said, relaying the information. "501 toward Durham. We think that's what Xavier saw."

Caine continued to talk with Tervain as he drove, navigating lane changes and easing around trucks with veteran driving skills. Part of her wanted to be driving, to be in control of the wheel. Then, at least, she'd have something to concentrate on besides how useless, how helpless she felt, trailing along behind her son's kidnapper.

Knowing Booth was heading for Donovan, Dana wanted to howl. Everything she'd prayed for, everything she'd been prepared to risk in this venture, was to keep Xavier out of the line of fire. Now, thanks to Booth, he was the bull's eye.

Caine suddenly tensed beside her, and her heart clenched.

"Gotta go, Tervain. Incoming call." He handed the phone to Dana. "You get it."

Her heart leapt up but tumbled just as quickly.

"False alarm," she said, cursing. "It's the school, calling about Xavier, I guess. Didn't Tervain call them?"

Adjusting her attitude, she answered. It took a few minutes to get the woman off the phone. She'd been calling about homework and PTA.

"What the fuck do I care?" Dana exploded, after hanging up. "I'm driving like a bat out of hell down a busy highway chasing a woman who has my son, and she wants to talk to me about PTA? Jesus, I'm going to scream. I'm preserving some useless fiction. And for what?" she turned on Caine. "Why? All this running and name-changing, what the hell has it gotten me? I'm still running, except this time I don't have my boy."

"Dana," he said, his voice firm. "You can't think about it that way. We have to take it one step at a time."

"You think I don't know that?" she raged. "I fucking *know* that."

"How much do you owe for saying fucking two times in a row without taking a breath?"

"Oh for Christ's sake," she said, half-laughing, half-crying. "I don't know." Burying her head in her hands, she struggled for composure. She couldn't lose it. Couldn't. Why the hell had she even answered the phone call? Caine's hand on her back was warm, possessive, comforting. Present.

With a deep breath, she mustered her scattered wits. "Fifty cents, I think."

"What?"

"For cursing, I owe fifty cents."

"You gonna pay up, or welch because Xavier didn't hear it?"

"Pay up. It goes into his college fund."

"Are you going to be okay, for now?" he asked softly, continuing to trace a reassuring pattern of warmth on her shirt.

"Yeah, but no guarantees on the time span between breakdowns," she warned, knowing he would understand.

Thankfully, he laughed. "You're entitled. I feel the same. He's an amazing kid, Dana, I hope you know that. I hate like hell that I let this happen."

Surprised at the admission, Dana whipped around to face him. "Caine, there's nothing you could have done. She'd have gotten us one way or the other. At the mountain house or at the hotel."

He remained silent, and Dana saw his jaw working, like he were chewing over difficult thoughts before he could speak them.

"When the doctor called me his dad, told me not to worry, I thought, 'yeah, buddy, tell that to me when your

kid's getting stitches,'" he admitted. "Scared the hell out
of me."

"I know." Whatever else Caine might have revealed was
forestalled by the vibration and trill of Dana's phone. She
checked the number.

"Xavy."

Chapter Twenty

Dana was as tense as piano wire. She was hunched forward in the seat, as if to make the car go faster and close the distance between her and her son.

Xavier had called twice more, once as he and Booth turned onto I-95, another as they crossed the South Carolina line. Tervain was in the Raleigh office gathering reinforcements. Until they knew a destination or a make and model on Booth's car, however, Tervain waited in limbo.

But, they were gaining. They'd passed a sign indicating they were one mile from the South Carolina line. Xavier and his kidnapper couldn't be far ahead.

Dana jolted as Xavier's voice came through the cell phone's speaker.

"Why're we getting off here? Oh, hey, food. I'm starving, and I gotta go to the bathroom."

"We're not getting out here," they heard Booth say. "No funny business, boy. I will shoot you. Donovan will be mad at me, but he'll be so glad to have you, he'll forgive me."

"I don't think he'll be happy if you hurt me," Xavy put an extra whine in his voice.

Dana grinned. *That's it,* she silently applauded, *go*

ahead, get on her last good nerve. Make her crazy as only a ten-year-old boy can.

"I'll bet he'll be pissed," Xavy continued. "Especially if you shoot me. I mean, you could really hurt me. What if I try to get away? You gonna whip out your gun in front of all these tourists? South of the Border's full of tourists, looks like," he made his voice more and more petulant, all the while giving them valuable information.

"South of the Border," Caine muttered. "Jesus, that place is huge."

"I've *really* got to pee," the boy reiterated, sounding four instead of ten.

"You'll pee when I tell you to," Booth sounded aggravated. "I'll pull off over there. You can go in the bushes. I'm not taking any chances with you, young Donovan."

"Oh, that'll tick him off," Dana murmured, cheering her boy in her heart, even as she clenched her hands in fear for him. "He hates that name."

"Where you going? You said you were going to let me pee."

"Lunch first. You hold it, you hear me?"

"I'm gonna pee on the seat if you don't hurry."

"I'll beat you black and blue if you do, you little twit."

Caine laughed softly. "Gotcha," he said. "Pushed her patience. Good boy."

Through the connection, they heard, "Welcome to South of the Border, Pedro's Place. How can I help you today?"

Booth ordered meals and drinks and had a brief conversation with the clerk as money changed hands. They heard the rattle of paper bags and Xavier's voice as he started in on Booth again.

"Now can I pee? Why'd you get burritos? I hate burritos,

they make me hurl. Oh, a cheeseburger. This doesn't have peppers in it, does it? I hate those."

"You'll eat the fucking cheeseburger, you little shitpot, or go hungry, dammit."

"Don't curse at me, my dad wouldn't like it."

"You don't know shit about your dad, so shut the fuck up."

"I do too. He loves me, he wants me. He's gonna teach me all about the business. That's what my mom said he wanted. A hair," Xavier protested.

"A what? Hair? Oh, an heir. Yeah, right. And loves you? You think?" She laughed at the boy, a grating, unpleasant sound. "You keep dreaming, little boy. I hope he whips your ass and locks you in a box."

"He won't," Xavy's reply was confident. "He wouldn't have worked so hard to get me if he was gonna lock me up."

"For God's sake, shut up. I gotta make a call." A different voice floated through the connection, still Booth, but a softer, more feminine version, totally unlike the tough, firm kidnapper. "Hey, honey. Yeah, I got the package. Aren't you proud of me? Where do you want me to . . ." she stopped.

Dana listened with bated breath. At the wheel, Caine drove like the Winston Cup leader at Talladega.

Finally, "Oh, you're . . . Oh, I'm one exit away. I wouldn't have gotten lunch if . . . well, of course he's fine." Her voice gained a sharper snap. "Yes. Yes. He's eager to see you, honey. Really. I got him a cheeseburger. It's what he wanted," she replied, then sighed. "I know. Yeah, you too. I'll wait for you there."

When she hung up Xavy started in on her again.

"Hey, stop. I really do gotta pee, lady," he said urgently. "You can't get on the road until I pee. Seriously. I gotta go so bad it's choking me." He made gagging sounds, and Booth cursed.

"We'll be there in five minutes. Wait."

"I can't. I'll pee myself. Honestly." He really sounded sincere, even to Dana. "C'mon, Agent. I don't wanna meet my dad, like, with pee all over me. Really. Please."

Somehow, the "please," clicked something with Booth that the whining had not. Tires squealed and Xavy gasped.

"Hey, warn a guy before you go tearing off the road that way. I spilled my drink."

"God dammit," Booth snarled. "Quit whining. Jesus, now I know why I hate kids. I'm coming to let you out. You pee on that bush. Then get in the damn car, you understand me?"

"Yeah, yeah. I get it. Thanks."

The door slammed and Xavy spoke quickly, his voice slightly muffled. "The phone's in my pocket. She's letting me out. I'm going to run for it. I see a radio tower. It's in some woods. I think I can make it there. Sign says Ranger Station or Forest Service or something, it's brown and green. I hope you're close 'cause she'll beat the hell out of me if she catches me. I made her really mad. Love you, Mom." The sound of a car door opening cut the flow of chatter.

Dana prayed with inarticulate fervor. *Please, God, please, watch over my boy.* A silly billboard with dancing sheep showed a grinning Pedro with shepherd's crook in hand. They were nearly at the exit.

Xavy's voice rang in the tense silence. "Okay, okay, don't push. Jeez, lady, give a guy some room."

"I'll step back," Booth said. "So I can get a better shot if you try anything stupid."

A zipper rasped and the distinct sound of water hitting the ground rang through the line.

"He's taking a leak," Caine said, amazed. "The cheeky devil."

"Shhhh," Dana was willing him to say something, anything.

And he did.

"I'm going for it. Hurry, Mom."

The roar of a semi-truck's horn blasted through the phone. Dana nearly dropped the phone, bobbling it twice before catching it securely. When they heard Xavy again, he was running.

"I did it, I got away. The horn distracted her. She's running after me, but she's slow. I'm zig-zagging like you told me, Mom."

Clicking the mute off, Dana called, "We're coming, honey, hang on."

"Big house, couple of barns. There's no cars. I'm going for the barn. Hurry."

The car swerved madly, spitting gravel, as Caine took the exit.

"Go, Xavy," Dana breathed. "Run."

"In the barn," the boy panted. "Trying to . . . Uh-oh. She's coming, in the car. There's another barn, way out. I'm runnin' for that. She can't shoot while she's driving."

"Where the hell is it?" Caine said frantically, looking for the ranger station.

"He said a radio tower," Dana cried, swiveling to search for it.

"There," Caine pointed. Spinning into a one-hundred-eighty degree turn, Caine headed for it, the tires squealing with the effort. Crouched low on the floorboard, Shadow whined in earnest, catching their fear and excitement.

Caine flipped open his cell, punched numbers, and slung the phone to the seat.

"Tervain, we're at the ranger station behind South of the Border. Look for the radio tower. Xavier got loose. There's a road behind it, a field, and a barn. Walker's close. He told Booth one exit. I can't let Booth get the boy."

The tires kicked out dirt and sod as Caine whipped into the grassy lane. Ahead of them, they saw Booth's car. The driver's side door was open, the car empty.

Tervain's voice came, tinny-small from the cell phone speaker, as he shouted. "Fuck Walker, protect that child."

"Read my mind," Caine shouted, as he threw the car in park and leapt from the truck, gun drawn.

Dana was out as well, weapon in hand. Releasing Shadow, she commanded, "Find Xavier. Protect. Full force."

Silent as his name, Shadow flew over the ground and into the barn. Booth's scream sounded and was cut short.

Then gunshots.

Dana's heart clenched. They pounded into the barn in time to see Shadow wiggle out the back wall through a hole low in the wood.

"Cover," Caine yelled as Booth swung out of hiding and fired.

"Give up, Booth," Caine yelled, peering around the frame of a stall. "I won't hurt you."

"I will," Dana growled, desperate to go after Xavier and Shadow. "C'mon, Booth."

The answer was another round, zinging out to burying itself in a beam with a solid whunk, right next to Caine's face. Then a door slammed, and a helicopter roared overhead.

"It's Donovan, he's out there," Dana cried, whipping

out to fire into the back of the barn, desperate to get past Booth.

There was no answering shot.

"She's out the back," Caine said, running for the rear of the building. A door banged in the light breeze, and they hit the wall next to it, one on either side, alternating looks to get a view of the territory.

A path led through scrubby pines; beyond them lay a field, its stubble greening in the warm South Carolina sunshine. An outbuilding lay a hundred yards into the field.

Booth was halfway to it, at a dead run.

Dana and Caine bolted through the door as a black Humvee appeared in the distance, tearing down a dirt road toward them. Was it Donovan or Tervain?

Dana ran, the phone to her ear, trying desperately to hear if Xavier was still on the line. "Xavy, are you there?"

"Mom? Mom?"

"I'm here. We're coming."

"Shadow's here. I locked the doors but Booth's trying to get in."

"We're coming," she repeated. "Stay down, keep Shadow with you."

She ran, saving her breath, eyes on Booth for the betraying body language that meant she was going to turn and shoot. She and Caine saw the warning at the same time.

"Hit the dirt," he yelled.

"Watch out," Dana called, diving for the ground.

As if they'd trained together, they flattened, then rose, one after the other, to return fire.

A puff of dust on the wall of the ramshackle building signaled a hit. It was within a foot of Booth's head.

"Yours or mine?" he called, heading out in a crouching zigzag for the barn.

"Yours, I was aiming lower."

As they closed in, Booth fired into the lock and the door swung open.

"Bloody hell, she's gotten in."

Running full out, they neared the barn. The Humvee, closer now, turned down the gravel road leading to the building. She heard the helicopter, but couldn't see it.

"Where the hell is Tervain?" Caine panted.

Dana was too busy sucking in air as she ran for the barn and her boy.

The Humvee screeched to a stop, and four men piled out, firing as they did. Dana and Caine threw themselves into the doorway just as Shadow broke cover to attack Booth.

The turncoat stumbled toward them and Dana flung herself to the side. Shadow body-slammed Booth, and his full-force attack sent the woman flying through the open door. The thrashing woman squealed as his teeth sliced into her gun arm. The shooting stopped for a moment, and the horrible growls and screams were the only sound.

"Xavy, stay where you are," Dana yelled, her heart rejoicing when she heard his answering shout. "Get behind something solid."

Booth screamed more sharply, and Dana shouted a release command. As the dog let loose, Booth kicked him away. He landed hard on the flap of the second door, swinging it wide. As it gave, Caine stumbled forward into the dirt in full view of the gunmen.

"It's him," one of them shouted. "Pollack."

"The traitor," another man yelled, firing at Caine.

"Kill him! Kill them all, but don't hit my son."

Dana froze. That was Donovan's voice. "You hit my boy, you assholes, I'll send you to hell."

Caine rolled and fired, yelling, "Dana, get back."

Booth, struggling to her feet, ran for the dubious protection of the Humvee.

Dark glasses glinting in the sun, Donovan left the protection of the Hummer's door and aimed at the running woman. "That's for failing me, bitch," he roared, firing.

In cold blood, Donovan shot his would-be paramour. Booth dropped, her left hand crumpling beneath her, her gun hand trailing the ground in front of her.

"And you, bitch of a wife," Walker shouted at Dana, firing shot after shot at the barn. "I'm gonna dance on your grave.

"Donny," he yelled. "Donny, I'll protect you. I'll take care of you, son." Walker shot at Dana with renewed fervor. Dana felt a rasp of pain as a bullet scored a path across her leg.

The other men resumed their wild barrage, but the shots were well shy of the barn, displacing more dirt and gravel than anything else. Shadow sprang forward, skimming along the ground. He moved so quickly that none of the men in the vehicle hit him. At the bumper he paused, gathering himself, then flew forward, locking his powerful jaws onto Donovan's arm, his ninety-five pound weight dragging the man nearly to the ground.

Walker shrieked like an old woman. Two of his men rushed to pull the dog from their leader's arm.

"Shoot the fucking dog," he yelled. Blood poured from Donovan's arm as his henchman took aim. Before his aide could fire, the man went down, screaming and clutching his leg.

Shaking off her paralysis, Dana fired as well, and the other henchman slumped to the ground. Donovan dragged himself toward the Humvee struggling with

Shadow for every inch of ground. He beat at the dog with the butt of his gun. The beastly growls and snarls rang in Dana's ears as she searched for an opening.

With a whup-whup-whup roar, the helicopter skimmed over the trees by the ranger station, and bore down on them. With superhuman effort, Donovan raised his gun arm, the dog swinging from it, blood gushing over Shadow's face and ears, and fired at the chopper. There was a whirring ping, as the bullet hit a rotor and was flung away.

Another shot rang out, and Donovan staggered. The beleaguered mobster swung round to fire at Caine, where the agent crouched in the doorway, gun perfectly balanced.

Dana screamed Caine's name, diving out of the barn to fire at the hated man before her. One remaining henchman staggered to his feet, gun pointed their way. She fired and he collapsed.

Donovan fell to his knees. Shadow still clung to his arm, and the force of the dog's pull wrenched Donovan onto his face, but not before Dana saw a small, round, bullet hole, right between his eyes.

Booth, who had crawled three more feet toward the Humvee, fell prone once more.

"Freeze! FBI, Sheriff, and US Marshals," a voice boomed from the copter's external speaker. Five shots rang out from behind the Humvee, a gunman Dana had yet to see. Answering fire from the helicopter sent a tall, gangly man stumbling into the field to sink to his knees. His arm fell, as did his body, and he lay still.

Dana squinted through the dust of the helicopter's landing.

"Dana, are you okay?" Caine crawled to where she knelt in the gravel still scanning for something, anything moving.

"I'm okay. You?"

"Grazed. My leg wound's open too. We need to get to Xavier."

"I'm here," a small voice said from behind her. Dana rolled to her feet, pushing him into the barn, sure someone would shoot him. She did it as well, to shield him from the sight of what lay outside.

"Where's Shadow? Can I call him?"

"Yes, but warn Caine."

"Mr. Caine," he called, "I'm going to call Shadow, okay?"

"Wait." They heard him yell out to the authorities who and what he was, relaying the information that the dog would be running through the scene.

"Call him, Xavy," Caine yelled.

"Shadow, return," he shouted, using the German commands.

The happy bark was a pealing ring of joy, and within seconds, the massive dog leaped onto Xavier. Shadow left a trail of blood in his wake as he bathed Xavier in enthusiastic affection. Hands buried in the dog's fur, Xavier raised one to caress him and gasped.

"Mom, there's blood all over him," the boy cried, frantic tears streaming from his eyes, as he urged the dog to be still. "Help me, Mom, help me. He can't be hurt, he can't die. Not Shadow. Maaaaaaamaa!" the boy wailed, the dog's huge head cradled in his arms.

"Let me see," she said, commanding the dog to lie down. She was terribly afraid the dog was mortally wounded, he'd been in the line of fire too long.

Shadow whined as she touched his flank. From his head and haunch, her hands came away wet and red.

"He's hurt, honey. I can't see how badly."

"Oh, Mom," she heard the tears in her son's voice. "I should have kept him with me."

"He saved our lives, honey," she said, checking further for injuries. "You did the right thing. It's what he's trained for—it's his job."

"But, there's so much blood," the boy wailed, staring in horror at his own red-coated hands. "He can't die. No, no, no." He frantically shook his head as Dana held him.

The light dimmed as someone blocked the door. It was Caine. Blood streaked his hands and face, and Xavier gasped, then leapt up, ran to him.

"Mr. Caine, Mr. Caine, are you okay? You're bloody, too. Are you hurt? Please say you're okay, Mr. Caine."

"Shhh, it's all right, Xavy," Caine soothed, going to one knee to hold the shaking boy. "I'm okay. We're going to get Shadow into the helicopter, take him to a vet, okay?"

"Okay, okay," Xavier was shaking, frantically moving between the two adults and Shadow, alternately hugging Caine, hugging Dana, and petting the dog. Outside, the sound of voices rose, the wail of sirens grew closer as more police, Sheriff, emergency vehicles, and federal agents arrived.

Xavier finally sat with the dog. Caine knelt in front of the boy, drawing his attention. "Xavy, I need you to do something for me, okay?"

Her son focused on Caine, nodded.

"What's outside is . . . pretty ugly. Some of the people are . . . dead."

"My . . . Walker?" the boy asked, his voice shaking.

"He didn't make it."

She saw Xavier's lip quiver, and her heart broke. His

next words allayed her pain. "I'm not glad, exactly," he
spoke in an unsteady, tear-filled voice. "But . . . but . . . since
he . . . if he . . . it means we won't have to run anymore," he
finally blurted. "We can go home. Right?" He turned to
her for confirmation. His tears made a dreadful effect on
a face streaked with blood and dirt, but she was so proud
of him.

"That's right, honey," Dana hugged him tightly. She
never wanted to let him go. She wanted to hang onto the
solid warmth, smell the unmistakable boy-child smell of
him, know he was alive.

Oh, God.

"Right," Caine confirmed. "I'll carry you out. Put your
head on my shoulder. I'll put a blanket over you, to
block your view. Okay?"

Dana knew he would do it whether Xavy agreed or
not, but the boy nodded and flung himself into Caine's
arms, eyes squeezed shut.

Struggling to stand with his own wounds and the
boy's weight, Caine staggered, then steadied. An offi-
cer appeared, a brawny Sheriff's deputy, who said he
would manage the dog. They walked out together, and
her stomach clenched at the awful tableau. Five dead
men sprawled out around the Humvee, including
Donovan.

Her ex-husband lay, mangled arm outstretched, gun
pointing her way. She shuddered at the view of his still-
handsome face and his fixed, sightless gaze. His features
were set in a rictus of hate, his true nature frozen in
place by death's hand. The bullet hole in his forehead
was no more than a black dot at this distance. It looked
as if you could take a cloth and wipe it away . . .

"Dana," Caine called from the helicopter.

She walked to him, took his hand, and climbed into the helicopter. As it rose into the air, leaving the past behind, Dana cuddled her boy in her arms and thanked God for second chances.

And freedom.

She didn't look back.

Epilogue

"You do understand that the censure has to go in before the commendation, Agent Bradley?" Agent Parlier said, a twinkle in his usually somber gaze.

"Of course," Caine replied, inwardly amused by the bureaucratic process. "Will it clear by the time my leave is over?"

"Of course. Can't have the Agency's newest senior instructor starting work under a cloud, can I?"

Caine laughed, and the two men shook hands. Parlier was pulling his wheelchair in to the table as Caine left. He never dreamed he'd actually look forward to teaching, to doing something other than serving his country in covert work. Once an agent chose that route, if they lived at all, they seldom returned to anything resembling normal life. It was a consequence Caine had lived with—even courted—for the last five years.

Not any more. Something about loving Dana and finding a way to avenge Carly, his partner who had died in Tijuana, had lifted that burden from his heart.

Driving south, Caine wondered if Parlier would ever walk again. He pondered that, and all the events of the

previous few weeks, until he turned into the long driveway at Dana's house.

The gate stood open, a welcome drawing him in. He'd
believed the promise of love was lost to him. Was it really
possible that all his deepest desires—a partner and lover
who accepted him, the freedom to have a family of his
own—were about to be fulfilled? If Dana agreed . . .

Fifty feet from the house, on the paved parking pad by
the garage, sat a huge RV, its streaming black and gold
metallic stripes glinting in the sun. An awning sheltered a
set of chairs, a table, and a large, round, fleece dog bed.

He heard the barking before he got out of the car and
grinned. Shadow, restrained by Dana, was greeting him.
Fixated on her, Caine felt his body stir, his blood race.
Hearing her voice on the phone as he worked out his
future, even discussing it with her and coming to love her
even more, wasn't the same as seeing her.

"Hey! Hey," Xavier shouted, running to the car. He
was practically vibrating with excitement as he waited for
Caine to get out. "You came, you really came."

"Of course I did, I don't go back on my promises."

"You gotta see," Xavy grabbed Caine's hand, dragged
him toward the camper, chattering all the way. "We got
this cool motor home to hang out in, while the house
gets fixed. You gotta see the shower. And the game stations," he enthused.

"That's awesome, we'll have a match. Hang on a sec,
though. Before we go over, I want to ask you something,"
Caine pulled the boy to one side and crouched down
until he and Xavier were eye to eye.

Standing at the RV, shading her eyes to block the glare,
Dana watched Caine drive in. Her heart started to pound

as he got out of the car. Everything within her leapt up, and she drank in every detail, from the flashing smile to his broad chest and long legs.

She smiled at the sight of her son, bouncing alongside as Caine walked her way.

Shadow stopped barking on her order. He also desisted in his efforts to go greet their visitor. His shaved leg was beginning to re-fuzz with dark fur, and the last of the stitches would come out within the week. Blessedly, the bullet hadn't done much damage where it had creased the dog's flank. Aside from a slice from Donovan's gun butt and a concussion, the dog had escaped with little other harm. The majority of the blood soaking him had been Donovan's.

The biggest surprise in the aftermath was that the bullet that killed Donovan, the head shot, had come from Booth's gun. She had redeemed herself with that final act.

Dana was about to run to meet Caine when he knelt down by Xavier. "What on earth are those two up to?" she wondered out loud.

The sound of hammering rang from the house as the contractors repaired the fire, water, and bullet damage. A landscaping crew bustled around the foundation, clearing out trampled trees and bushes. It had taken her two days to disable and dispose of the rest of her booby traps before she let them come in.

Xavier was nodding and grinning as he and Caine continued toward her. It lifted her heart. She wanted to fling herself at Caine, but seeing him again had her tied in knots.

"Hey," Caine said, coming over to her. His eyes were hot, full of promises, but instead of taking her in his arms, he bent and brushed a brotherly kiss over her cheek in greeting. Was his hand, resting on her back, shaking? Or was she? Her knees felt weak as her insecurities reared ugly questions within her.

Doubt flooded through her. Had he changed his mind? Was he too addicted to the adrenaline rush of his double life?

"Hey, Xav," Caine turned to the boy. His voice sounded strange, tight and strained. "Why don't you take Shadow for a slow walk, let him stretch that leg."

"Okay," Xavier said with an exaggerated expression of innocence. "That's a great idea, Mr. Caine."

Confused by the interplay, Dana searched both their faces, trying to ferret out what she was dealing with. The boy snapped on Shadow's leash and released him from the wire exercise pen.

"We'll be over there," he said, pointing across the yard at a stand of fading dogwoods and flowering cherries.

"Okay," Dana said, watching them go with a sense of foreboding.

"He's helping me out."

"Oh, really?" she said, whipping her gaze to Caine's face. "Why would he need to do that?"

"Because I'm going to ask his mom a really important question."

"*What*? Why? What question?"

"Why don't we sit down," Caine went on, ignoring her distress as he pulled a chair out from the table. He nearly tipped it over in his haste to urge her into it. "I, uh, want to set the stage here."

Nervous, she sat, hands in her lap.

"So?" she said, when it seemed as if he wasn't going to say anything. What was this?

"I'm working on it," he muttered. Clearing his throat, he started to speak. "Dana, I . . ."

"Yes?"

"Jeez, this is hard."

Her heart fell, was he about to say that this was the last time they would see him? They'd talked over the phone virtually every night during the last three weeks, long, endlessly fascinating conversations. Intimate explorations of their feelings, their dreams.

They'd talked about a future. It had been tentative, provisional, hemmed in with all sorts of "if we like it" and "if it works out", but . . . Was he going to thank her now and leave? But no, he'd said something about asking her . . . was he going to . . .

"What I want to say is I really care about you, and Xavy . . . I lo—"

"Are you saying goodbye? Leaving?" She blurted the questions.

"What? No," he said, looking annoyed. "Let me talk, woman. I'm trying to be gallant here."

"Skip gallant," she cut in. "You're killing me."

"Oh, for heaven's sake," he said, sounding like a testy grandmother. "I want you to be engaged to me. Go steady. Something. Time together. Think about making it permanent. The relationship thing. Dammit, I screwed it up." Visibly disgusted with himself, he ran a hand through his hair in agitation. "I wanted that to come out better."

"I think it's a grand idea," Dana said, beaming at him, joy flooding through her. "The relationship thing. Being engaged." Thank God. He wanted her, he wanted them. "But we'll have to ask Xavier."

"I already did. He's all for it."

"Oh. Well." Tears sprang to her eyes. Their earlier powwow made sense. That he had thought to go to Xavier first, man to man, was just one more reason to love him.

"What about you?" he said, looking at her so intently she wanted to explode.

"I think it's a wonderful, wonderful idea." Unable to contain herself any longer, she grabbed him and kissed him, nearly toppling them both to the ground.

"Will you wear this, then?" he said, a smile blooming on his face, turning her knees to jelly. He plopped a leather jeweler's box into her hand. "See if it fits."

She opened the box and gasped. The square, princess cut diamond glittered in the sunlight, the emeralds flanking it glowed as if lit from within.

"Oh, my God," she breathed.

"I have a new job," he blurted. "Teaching. I'll have to travel some."

"You didn't quit then?"

"No, but I still want us to live here," he paused, "that is, if you still want—"

"The RV's huge," she said, still focused on the diamond. "This is gorgeous, Caine."

"It suits you," he said, relief in his voice. "Did you hear what I said, about the job?"

"Yes," she looked at him as she slipped the ring on her finger. "The guy I'm engaged to has a job as an instructor for the FBI, and he may have to travel some. His fiancée and her son will have to travel too, and we're hoping you'll come with us, when you can."

"Why? I mean, why do you have to travel?"

"You know all the stuff that came out, after . . . after Donovan . . . when they raided his house, office, and warehouse?"

"You mean that virtually all his holdings were held within corporations in either your name or Xavier's?"

"And everything went to Xavier on Donovan's death.

Whatever else he did, he was thorough with his will."
When the document had been presented by the team of
lawyers, the shit had really hit the fan. Washington was
still untangling the legalities.

"So, you know how much Xavy owns now. Even if half
of it goes to the government, the estate is still humongous, the amounts are mind boggling. Lord, the property
alone is worth millions . . ." she trailed off, shaking her
head in bafflement.

"Anyway, we don't know anything about these houses
and businesses. And there are about thirty cars garaged in
Miami. Xavy wants to see everything before we sell it. He
says he wants to keep one car for when he can drive. He
wanted to give one to you, and one to his Uncle Jimmy.
Said he wanted to give one of the houses to Jimmy, too."

Caine reached for her, pulling her into his embrace.
"Have I told you what a great kid you've raised, Dana
Markham?"

"Never hurts to hear it again," she said, raising her
face to his.

Kissing her and wrapping his arms around her, Caine
closed his eyes and let the reality of her love, the surety of
her welcome bathe him in relief. Throughout the drive
from DC he'd worried that she'd changed her mind.

He'd never believed he could have this. Never thought
he could atone for the darkness he'd lived in the name of
justice. Dana accepted him, a trusted partner in every
sense of the word.

And then there was Xavier. A son.

Although Donovan's motives had been twisted, Caine
understood the powerful bond that drove the dead mobster to risk everything for Xavier.

"Did'ja ask her yet?" Xavy bounded over, swiveling from Dana to Caine. "'Cause Shadow and I are hungry."

Caine laughed, and hooked an arm around the boy, pulling him into a three-way hug. Shadow barked happily and sat as close to them as he could.

"So did he ask ya', Mom? Did he? What did you say?"

With Dana tucked near his heart, and her boy hugged close, he was about to answer when Dana beat him to it.

"He asked me, Xavier," she beamed at the grinning boy. "I said yes, we'll be engaged and we'll see about becoming a real family. That suit you?"

"Suits me. Now you can, like, bill and coo for real. You know?" came the surprising reply. Then, a more typical, "Can we eat now?"

"You bet."

"We'll hunt up some grub, big guy. There's one thing I have to do first."

"What?"

"This," he said, pulling Dana into his chest, kissing her, long and hard. He put everything he was, all his love, into that kiss.

"I love you, Dana Markham," he said, kissing her cheeks before returning to her lips. "I'm going to do everything in my power to make you happy, to prove to you that I'm worthy of you and your wonderful son."

The smile she gave him washed away every doubt, every fear.

"You already have. You've been my black knight in shining armor," she said, returning the kiss with interest. "Let's go, get yon starving boy and his dragon some food."

They went in, pulling the door shut behind them.

A family.